THE DAUGHTER
OF ANDERSON CROW

BY

GEORGE BARR McCUTCHEON

Author of
"Beverly of Graustark," "Jane Cable," etc.

WITH ILLUSTRATIONS BY
B. MARTIN JUSTICE

NEW YORK
DODD, MEAD AND COMPANY
1907

CONTENTS

CHAPTER		PAGE
I	ANDERSON CROW, DETECTIVE	1
II	THE PURSUIT BEGINS	14
III	THE CULPRITS	25
IV	ANDERSON RECTIFIES AN ERROR	36
V	THE BABE ON THE DOORSTEP	49
VI	REFLECTION AND DEDUCTION	61
VII	THE MYSTERIOUS VISITOR	68
VIII	SOME YEARS GO BY	75
IX	THE VILLAGE QUEEN	84
X	ROSALIE HAS PLANS OF HER OWN	91
XI	ELSIE BANKS	98
XII	THE SPELLING-BEE	107
XIII	A TINKLETOWN SENSATION	115
XIV	A CASE OF MISTAKEN IDENTITY	124
XV	ROSALIE DISAPPEARS	131
XVI	THE HAUNTED HOUSE	143
XVII	WICKER BONNER, HARVARD	154
XVIII	THE MEN IN THE SLEIGH	165
XIX	WITH THE KIDNAPERS	173
XX	IN THE CAVE	183
XXI	THE TRAP-DOOR	192
XXII	JACK, THE GIANT KILLER	199
XXIII	TINKLETOWN'S CONVULSION	208
XXIV	THE FLIGHT OF THE KIDNAPERS	217

Contents

CHAPTER		PAGE
XXV	As the Heart Grows Older	227
XXVI	The Left Ventricle	236
XXVII	The Grin Derisive	245
XXVIII	The Blind Man's Eyes	255
XXIX	The Mysterious Questioner	263
XXX	The Hemisphere Train Robbery	273
XXXI	"As You Like It"	285
XXXII	The Luck of Anderson Crow	297
XXXIII	Bill Briggs Tells a Tale	309
XXXIV	Elsie Banks Returns	319
XXXV	The Story is Told	330
XXXVI	Anderson Crow's Resignation	341

ILLUSTRATIONS

Anderson Crow .... Frontispiece

" 'Safe for a minute or two at least,' he whispered" Facing page 28

"A baby, alive and warm, lay packed in the blankets" " " 54

" September brought Elsie Banks " " " 96

" The teacher was amazingly pretty on this eventful
night " " " 110

" ' What is the meaning of all this ? ' " " " 126

The haunted house " " 146

Wicker Bonner " " 156

" Rosalie was no match for the huge woman " " " 174

" She shrank back from another blow which seemed
impending " " " 184

" Left the young man to the care of an excellent
nurse " " " 222

" ' I think I understand, Rosalie ' " " " 252

" ' I beg your pardon,' he said humbly " " " 260

" It was a wise, discreet old oak " " " 270

" The huge automobile had struck the washout " " " 304

THE DAUGHTER OF ANDERSON CROW

CHAPTER I

Anderson Crow, Detective

HE was imposing, even in his pensiveness. There was
no denying the fact that he was an important personage in Tinkletown, and to the residents of Tinkletown
that meant a great deal, for was not their village a
perpetual monument to the American Revolution?
Even the most generalising of historians were compelled to devote at least a paragraph to the battle of
Tinkletown, while some of the more enlightened gave
a whole page and a picture of the conflict that brought
glory to the sleepy inhabitants whose ancestors were
enterprising enough to annihilate a whole company of
British redcoats, once on a time.

Notwithstanding all this, a particularly disagreeable
visitor from the city once remarked, in the presence of half a dozen descendants (after waiting
twenty minutes at the post-office for a dime's worth of
stamps), that Tinkletown was indeed a monument, but
he could not understand why the dead had been left
unburied. There was excellent cause for resentment,
but the young man and his stamps were far away before the full force of the slander penetrated the brains
of the listeners.

Anderson Crow was as imposing and as rugged as the tallest shaft of marble in the little cemetery on the edge of the town. No one questioned his power and authority, no one misjudged his altitude, and no one overlooked his dignity. For twenty-eight years he had served Tinkletown and himself in the triple capacity of town marshal, fire chief and street commissioner. He had a system of government peculiarly his own; and no one possessed the heart or temerity to upset it, no matter what may have been the political induce-ments. It would have been like trying to improve the laws of nature to put a new man in his place. He had become a fixture that only dissolution could remove. Be it said, however, that dissolution did not have its com-mon and accepted meaning when applied to Anderson Crow. For instance, in discoursing upon the ob-noxious habits of the town's most dissolute rake—Alf Reesling—Anderson had more than once ven-tured the opinion that "he was carrying his dissolution entirely too far."

And had not Anderson Crow risen to more than local distinction? Had not his fame gone abroad throughout the land? Not only was he the Marshal of Tinkletown at a salary of $200 a year, but he was president of the County Horse-thief Detectives' As-sociation and also a life-long delegate to the State Convention of the Sons of the Revolution. Along that line, let it be added, every parent in Tinkletown bemoaned the birth of a daughter, because that simple circumstance of origin robbed the society's roster of a new name.

Anderson Crow, at the age of forty-nine, had a proud official record behind him and a guaranteed future ahead. Doubtless it was of this that he was thinking, as he leaned pensively against the town hitching-rack and gingerly chewed the blade of wire-grass which dangled even below the chin whiskers that had been with him for twenty years. The far-away expression in his watery-blue eyes gave evidence that he was as great reminiscently as he was personally. So successful had been his career as a law preserver, that of late years no evil-doer had had the courage to ply his nefarious games in the community. The town drunkard, Alf

Reesling, seldom appeared on the streets in his habitual condition, because, as he dolefully remarked, he would deserve arrest and confinement for "criminal negligence," if for nothing else. The marshal's fame as a detective had long since escaped from the narrow confines of Tinkletown. He was well known at the county seat, and on no less than three occasions had his name mentioned in the "big city" papers in connection with the arrest of notorious horse-thieves.

And now the whole town was trembling with a new excitement, due to the recognition accorded her triple official. On Monday morning he had ventured forth from his office in the long-deserted "calaboose," resplendent in a brand-new nickel-plated star. By noon everybody in town knew that he was a genuine "detective," a member of the great organisation known as the New York Imperial Detective Association; and that fresh honour had come to Tinkletown through the agency of a post-revolution generation. The beauty of it all was that Anderson never lost a shred of his serenity in explaining how the association had implored him to join its forces, even going so far as to urge him to come to New York City, where he could assist and advise in all of its large operations. And, moreover, he had been obliged to pay but ten dollars membership fee, besides buying the blazing star for the paltry sum of three dollars and a quarter.

Every passer-by on this bright spring morning offered a respectful "Howdy" to Anderson Crow, whose only recognition was a slow and imposing nod of the head. Once only was he driven to relinquish his pensive attitude, and that was when an impertinent blue-bottle fly undertook to rest for a brief spell upon the nickel-plated star. Never was blue-bottle more energetically put to flight.

But even as the Tinkletown Pooh-Bah posed in restful supremacy there were rushing down upon him affairs of the epoch-making kind. Up in the clear, lazy sky a thunderbolt was preparing to hurl itself into the very heart of Tinkletown, and at the very head of Anderson Crow.

Afterward it was recalled by observing citizens that just before noon—seven minutes to twelve, in fact—a small cloud no bigger than the proverbial hand crossed the sun hurriedly as if afraid to tarry. At that very instant a stranger drove up to the hitching-rack, bringing his sweat-covered horse to a standstill so abruptly in front of the marshal's nose that that dignitary's hat fell off backward.

"Whoa!" came clearly and unmistakably from the lips of the stranger who held the reins. Half a dozen loafers on the post-office steps were positive that he said nothing more, a fact that was afterward worth remembering.

"Here!" exclaimed Anderson Crow wrathfully. "Do you know what you're doin', consarn you?"

"I beg pardon," everybody within hearing heard the young man say. "Is this the city of Tinkletown?" He said "city," they could swear, every man's son of them.

"Yes, it is," answered the marshal severely. "What of it?"

"That's all. I just wanted to know. Where's the store?"

"Which store?" quite crossly. The stranger seemed nonplussed at this.

"Have you more than—oh, to be sure. I should say, where is the *nearest* store?" apologised the stranger.

"Well, this is a good one, I reckon," said Mr. Crow laconically, indicating the post-office and general store.

"Will you be good enough to hold my horse while I run in there for a minute?" calmly asked the new arrival in town, springing lightly from the mud-spattered buggy. Anderson Crow almost staggered beneath this indignity. The crowd gasped, and then waited breathlessly for the withering process.

"Why—why, dod-gast you, sir, what do you think I am—a hitchin'-post?" exploded on the lips of the new detective. His face was flaming red.

"You'll have to excuse me, my good man, but I thought I saw a hitching-rack as I drove up. Ah, here it is. How careless of me. But say, I won't be in the store more than a second, and it doesn't seem worth while to tie the old crow-bait. If you'll just watch him—or her—for a minute I'll be greatly obliged, and——"

"Watch your own horse," roared the marshal thunderously.

"Don't get huffy," cried the young man cheerily. "It will be worth a quarter to you."

"Do you know who I am?" demanded Anderson Crow, purple to the roots of his goatee.

"Yes, sir; I know perfectly well, but I refuse to give it away. Here, take the bit, old chap, and hold Dobbin for about a minute and half," went on the stranger ruthlessly; and before Anderson Crow knew what

had happened he was actually holding the panting nag by the bit. The young man went up the steps three at a time, almost upsetting Uncle Gideon Luce, who had not been so spry as the others in clearing the way for him. The crowd had ample time in which to study the face, apparel and manner of this energetic young man.

That he was from the city, good-looking and well dressed, there was no doubt. He was tall and his face was beardless; that much could be seen at a glance. Somehow, he seemed to be laughing all the time—a fact that was afterward recalled with some surprise and no little horror. At the time, the loungers thought his smile was a merry one, but afterward they stoutly maintained there was downright villainy in the leer. His coat was very dusty, proving that he had driven far and swiftly. Three or four of the loungers followed him into the store. He was standing before the counter over which Mr. Lamson

served his soda-water. In one hand he held an envelope and in the other his straw hat. George Ray, more observant than the rest, took note of the fact that it was with the hat that he was fanning himself vigorously.

"A plain vanilla—please rush it along," commanded the stranger. Mr. Lamson, if possible slower than the town itself, actually showed unmistakable signs of acceleration. Tossing off the soda, the stranger dried his lips with a blue-hemmed white handkerchief. "Is this the post-office?" he asked.

"Yep," said Mr. Lamson, who was too penurious to waste words.

"Anything here for me?" demanded the new-comer.

"I'll see," said the postmaster, and from force of habit began looking through the pile of letters without asking the man's name. Mr. Lamson knew everybody in the county.

"Nothing here," taking off his spectacles conclusively.

"I didn't think there was," said the other complacently. "Give me a bottle of witch hazel, a package of invisible hair-pins and a box of parlor matches. Quick; I'm in a hurry!"

"Did you say hat-pins?"

"No, sir; I said hair-pins."

"We haven't any that ain't visible. How would safety-pins do?"

"Never mind; give me the bottle and the matches," said the other, glancing at a very handsome gold watch. "Is the old man still holding my horse?" he called to a citizen near the door. Seven necks stretched simultaneously to accommodate him, and seven voices answered in the affirmative. The stranger calmly opened the box of matches, filled his silver match-safe, and then threw the box back on the counter, an unheard-of piece of profligacy in those parts. "Needn't mind wrapping up the bottle," he said.

"Don't you care for these matches?" asked Mr. Lamson in mild surprise.

"I'll donate them to the church," said the other, tossing a coin upon the counter and dashing from the store. The crowd ebbed along behind him. "Gentle as a lamb, isn't he?" he called to Anderson Crow, who still clutched the bit. "Much obliged, sir; I'll do as much for you some day. If you're ever in New York, hunt me up and I'll see that you have a good time. What road do I take to Crow's Cliff?"

"Turn to your left here," said Anderson Crow before he thought. Then he called himself a fool for being so obliging to the fellow.

"How far is it from here?"

"Mile and a half," again answered Mr. Crow helplessly. This time he almost swore under his breath.

"But he can't get there," volunteered one of the bystanders.

"Why can't he?" demanded the marshal.

"Bridge over Turnip Creek is washed out. Did you forget that?"

"Of course not," promptly replied Mr. Crow, who *had* forgotten it. "But, dang it, he c'n swim, can't he?"

"You say the bridge is gone?" asked the stranger, visibly excited.

"Yes, and the crick's too high to ford, too."

"Well, how in thunder am I to get to Crow's Cliff?"

"There's another bridge four miles upstream. It's

still there," said George Ray. Anderson Crow had
scornfully washed his hands of the affair.

"Confound the luck! I haven't time to drive that
far. I have to be there at half-past twelve. I'm
late now! Is there no way to get across this miserable creek?" He was in the buggy now, whip in
hand, and his eyes wore an anxious expression. Some
of the men vowed later that he positively looked
frightened.

"There's a foot-log high and dry, and you can walk
across, but you can't get the horse and buggy over,"
said one of the men.

"Well, that's just what I'll have to do. Say, Mr.
Officer, suppose you drive me down to the creek and
then bring the horse back here to a livery stable. I'll
pay you well for it. I must get to Crow's Cliff in
fifteen minutes."

"I'm no errant-boy!" cried Anderson Crow so
wrathfully that two or three boys snickered.

"You're a darned old crank, that's what you are!"
exclaimed the stranger angrily. Everybody gasped,
and Mr. Crow staggered back against the hitching-
rail.

"See here, young man, none o' that!" he sputtered.
"You can't talk that way to an officer of the law.
I'll——"

"You won't do anything, do you hear that? But if
you knew who I am you'd be doing something
blamed quick." A dozen men heard him say it, and
they remembered it word for word.

"You go scratch yourself!" retorted Anderson Crow

scornfully. That was supposed to be a terrible challenge, but the stranger took no notice of it.

"What am I to do with this horse and buggy?" he growled, half to himself. "I bought the darned thing outright up in Boggs City, just because the liveryman didn't know me and wouldn't let me a rig. Now I suppose I'll have to take the old plug down to the creek and drown him in order to get rid of him."

Nobody remonstrated. He looked a bit dangerous with his broad shoulders and square jaw.

"What will you give me for the outfit, horse, buggy, harness and all? I'll sell cheap if some one makes a quick offer." The bystanders looked at one another blankly, and at last the concentrated gaze fell upon the Pooh-Bah of the town. The case seemed to be one that called for his attention; truly, it did not look like public property, this astounding proposition.

"What you so derned anxious to sell for?" demanded Anderson Crow, listening from a distance to see if he could detect a blemish in the horse's breathing gear. At a glance, the buggy looked safe enough.

"I'm anxious to sell for cash," replied the stranger; and Anderson was floored. The boy who snickered this time had cause to regret it, for Mr. Crow arrested him half an hour later for carrying a bean-shooter. "I paid a hundred dollars for the outfit in Boggs City," went on the stranger nervously. "Some one make an offer—and quick! I'm in a rush!"

"I'll give five dollars!" said one of the onlookers with an apologetic laugh. This was the match that

started fire in the thrifty noddles of Tinkletown's
best citizens. Before they knew it they were bidding
against each other with the true "horse-swapping"
instinct, and the offers had reached $21.25 when the
stranger unceremoniously closed the sale by crying
out, "Sold!" There is no telling how high the bids
might have gone if he could have waited half an hour
or so. Uncle Gideon Luce afterward said that he
could have had twenty-four dollars "just as well as
not." They were bidding up a quarter at a time, and
no one seemed willing to drop out. The successful
bidder was Anderson Crow.

"You can pay me as we drive along. Jump in!"
cried the stranger, looking at his watch with considerable agitation. "All I ask is that you drive me
to the foot-log that crosses the creek."

CHAPTER II

The Pursuit Begins

FIFTEEN minutes later Anderson Crow was parading proudly about the town. He had taken the stranger to the creek and had seen him scurry across the log to the opposite side, supplied with directions that would lead him to the nearest route through the swamps and timberland to Crow's Cliff. The stranger had Anderson's money in his pocket; but Anderson had a very respectable sort of driving outfit to show for it. His wife kept dinner for him until two o'clock, and then sent the youngest Crow out to tell her father that he'd have to go hungry until supper-time.

It is no wonder that Anderson failed to reach home in time for the midday meal. He started home properly enough, but what progress could he make when everybody in town stopped him to inquire about the remarkable deal and to have a look at the purchase. Without a single dissenting voice, Tinkletown said Anderson had very much the "best of the bargain." George Ray meant all right when he said, "A fool for luck," but he was obliged to explain thoroughly the witticism before the proud Mr. Crow could consider himself appeased.

It was not until he pulled up in front of the *Weekly Banner* establishment to tell the reporter "the news" that his equanimity received its first jar. He was quite proud of the deal, and, moreover, he enjoyed seeing his name in the paper. In the meantime almost everybody in Tinkletown was discussing the awful profligacy of the stranger. It had not occurred to anybody to wonder why he had been in such a hurry to reach Crow's Cliff, a wild, desolate spot down the river.

"The hoss alone is worth fifty dollars easy," volunteered Mr. Crow triumphantly. The detective's badge on his inflated chest seemed to sparkle with glee.

"Say, Anderson, isn't it a little queer that he should sell out so cheap?" asked Harry Squires, the local reporter and pressfeeder.

"What's that?" demanded Anderson Crow sharply.

"Do you think it's really true that he bought the nag up at Boggs City?" asked the sceptic. Mr. Crow wallowed his quid of tobacco helplessly for a minute or two. He could feel himself turning pale.

"He said so; ain't that enough?" he managed to bluster.

"It seems to have been," replied Harry, who had gone to night school in Albany for two years.

"Well, what in thunder are you talking about then?" exclaimed Anderson Crow, whipping up.

"I'll bet three dollars it's a stolen outfit!"

"You go to Halifax!" shouted Anderson, but his heart was cold. Something told him that Harry Squires was right. He drove home in a state of dire uncertainty and distress. Somehow, his enthusiasm was gone.

"Dang it!" he said, without reason, as he was unhitching the horse in the barn lot.

"Hey, Mr. Crow!" cried a shrill voice from the street. He looked up and saw a small boy coming on the run.

"What's up, Toby?" asked Mr. Crow, all a-tremble. He knew!

"They just got a telephone from Boggs City," panted the boy, "down to the *Banner* office. Harry Squires says for you to hurry down—buggy and all. It's been stole."

"Good Lord!" gasped Anderson. His badge danced before his eyes and then seemed to shrivel.

Quite a crowd had collected at the *Banner* office. There was a sudden hush when the marshal drove up. Even the horse felt the intensity of the moment. He shied at a dog and then kicked over the dashboard, upsetting Anderson Crow's meagre dignity and almost doing the same to the vehicle.

"You're a fine detective!" jeered Harry Squires; and poor old Anderson hated him ever afterward.

"What have you heerd?" demanded the marshal.

"There's been a terrible murder at Boggs City, that's all. The chief of police just telephoned to us that a farmer named Grover was found dead in a ditch just outside of town—shot through the head, his pockets rifled. It is known that he started to town to deposit four hundred dollars hog-money in the bank. The money is missing, and so are his horse and buggy. A young fellow was seen in the neighbourhood early this morning—a stranger. The chief's description corresponds with the man who sold that rig to you. The murderer is known to have driven in this direction. People saw him going almost at a gallop."

It is not necessary to say that Tinkletown thoroughly turned inside out with excitement. The whole population was soon at the post-office, and everybody was trying to supply Anderson Crow with wits. He had lost his own.

"We've got to catch that fellow," finally resolved the marshal. There was a dead silence.

"He's got a pistol," ventured some one.

"How do you know?" demanded Mr. Crow keenly. "Did y' see it?"

"He couldn't ha' killed that feller 'thout a gun."

"That's a fact," agreed Anderson Crow. "Well, we've got to get him, anyhow. I call for volunteers! Who will join me in the search?" cried the marshal bravely.

"I hate to go to Crow's Cliff after him," said George Ray. "It's a lonesome place, and as dark as night 'mong them trees and rocks."

"It's our duty to catch him. He's a criminal, and besides, he's killed a man," said Crow severely.

"And he has twenty-one dollars of your money," added Harry Squires. "I'll go with you, Anderson. I've got a revolver."

"Look out there!" roared Anderson Crow. "The blamed thing might go off!" he added as the reporter drew a shiny six-shooter from his pocket.

The example set by one brave man had its influence

on the crowd. A score or more volunteered, despite the objections of their wives, and it was not long before Anderson Crow was leading his motley band of sleuths down the lane to the foot-log over which the desperado had gone an hour before.

It was at the beginning of the man-hunt that various citizens recalled certain actions and certain characteristics of the stranger which had made them suspicious from the start. His prodigal disposition of the box of matches impressed most of them as reckless daredevilism; his haste, anxiety, and a single instance of mild profanity told others of his viciousness. One man was sure he had seen the stranger's watch chain in farmer Grover's possession; and another saw something black on his thumb, which he now remembered was a powder stain.

"I noticed all them things," averred Anderson Crow, supreme once more.

"But what in thunder did he want with those hairpins?" inquired George Ray.

"Never mind," said Anderson mysteriously. "You'll find out soon enough."

"Do you know, Anderson?" some one asked.

"Of course I do," responded the marshal loftily.

"Well, what were they for, then?"

"I'm not givin' any clews away. You just wait a while and see if I'm not right."

And they were satisfied that the detective knew all about it. After crossing the foot-log the party was divided as to which direction it should take. The marshal said the man had run to the southeast, but for some inexplicable reason quite a number of the pursuers wanted to hunt for him in the northwest. Finally it was decided to separate into posses of ten, all to converge at Crow's Cliff as soon as possible. There were enough double-barrelled shotguns in the party to have conquered a pirate crew.

At the end of an hour Anderson Crow and his delegation came to the narrow path which led to the summit of Crow's Cliff. They were very brave by this time. A small boy was telling them he had seen the fugitive about dinner-time "right where you fellers are standin' now."

"Did he have any blood on him?" demanded Anderson Crow.

"No, sir; not 'less it was under his clothes."

"Did he say anythin' to you?"

"He ast me where this path went to."

"See that, gentlemen!" cried Anderson. "I knew I was right. He wanted——"

"Well, where did he go?" demanded Harry Squires.

"I said it went to the top of the clift. An' then he said, 'How do you git to the river?' I tole him to go down this side path here an' 'round the bottom of the hill."

"Didn't he go up the cliff?" demanded the marshal. "No, sir."

"Well, what in thunder did he ask me where the cliff was if he——"

"So he went to the river, eh?" interrupted Squires. "Come on, men; he went down through this brush and bottomland."

"He got lost, I guess," volunteered the boy.

"What!"

"'Cause he yelled at me after he'd gone in a-ways an' ast—an' ast——" The boy paused irresolutely.

"Asked what?"

"He ast me where in h—— the path was."

"By ginger, that's him, right out an' out!" exclaimed Mr. Crow excitedly.

"'Nen he said he'd give me a quarter if I'd show him the way; so I——"

"Did he give you the quarter?" questioned one of the men.

"Yep. He'd a roll of bills as big as my leg."
Everybody gasped and thought of Grover's hog-
money.

"You went to the river with him?" interrogated
the reporter.

"I went as fur as the clearin', an' then he tole me
to stop. He said he could find the way from there.
After that he run up the bank as if some one was
after him. There was a boat waitin' fer him under
the clift."

"Did he get into it?" cried Squires.

"He tole me not to look or he'd break my neck,"
said the boy. The posse nervously fingered its
arsenal.

"But you *did* look?"

"Yep. I seen 'em plain."

"Them? Was there more than one?"

"There was a woman in the skift."

"You don't say so!" gasped Squires.

"Dang it, ain't he tellin' you!" Anderson ejaculated
scornfully.

The boy was hurried off at the head of the posse,
which by this time had been reinforced. He led the
way through the dismal thickets, telling his story as
he went.

"She was mighty purty, too," he said. "The feller
waved his hat when he seen her, an' she waved back.
He run down an' jumped in the boat, an' 'nen—
'nen——"

"Then what?" exploded Anderson Crow.

"He kissed her!"

"The d—— murderer!" roared Crow.

"He grabbed up the oars and rowed 'cross an' down-stream. An' he shuck his fist at me when he see I'd been watchin'," said the youngster, ready to whimper now that he realised what a desperate character he had been dealing with.

"Where did he land on the other side?" pursued the eager reporter.

"Down by them willer trees, 'bout half a mile down. There's the skiff tied to a saplin'. Cain't you see it?"

Sure enough, the stern of a small boat stuck out into the deep, broad river, the bow being hidden by the bushes.

"Both of 'em hurried up the hill over yender, an' that's the last I seen of 'em," concluded the lad.

Anderson Crow and his man-hunters stared help-lessly at the broad, swift river, and then looked at each other in despair. There was no boat in sight except the murderer's, and there was no bridge within ten miles.

While they were growling a belated detachment of hunters came up to the river bank greatly agitated.

"A telephone message has just come to town sayin' there would be a thousand dollars reward," announced one of the late arrivals; and instantly there was an imperative demand for boats.

"There's an old raft upstream a-ways," said the boy, "but I don't know how many it will kerry. They use it to pole corn over from Mr. Knoblock's farm to them big summer places in the hills up yender."

"Is it sound?" demanded Anderson Crow.

"Must be or they wouldn't use it," said Squires sarcastically. "Where is it, kid?"

The boy led the way up the river bank, the whole company trailing behind.

"Sh! Not too loud," cautioned Anderson Crow.

Fifteen minutes later a wobbly craft put out to sea, manned by a picked crew of determined citizens of Tinkletown. When they were in midstream a loud cry came from the bank they had left behind. Looking back, Anderson Crow saw excited men dashing about, most of them pointing excitedly up into the hills across the river. After a diligent search the eyes of the men on the raft saw what it was that had created such a stir at the base of Crow's Cliff.

"There he is!" cried Anderson Crow in awed tones. There was no mistaking the identity of the coatless man on the hillside. A dozen men recognised him as the man they were after. Putting his hands to his mouth, Anderson Crow bellowed in tones that savoured more of fright than command:

"Say!"

There was no response.

"Will you surrender peaceably?" called the captain of the craft.

There was a moment of indecision on the part of the fugitive. He looked at his companion, and she shook her head—they all saw her do it.

Then he shouted back his reply.

THEN HE SHOUTED BACK HIS REPLY

CHAPTER III

The Culprits

"SHIP ahoy!" shouted the coatless stranger between his palms.

"Surrender or we'll fill you full of lead!" called Anderson Crow.

"Who are you—pirates?" responded the fugitive with a laugh that chilled the marrow of the men on the raft.

"I'll show you who we are!" bellowed Anderson Crow. "Send her ashore, boys, fast. The derned scamp sha'n't escape us. Dead er alive, we must have him."

As they poled toward the bank the woman grasped the man by the arm, dragging him back among the trees. It was observed by all that she was greatly terrified. Moreover, she was exceedingly fair to look upon—young, beautiful, and a most incongruous companion for the bloody rascal who had her in his power. The raft bumped against the reedy bank, and Anderson Crow was the first man ashore.

"Come on, boys; follow me! See that your guns are all right! Straight up the hill now, an' spread out a bit so's we can surround him!" commanded he in a high treble.

"But supposin' he surrounds us," panted a cautious pursuer, half way up the hill.

"That's what we've got to guard against," retorted Anderson Crow. The posse bravely swept up to and across the greensward; but the fox was gone. There was no sight or sound of him to be had. It is but just to say that fatigue was responsible for the deep breath that came from each member of the pursuing party.

"Into the woods after him!" shouted Anderson Crow. "Hunt him down like a rat!"

In the meantime a coatless young man and a most enticing young woman were scampering off among the oaks and underbrush, consumed by excitement and no small degree of apprehension.

"They really seem to be in earnest about it, Jack," urged the young woman insistently, to offset his somewhat sarcastic comments.

"How the dickens do you suppose they got onto me?" he groaned. "I thought the tracks were beautifully covered. No one suspected, I'm sure."

"I told you, dear, how it would turn out," she cried in a panic-stricken voice.

"Good heavens, Marjory, don't turn against me! It all seemed so easy and so sure, dear. There wasn't a breath of suspicion. What are we to do? I'll stop and fight the whole bunch if you'll just let go my arm."

"No, you won't, Jack Barnes!" she exclaimed resolutely, her pretty blue eyes wide with alarm. "Didn't you hear them say they'd fill you full of lead? They had guns and everything. Oh, dear! oh, dear! isn't it horrid?"

"The worst of it is they've cut us off from the river," he said miserably. "If I could have reached the boat ahead of them they never could have caught us. I could distance that old raft in a mile."

"I know you could, dear," she cried, looking with frantic admiration upon his broad shoulders and brawny bare arms. "But it is out of the question now."

"Never mind, sweetheart; don't let it fuss you so. It will turn out all right, I know it will."

"Oh, I can't run any farther," she gasped despairingly.

"Poor little chap! Let me carry you?"

"You big ninny!"

"We are at least three miles from your house, dear, and surrounded by deadly perils. Can you climb a tree?"

"I can—but I won't!" she refused flatly, her cheeks very red.

"Then I fancy we'll have to keep on in this manner. It's a confounded shame—the whole business. Just as I thought everything was going so smoothly, too. It was all arranged to a queen's taste—nothing was left undone. Bracken was to meet us at his uncle's boathouse down there, and—good heavens, there was a shot!"

The sharp crack of a rifle broke upon the still, balmy air, as they say in the "yellow-backs," and the fugitives looked at each other with suddenly awakened dread.

"The fools!" grated the man.

"What do they mean?" cried the breathless girl, very white in the face.

"They are trying to frighten us, that's all. Hang it! If I only knew the lay of the land. I'm completely lost, Marjory. Do you know precisely where we are?"

"Our home is off to the north about three miles. We are almost opposite Crow's Cliff—the wildest part of the country. There are no houses along this part of the river. All of the summer houses are farther up or on the other side. It is too hilly here. There is a railroad off there about six miles. There isn't a boathouse or fisherman's hut nearer than two miles. Mr. Bracken keeps his boat at the point—two miles south, at least."

"Yes; that's where we were to have gone—by boat. Hang it all! Why did we ever leave the boat? You can never scramble through all this brush to Bracken's place; it's all I can do. Look at my arms! They are scratched to——"

"Oh, dear! It's dreadful, Jack. You poor fellow, let me——"

"We haven't time, dearest. By thunder, I wouldn't have those Rubes head us off now for the whole county. The jays! How could they have found us out?"

"Some one must have told."

"But no one knew except the Brackens, you and I."

"I'll wager my head Bracken is saying hard things for fair down the river there."

"He—he—doesn't swear, Jack," she panted.

"Why, you are ready to drop! Can't you go a step

"'SAFE FOR A MINUTE OR TWO AT LEAST,' HE WHISPERED"

farther? Let's stop here and face 'em. I'll bluff 'em
out and we'll get to Bracken's some way. But I *won't*
give up the game! Not for a million!"

"Then we can't stop. You forget I go in for gym-
nasium work. I'm as strong as anything, only I'm—
I'm a bit nervous. Oh, I knew something would go
wrong!" she wailed. They were now standing like
trapped deer in a little thicket, listening for sounds of
the hounds.

"Are you sorry, dear?"

"No, no! I love you, Jack, and I'll go through
everything with you and for you. Really," she cried
with a fine show of enthusiasm, "this is jolly good fun,
isn't it? Being chased like regular bandits——"

"Sh! Drop down, dear! There's somebody passing above us—hear him?"

They crawled into a maze of hazel bushes with much
less dignity than haste. Two men sped by an instant
later, panting and growling.

"Safe for a minute or two at least," he whispered as
the crunching footsteps were lost to the ear. "They
won't come back this way, dear."

"They had guns, Jack!" she whispered, terrified.

"I don't understand it, hanged if I do," he said, pulling his brows into a mighty scowl. "They are after
us like a pack of hounds. It must mean something.
Lord, but we seem to have stirred up a hornet's nest!"

"Oh, dear, I wish we were safely at——" she
paused.

"At home?" he asked quickly.

"At Bracken's," she finished; and if any of the pur-

suers had been near enough he might have heard the unmistakable suggestion of a kiss.

"I feel better," he said, squaring his shoulders. "Now, let me think. We must outwit these fellows, whoever they are. By George, I remember one of them! That old fellow who bought the horse is with them. That's it! The horse is mixed up in this, I'll bet my head." They sat upon the ground for several minutes, he thinking deeply, she listening with her pretty ears intent.

"I wonder if they've left anybody to guard our boat?" he said suddenly. "Come on, Marjory; let's investigate! By George, it would be just like them to leave it unprotected!"

Once more they were moving cautiously through the brush, headed for the river. Mr. Jack Barnes, whoever he was and whatever his crime, was a resourceful, clever young man. He had gauged the intelligence of the pursuers correctly. When he peered through the brush along the river bank he saw the skiff in the reeds below, just as they had left it. There was the lunch basket, the wee bit of a steamer trunk with all its labels, a parasol and a small handbag.

"Goody, goody!" Marjory cried like a happy child.

"Don't show yourself yet, dearie. I'll make sure. They may have an ambuscade. Wait here for me."

He crept down the bank and back again before she could fully subdue the tremendous thumping his temerity had started in her left side.

"It's safe and sound," he whispered joyously. "The idiots have forgotten the boat. Quick, dear; let's make a dash for it! Their raft is upstream a hundred yards, and it is also deserted. If we can once get well across the river we can give them the laugh."

"But they may shoot us from the bank," she protested as they plunged through the weeds.

"They surely wouldn't shoot a woman!" he cried gayly.

"But you are not a woman!"

"And I'm not afraid of mice or men. Jump in!"

Off from the weeds shot the light skiff. The water splashed for a moment under the spasmodic strokes of the oarsman, and then the little boat streaked out into the river like a thing of life. Marjory sat in the stern and kept her eyes upon the bank they were leaving. Jack Barnes drove every vestige of his strength into the stroke; somehow he pulled like a man who had learned how on a college crew. They were half way across the broad river before they were seen from the hills. The half dozen men who lingered at the base of Crow's Cliff had shouted the alarm to their friends on the other side, and the fugitives were sighted once more. But it was too late. The boat was well out of gunshot range and making rapid progress downstream in the shelter of the high bluffs below Crow's Cliff. Jack Barnes was dripping with perspiration, but his stroke was none the feebler.

"They see us!" she cried.

"Don't wriggle so, Marjory—trim boat!" he panted. "They can't hit us, and we can go two miles to their one."

"And we can get to Bracken's!" she cried triumphantly. A deep flush overspread her pretty face.

"Hooray!" he shouted with a grin of pure delight. Far away on the opposite bank Anderson Crow and his sleuths were congregating, their baffled gaze upon the man who had slipped out of their grasp. The

men of the posse were pointing at the boat and argu-
ing frantically; there were decided signs of dispute
among them. Finally two guns flew up, and then
came the puffs of smoke, the reports and little splashes
of water near the flying skiff.

"Oh, they are shooting!" she cried in a panic.

"And rifles, too," he grated, redoubling his pull on
the oars. Other shots followed, all falling short.
"Get down in the bottom of the boat, Marjory.
Don't sit up there and be——"

"I'll sit right where I am," she cried defiantly.

Anderson Crow waved to the men under Crow's
Cliff, and they began to make their arduous way along
the bank in the trail of the skiff. Part of the armed
posse hurried down and boarded the raft, while others
followed the chase by land.

"We'll beat them to Bracken's by a mile," cried Jack
Barnes.

"If they don't shoot us," she responded. "Why,
oh, why are they so intent upon killing us?"

"They don't want you to be a widow and—break
a—lot of hearts," he said. "If they—hit me now
you—won't be—dangerous as a—widow."

"Oh, you heartless thing! How can you jest about
it? I'd—I'd go into mourning, anyway, Jack," she
concluded, on second thought. "We are just as good
as married, you see."

"It's nice—of you to say it, dear—but we're a long
—way from—Bracken's. Gee! That was close!"
A bullet splashed in the water not ten feet from the
boat. "The cowards! They're actually trying to

kill us!" For the first time his face took on a look of alarm and his eyes grew desperate. "I can't let them shoot at you, Marjory, dear! What the dickens they want I don't know, but I'm going to surrender." He had stopped rowing and was making ready to wave his white handkerchief on high.

"Never!" she cried with blazing eyes. "Give me the oars!" She slid into the other rowing seat and tried to snatch the oars from the rowlocks.

"Bravo! I could kiss you a thousand times for that. Come on, you Indians! You're a darling, Marjory." Again the oars caught the water, and Jack Barnes's white handkerchief lay in the bottom of the boat. He was rowing for dear life, and there was a smile on his face.

The raft was left far behind and the marksmen were put out of range with surprising ease. Fifteen minutes later the skiff shot across the river and up to the landing of Bracken's boathouse, while a mile back in the brush Anderson Crow and his men were wrathfully scrambling in pursuit.

"Hey, Bracken! Jimmy!" shouted Jack Barnes, jumping out upon the little wharf. Marjory gave him her hands and was whisked ashore and into his arms. "Run into the boathouse, dear. I'll yank this stuff ashore. Where the dickens is Bracken?"

The boathouse door opened slowly and a sleepy young man looked forth.

"I thought you'd never come," he yawned.

"Wake up, you old loafer! We're here and we are pursued! Where are George and Amy?" cried

Mr. Barnes, doing herculean duty as a baggage smasher.

"Pursued?" cried the sleepy young man, suddenly awake.

"Yes, and shot at!" cried Marjory, running past him and into the arms of a handsome young woman who was emerging from the house.

"We've no time to lose, Jimmy! They are on to us, Heaven knows how. They are not more than ten minutes behind us. Get it over with, Jimmy, for Heaven's sake! Here, George, grab this trunk!"

CHAPTER IV

Anderson Rectifies an Error

IN a jiffy the fugitives and their property were transferred to the interior of the roomy boathouse, the doors bolted, and George Crosby stationed at a window to act as lookout.

"Is it your father?" demanded the Rev. James Bracken, turning to Marjory. Young Mrs. Crosby was looking on eagerly.

"Mr. Brewster is at home and totally oblivious to all this," cried Jack Barnes. "I don't know what it means. Here's the license, Jimmy. Are you ready, Marjory?"

"This is rather a squeamish business, Jack——" began the young minister in the negligée shirt. He was pulling on his coat as he made the remark.

"Oh, hurry, Jimmy; please hurry!" cried Marjory Brewster.

"Don't wait a second, Jimmy Bracken!" cried Amy Crosby, dancing with excitement. "You can't go back on them now!"

Three minutes later there was no Marjory Brewster, but there was a Mrs. John Ethelbert Barnes—and she was kissing her husband rapturously.

"Now, tell us everything," cried Mrs. Crosby after the frantic congratulations. The Reverend "Jimmy" Bracken, of the Eleventh Presbyterian Church, was the only one who seemed uncertain as to his position. In the first place, old Judge Brewster was a man of influence in the metropolis, from which all had fled for a sojourn in the hills. He and his daughter were Episcopalians, but that made them none the less important in the eyes of "Jimmy" Bracken. In the second place, Jack Barnes was a struggling lawyer, in the Year of our Lord 1880, and possessed of objectionable poverty. The young men had been roommates at college. Friendship had overcome discretion in this instance, at least. The deed being done, young Mr. Bracken was beginning to wonder if it had not been overdone, so to speak.

"I wish somebody would tell me!" exclaimed Jack Barnes, with a perplexed frown. "The beastly jays shot at us and all that. You'd think I was an outlaw. And they blazed away at Marjory, too, hang them!"

Marjory, too excited to act like a blushing bride, took up the story and told all that had happened. George Crosby became so interested that he forgot to keep guard.

"This is a funny mess!" he exclaimed. "There's something wrong———"

"Hey, you!" came a shout from the outside.

"There they are!" cried Marjory, flying to her husband's side. "What are we to do?"

"You mean, what are they to do? We're married, and they can't get around that, you know. Let 'em come!" cried the groom exultantly. "You don't regret it, do you, sweetheart?" quite anxiously.

She smiled up into his eyes, and he felt very secure.

"What do you fellows want?" demanded Crosby from the window. Anderson Crow was standing on the river bank like a true Napoleon, flanked by three trusty riflemen.

"Who air you?" asked Anderson in return. He was panting heavily, and his legs trembled.

"None of your business! Get off these grounds at once; they're private!"

"None o' your sass, now, young man; I'm an officer of the law, an' a detective to boot! We sha'n't stand any nonsense. The place is surrounded and he can't escape! Where is he?"

"That's for you to find out if you're such a good detective! This is David Bracken's place, and you can find him at his home on the hilltop yonder!"

"Ask him what we've done, George," whispered Barnes.

"We ain't after Mr. Bracken, young feller, but you know what we *do* want! He's in there—you're shielding him—we won't parley much longer! Send him out!" said Anderson Crow.

"If you come a foot nearer you'll get shot into the middle of kingdom come!" shouted Crosby defiantly.

The inmates gasped, for there was not a firearm on the place.

"Be careful!" warned the Reverend "Jimmy" nervously.

"Goin' to resist, eh? Well, we'll get him; don't you worry; an' that ornery female o' hisn', too!"

"Did you hear that?" exclaimed Jack Barnes. "Let me get at the old rat." He was making for the door when the two women obstructed the way. Both were frantic with fear.

"But he called you a female!" roared he.

"Well, I *am!*" she wailed miserably.

"Who is it you want?" asked Crosby from the window.

"That's all right," roared Anderson Crow; "purduce him at once!"

"Is this the fellow?" and Crosby dragged the Reverend "Jimmy" into view. There was a moment's inspection of the cadaverous face, and then the sleuths shook their heads.

"Not on your life!" said Mr. Crow. "But he's in there—Ike Smalley seen him an' his paramount go up the steps from the landin'! 'Twon't do no good to hide him, young feller; he's——"

"Well, let me tell you something. You are too late —they're married!" cried Crosby triumphantly.

"I don't give a cuss if they're married and have sixteen children!" shouted the exasperated Crow, his badge fairly dancing. "He's got to surrender!"

"Oh, he does, eh?"

"Yes, sir-ee-o-bob; he's got to give up, dead or alive! Trot him out lively, now!"

"I don't mind telling you that Mr. Barnes is here; but I'd like to know why you're hunting him down like a wild beast, shooting at him and Miss—I mean Mrs. Barnes. It's an outrage!"

"Oh, we ain't the on'y people that can kill and

slaughter! She's just as bad as he is, for that matter —an' so are you and that other lantern-jawed outlaw in there." The Reverend "Jimmy" gasped and turned a fiery red.

"Did he call me a— say!" and he pushed Crosby aside. "I'd have you to understand that I'm a minister of the gospel—I am the Reverend James Bracken, of——."

A roar of laughter greeted his attempt to explain; and there were a few remarks so uncomplimentary that the man of cloth sank back in sheer hopelessness.

"Well, I'll give them reason to think that I'm something of a desperado," grated the Reverend "Jimmy," squaring his shoulders. "If they attempt to put foot inside my uncle's house I'll—I'll smash a few heads."

"Bravo!" cried Mrs. Crosby. She was his cousin, and up to that time had had small regard for her mild-mannered relative.

"He can preach the funeral!" shouted Ike Smalley. By this time there were a dozen men on the bank below.

"I give you fair warning," cried Anderson Crow

impressively. "We're goin' to surround the house, an' we'll take that rascal if we have to shoot the boards into sawdust!"

"But what has he done, except to get married?" called Crosby as the posse began to spread out.

"Do you s'pose I'm fool enough to tell you if you don't

know?" said Anderson Crow. "Just as like as not you'd be claimin' the thousand dollars reward if you knowed it had been offered! Spread out, boys, an' we'll show 'em dern quick!"

There was dead silence inside the house for a full minute. Every eye was wide and every mouth was open in surprise and consternation.

"A thousand dollars reward!" gasped Jack Barnes. "Then, good Lord, I *must* have done something!"

"What *have* you been doing, Jack Barnes?" cried his bride, aghast.

"I must have robbed a train," said he dejectedly.

"Well, this *is* serious, after all," said Crosby. "It's not an eloper they're after, but a desperado."

"A kidnaper, perhaps," suggested his wife.

"What are we to do?" demanded Jack Barnes.

"First, old man, what have you actually done?" asked the Reverend "Jimmy."

"Nothing that's worth a thousand dollars, I'm dead sure," said Barnes positively. "By George, Marjory, this is a nice mess I've led you into!"

"It's all right, Jack; I'm happier than I ever was before in my life. We ran away to get married, and I'll go to jail with you if they'll take me."

"This is no time for kissing," objected Crosby sourly. "We must find out what it all means. Leave it to me."

It was getting dark in the room, and the shadows were heavy on the hills. While the remaining members of the besieged party sat silent and depressed upon the casks and boxes, Crosby stood at the window calling to the enemy.

"Is he ready to surrender?" thundered Anderson Crow from the shadows.

Then followed a brief and entirely unsatisfactory dialogue between the two spokesmen. Anderson Crow was firm in his decision that the fugitive did not have to be told what he had done; and George Crosby was equally insistent that he had to be told before he could decide whether he was guilty or innocent.

"We'll starve him out!" said Anderson Crow.

"But there are ladies here, my good man; you won't subject them to such treatment!"

"You're all of a kind—we're going to take the whole bunch!"

"What do you think will happen to you if you are mistaken in your man?"

"We're not mistaken, dang ye!"

"He could sue you for every dollar you possess. I know, for I'm a lawyer!"

"Now, I'm sure you're in the job with him. I s'pose you'll try to work in the insanity dodge! It's a nest of thieves and robbers! Say, I'll give you five minutes to surrender; if you don't, we'll set fire to the derned shanty!"

"Look here, boys," said Jack Barnes suddenly, "I've done nothing and am not afraid to be arrested. I'm going to give myself up." Of course there was a storm of protest and a flow of tears, but the culprit was firm. "Tell the old fossil that if he'll guarantee safety to me I'll give up!"

Anderson was almost too quick in promising protection.

"Ask him if he will surrender and make a confession to me—I am Anderson Crow, sir!" was the marshal's tactful suggestion.

"He'll do both, Mr. Crow!" replied Crosby.

"We've got to take the whole bunch of you, young man. You're all guilty of conspiracy, the whole caboodle!"

"But the ladies, you darned old Rube—they can't——"

"Looky here, young feller, you can't dictate to me. I'll have you to——"

"We'll all go!" cried Mrs. Crosby warmly.

"To the very end!" added the new Mrs. Barnes.

"What will your father say?" demanded the groom.

"He'll disown me anyway, dear, so what's the difference?"

"It's rather annoying for a minister——" began the Reverend "Jimmy," putting on his hat.

"We'll beg off for you!" cried Mrs. Crosby ironically.

"But I'm going to jail, too," finished he grimly.

"All right," called Crosby from the window; "here we come!"

And forth marched the desperate quintet, three strapping young men and two very pretty and nervous young women. They were met by Anderson Crow and a dozen armed men from Tinkletown, every one of them shaking in his boots. The irrepressible Mrs. Crosby said "Boo!" suddenly, and half the posse jumped as though some one had thrown a bomb at them.

"Now, I demand an explanation of this outrage," said Jack Barnes savagely. "What do you mean by shooting at me and my—my wife and arresting us, and all that?"

"You'll find out soon enough when you're strung up fer it," snarled Anderson Crow. "An' you'll please hand over that money I paid fer the hoss and buggy. I'll learn you how to sell stolen property to me."

"Oh, I'm a horse-thief, am I? This is rich. And they'll string me up, eh? Next thing you'll be accusing me of killing that farmer up near Boggs City."

"Well, by gosh! you're a cool one!" ejaculated Anderson Crow. "I s'pose you're goin' ter try the insanity dodge."

"It's lucky for me that they caught him," said Barnes as the herd of prisoners moved off toward the string of boats tied to Mr. Bracken's wharf.

"Come off!" exclaimed Squires, the reporter, scornfully. "We're onto you, all right, all right."

"What! Do you think I'm the man who—well, holy mackerel! Say, you gravestones, don't you ever hear any news out here? Wake up! They caught the murderer at Billsport, not more than five miles from your jay burg. I was driving through the town when they brought him in. That's what made me late, dear," turning to Marjory.

"Yes, and I'll bet my soul that here comes some one with the news," cried George Crosby, who had heard nothing of the tragedy until this instant.

A rowboat containing three men was making for the landing. Somehow, Anderson Crow and his posse felt the ground sinking beneath them. Not a man uttered a sound until one of the newcomers called out from the boat:

"Is Anderson Crow there?"

"Yes, sir; what is it?" demanded Crow in a wobbly voice.

"Your wife wants to know when in thunder you're

comin' home." By this time the skiff was bumping against the landing.

"You tell her to go to Halifax!" retorted Anderson Crow. "Is that all you want?"

"They nabbed that murderer up to Billsport long 'bout 'leven o'clock," said Alf Reesling, the town drunkard. "We thought we'd row down and tell you so's you wouldn't be huntin' all night for the feller who—hello, you got him, eh?"

"Are you fellers lyin'?" cried poor Anderson Crow.

"Not on your life. We knowed about the captcher over in town just about half an hour after you started 'cross the river this afternoon."

"You—four hours ago? You—you——" sputtered the marshal. "An' why didn't you let us know afore this?"

"There was a game o' baseball in Hasty's lot, an'——" began one of the newcomers sheepishly.

"Well, I'll be gosh-whizzled!" gasped Anderson Crow, sitting down suddenly.

An hour and a half later Mr. and Mrs. John Ethelbert Barnes were driven up to Judge Brewster's country place in Mr. David Bracken's brake. They were accompanied by Mr. and Mrs. George Crosby, and were carrying out the plans as outlined in the original programme.

"Where's papa?" Marjory tremulously inquired of the footman in the hallway.

"He's waitin' for you in the library, miss—I should say Mrs. Barnes," replied the man, a trace of excitement in his face.

"Mrs. Barnes!" exclaimed four voices at once.

"Who told you, William?" cried Marjory, leaning upon Jack for support.

"A Mr. Anderson Crow was here not half an hour ago, ma'am, to assure Mr. Brewster as to how his new son-in-law was in nowise connected with the murder up the way. He said as how he had personally investigated the case, miss—ma'am, and Mr. Brewster could rely on his word for it, Mr. Jack was not the man. He told him as how you was married at the boathouse."

"Yes—and then?" cried Marjory eagerly.

"Mr. Brewster said that Mr. Jack wasn't born to be hanged, and for me to have an extry plate laid at the table for him to-night," concluded William with an expressive grin.

CHAPTER V

The Babe on the Doorstep

It was midnight in Tinkletown, many months after the events mentioned in the foregoing chapters, and a blizzard was raging. The February wind rasped through the bare trees, shrieked around the corners of lightless houses and whipped its way through the scurrying snow with all the rage of a lion. The snow, on account of the bitter cold in the air, did not fly in big flakes, but whizzed like tiny bullets, cutting the flesh of men and beasts like the sting of wasps. It was a good night to be indoors over a roaring fire or in bed between extra blankets. No one, unless commanded by emergency, had the temerity to be abroad that night.

The Crow family snoozed comfortably in spite of the calliope shrieks of the wind. The home of the town marshal was blanketed in peace and the wind had no terrors for its occupants. They slept the sleep of the toasted. The windows may have rattled a bit, perhaps, and the shutters may have banged a trifle too remorselessly, but the Crows were not to be disturbed.

The big, old-fashioned clock in the hall downstairs was striking twelve when Anderson Crow awoke with a start. He was amazed, for to awake in the middle of the night was an unheard-of proceeding for him.

He caught the clang of the last five strokes from the clock, however, and was comforting himself with the belief that it was five o'clock, after all, when his wife stirred nervously.

"Are you awake, Anderson?" she asked softly.

"Yes, Eva, and it's about time to get up. It jest struck five. Doggone, it's been blowin' cats and dogs outside, ain't it?" he yawned.

"Five? It's twelve—now, don't tell me you counted the strokes, because I did myself. Ain't it queer we should both git awake at this unearthly hour?"

"Well," murmured he sleepily now that it was not five o'clock, "it's a mighty good hour to go back to sleep ag'in, I reckon."

"I thought I heard a noise outside," she persisted.

"I don't blame you," he said, chuckling. "It's been out there all night."

"I mean something besides the wind. Sounded like some one walkin' on the front porch."

"Now, look here, Eva, you ain't goin' to git me out there in this blizzard—in my stockin' feet—lookin' fer robbers——"

"Just the same, Anderson, I'm sure I heard some one. Mebby it's some poor creature freezin' an' in distress. If I was you, I'd go and look out there. Please do."

"Doggone, Eva, if you was me you'd be asleep instid of huntin' up trouble on a night like this. They ain't nothin' down there an' you—but, by cracky! mebby you're right. Supposin' there is some poor cuss out there huntin' a place to sleep. I'll go and look;" and Mr. Crow, the most tender-hearted man in the world, crawled shiveringly but quickly from the warm bed. In his stocking feet—Anderson slept in his socks on those bitter nights—he made his way down the front stairs, grumbling but determined. Mrs. Crow followed close behind, anxious to verify the claim that routed him from his nest.

"It may be a robber," she chattered, as he pulled aside a front window curtain. Anderson drew back hastily.

"Well, why in thunder didn't you say so before?" he gasped. "Doggone, Eva, that's no way to do! He might 'a' fired through the winder at me."

"But he's in the house by this time, if it was a robber," she whispered. "He wouldn't stand out on the porch all night."

"That's right," he whispered in reply. "You're a good deducer, after all. I wish I had my dark lantern. Thunderation!" He stubbed his toe against the sewing machine. There is nothing that hurts more than unintentional contact with a sewing machine. "Why in sixty don't you light a light, Eva? How can I——"

"Listen!" she whispered shrilly. "Hear that? Anderson, there's some one walkin' on the porch!"

" 'y gosh!" faltered he. "Sure as Christmas! You wait here, Eva, till I go upstairs an' put on my badge and I'll——"

"I'll do nothing of the kind. You don't ketch me stayin' down here alone," and she grabbed the back of his nightshirt as he started for the stairs.

"Sho! What air you afeerd of? I'll get my revolver, too. I never did see such a coward'y calf as——"

Just then there was a tremendous pounding on the front door, followed by the creaking of footsteps on the frozen porch, a clatter down the steps, and then the same old howling of the wind. The Crows jumped almost out of their scanty garments, and then settled down as if frozen to the spot. It was a full minute before Anderson found his voice—in advance of Mrs. Crow at that, which was more than marvellous.

"What was that?" he chattered.

"A knock!" she gasped.

"Some neighbour's sick."

"Old Mrs. Luce. Oh, goodness, how my heart's going!"

"Why don't you open the door, Eva?"

"Why don't you? It's your place."

"But, doggone it, cain't you see—I mean feel—that I ain't got hardly any clothes on? I'd ketch my death o' cold, an' besides——"

"Well, I ain't got as much on as you have. You got socks on an'——"

"But supposin' it's a woman," protested he. "You wouldn't want a woman to see me lookin' like this, would you? Go ahead an'——"

"I suppose you'd like to have a man see me like this. I ain't used to receivin' men in—but, say, whoever it was, is gone. Didn't you hear the steps? Open the door, Anderson. See what it is."

And so, after much urging, Anderson Crow unbolted his front door and turned the knob. The wind did the rest. It almost blew the door off its hinges, carrying Mr. and Mrs. Crow back against the wall. A gale of snow swept over them.

"Gee!" gasped Anderson, crimping his toes. Mrs. Crow was peering under his arm.

"Look there!" she cried. Close to the door a large bundle was lying.

"A present from some one!" speculated Mr. Crow; but some seconds passed before he stooped to pick it up. "Funny time fer Santy to be callin' 'round. Wonder if he thinks it's next Christmas."

"Be careful, Anderson; mebby it's an infernal machine!" cried his wife.

"Well, it's loaded, 'y ginger," he grunted as he straightened up in the face of the gale. "Shut the door, Eva! Cain't you see it's snowin'?"

"I'll bet it was Joe Ramsey leavin' a sack o' hickor' nuts fer us," she said eagerly, slamming the door.

"You better bolt the door. He might change his mind an' come back fer 'em," observed her husband. "It don't feel like hickor' nuts. Why, Eva, it's a baskit—a reg'lar clothes baskit. What in thunder do——"

"Let's get a light out by the kitchen fire. It's too cold in here."

Together they sped to the kitchen with the mysterious offering from the blizzard. There was a fire in the stove, which Anderson replenished, while Eva began to remove the blankets and packing from the basket, which she had placed on the hearth. Anderson looked on eagerly.

"Lord!" fell from the lips of both as the contents of the basket were exposed to their gaze.

A baby, alive and warm, lay packed in the blankets, sound asleep and happy. For an interminable length of time the Crows, *en dishabille,* stood and gazed open-mouthed and awed at the little stranger. Ten minutes later, after the ejaculations and surmises, after the tears and expletives, after the whole house had been aroused, Anderson Crow was plunging amiably but aimlessly through the snowstorm in search of the heartless wretch who had deposited the infant on his doorstep. His top boots scuttled up and down the street, through yards and barn lots for an

"A BABY, ALIVE AND WARM, LAY PACKED IN THE BLANKETS"

hour, but despite the fact that he carried his dark lantern and trailed like an Indian bloodhound, he found no trace of the wanton visitor. In the meantime, Mrs. Crow, assisted by the entire family, had stowed the infant, a six-weeks-old girl, into a warm bed, ministering to the best of her ability to its meagre but vociferous wants. There was no more sleep in the Crow establishment that night. The head of the house roused a half dozen neighbours from their beds

to tell them of the astounding occurrence, with the perfectly natural result that one and all hurried over to see the baby and to hear the particulars.

Early next morning Tinkletown wagged with an excitement so violent that it threatened to end in a municipal convulsion. Anderson Crow's home was besieged. The snow in his front yard was packed to an icy consistency by the myriad of footprints that fell upon it; the interior of the house was "tracked" with mud

and slush and three window panes were broken
by the noses of curious but unwelcome spectators.
Altogether, it was a sensation unequalled in the history of the village. Through it all the baby blinked
and wept and cooed in perfect peace, guarded by
Mrs. Crow and the faithful progeny who had been
left by the stork, and not by a mysterious stranger.

The missionary societies wanted to do something
heroic, but Mrs. Crow headed them off; the sewing
circle got ready to take charge of affairs, but Mrs.
Crow punctured the project; figuratively, the churches
ached for a chance to handle the infant, but Mrs.
Crow stood between. And all Tinkletown called
upon Anderson Crow to solve the mystery before it
was a day older.

"It's purty hard to solve a mystery that's got six
weeks' start o' me," said Anderson despairingly, "but
I'll try, you bet. The doggone thing's got a parent
or two somewhere in the universe, an' I'll locate 'em
er explode somethin'. I've got a private opinion
about it myself."

Whatever this private opinion might have been, it
was not divulged. Possibly something in connection
with it might have accounted for the temporary
annoyance felt by nearly every respectable woman in
Tinkletown. The marshal eyed each and every one
of them, irrespective of position, condition or age,
with a gleam so accusing that the Godliest of them
flushed and then turned cold. So knowing were these
equitable looks that before night every woman in the
village was constrained to believe the worst of her

neighbour, and almost as ready to look with suspicion upon herself.

One thing was certain—business was at a standstill in Tinkletown. The old men forgot their chess and checker games at the corner store; young men neglected their love affairs; women forgot to talk about each other; children froze their ears rather than miss any of the talk that went about the wintry streets; everybody was asking the question, "Whose baby is it?"

But the greatest sensation of all came late in the day when Mrs. Crow, in going over the garments worn by the babe, found a note addressed to Anderson Crow. It was stitched to the baby's dress, and proved beyond question that the strange visitor of the night before had selected not only the house, but the individual. The note was to the point. It said:

"February 18, 1883.

"ANDERSON CROW: To your good and merciful care an unhappy creature consigns this helpless though well-beloved babe. All the world knows you to be a tender, loving, unselfish man and father. The writer humbly, prayerfully implores you to care for this babe as you would for one of your own. It is best that her origin be kept a secret. Care for her, cherish her as your own, and at the end of each year the sum of a thousand dollars will be paid to you as long as she lives in your household as a member thereof. Do not seek to find her parents. It would be a fool's errand. May God bless you and yours, and may God care for and protect Rosalie—the name she shall bear."

Obviously, there was no signature and absolutely no clew to the identity of the writer. Two telegraph line repairers who had been working near Crow's house during the night, repairing damage done by the blizzard, gave out the news that they had seen a cloaked and mysterious-looking woman standing near the Methodist Church just before midnight, evidently disregarding the rage of the storm. The sight was so unusual that the men paused and gazed at her for several minutes. One of them was about to approach her when she turned and fled down the side street near by.

"Was she carryin' a big bundle?" asked Anderson Crow.

The men replied in the negative.

"Then she couldn't have been the party wanted. The one we're after certainly had a big bundle."

"But, Mr. Crow, isn't it possible that these men saw her after she left the basket at—" began the Presbyterian minister.

"That ain't the way I deduce it," observed the town detective tartly. "In the first place, she wouldn't 'a' been standin' 'round like that if the job was over, would she? Wouldn't she 'a' been streakin' out fer home? 'Course she would."

"She may have paused near the church to see whether you took the child in," persisted the divine.

"But she couldn't have saw my porch from the back end of the church."

"Nobody said she was standing back of the church," said the lineman.

"What's that? You don't mean it?" cried Anderson, pulling out of a difficulty bravely. "That makes all the difference in the world. Why didn't you say she was in front of the church? Cain't you see we've wasted time here jest because you didn't have sense 'nough to——"

"Anybody ought to know it 'thout being told, you old Rube," growled the lineman, who was from Boggs City.

"Here, now, sir, that will do you! I won't 'low no man to——"

"Anderson, be quiet!" cautioned Mrs. Crow. "You'll wake the baby!" This started a new train of thought in Anderson's perplexed mind.

"Mebby she was waitin' there while some one—her husband, fer instance—was leavin' the baskit," volunteered Isaac Porter humbly.

"Don't bother me, Ike; I'm thinkin' of somethin' else," muttered Anderson. "Husband nothin'! Do you s'pose she'd 'a' trusted that baby with a fool husband on a terrible night like that? Ladies and gentlemen, this here baby was left by a *female* resident of this very town." His hearers gasped and looked at him wide-eyed. "If she has a husband, he don't know he's the father of this here baby. Don't you see that a woman couldn't 'a' carried a heavy baskit any great distance? She couldn't 'a' packed it from Boggs City er New York er Baltimore, could she? She wouldn't 'a' been strong enough. No, siree; she didn't have far to come, folks. An' she was a woman, 'cause ain't all typewritin' done by women? You don't hear of men type-writers, do you? People wouldn't have 'em. Now, the thing fer me to do first is to make a house-to-house search to see if I c'n locate a typewritin' machine anywheres. Get out of the way, Toby. Dog-gone you boys, anyhow; cain't you see I want ter get started on this job?"

"Say, Anderson," said Harry Squires, the reporter, "I'd like to ask if there is any one in Tinkletown, male or female, who can afford to pay you a thousand dollars a year for taking care of that kid?"

"What's that?" slowly oozed from Anderson's lips.

"You heard what I said. Say, don't you know you can bring up a kid in this town for eleven or twelve dollars a year?"

"You don't know what you're talkin' about," burst from Anderson's indignant lips, but he found instant excuse to retire from the circle of speculators. A few minutes later he and his wife were surreptitiously re-reading the note, both filled with the fear that it said $10.00 instead of $1000.

CHAPTER VI

Reflection and Deduction

"By gum, it does say a thousand," cried Anderson, mightily relieved. "Harry Squires is a fool. He said jest now that it could be did fer eleven or twelve dollars. Don't you suppose, Eva, that the mother of this here child knows what it costs to bring 'em up? Of course she does. When I find her I'll prove it by her own lips that she knows. But don't bother me any more, Eva; I got to git out an' track her down. This is the greatest job I've had in years."

"See here, Anderson," said his wife thoughtfully and somewhat stealthily, "let's go slow about this thing. What do you want to find her for?"

"Why—why, doggone it, Eva, what air you talkin' about?" began he in amazement.

"Well, it's just this way: I don't think we can earn a thousand dollars a year easier than takin' care of this child. Don't you see? Suppose we keep her fer twenty years. That means twenty thousand dollars, don't it? It beats a pension all to pieces."

"Well, by ginger!" gasped Anderson, vaguely comprehending. "Fifty years would mean fifty thousand dollars, wouldn't it Gee whiz, Eva!"

"I don't imagine we can keep her that long."

"No," reflectively; "the chances are she'd want ter git married inside of that time. They always

" 'Tain't that, Anderson. You an' me'd have to live to be more'n a hundred years old."

"That's so. We ain't spring chickens, are we, deary?"

She put her hard, bony hand in his and there was a suspicion of moisture in the kindly old eyes.

"I love to hear you call me 'deary,' Anderson. We never get too old for that."

He coughed and then patted her hand rather confusedly. Anderson had long since forgotten the meaning of sentiment, but he was surprised to find that he had not forgotten how to love his wife.

"Shucks!" he muttered bravely. "We'll be kissin' like a couple of young jay birds first thing we know. Doggone if it ain't funny how a baby, even if it is some one else's, kinder makes a feller foolisher'n he intends to be." Hand in hand they watched the sleeping innocent for several minutes. Finally the detective shook himself and spoke:

"Well, Eva, I got to make a bluff at findin' out whose baby it is, ain't I? My reputation's at stake. I jest have to investigate."

"I don't see that any harm can come from that, Anderson," she replied, and neither appreciated the sarcasm unintentionally involved.

"I won't waste another minute," he announced promptly. "I will stick to my theory that the parents live in Tinkletown."

"Fiddlesticks!" snorted Mrs. Crow disgustedly, and then left him to cultivate the choleric anger her exclamation had inspired.

"Doggone, I wish I hadn't patted her hand," he lamented. "She didn't deserve it. Consarn it, a woman's always doin' something to spoil things."

And so he fared forth with his badges and stars, bent on duty, but not accomplishment. All the town soon knew that he was following a clew, but all the town was at sea concerning its character, origin, and plausibility. A dozen persons saw him stop young Mrs. Perkins in front of Lamson's store, and the same spectators saw his feathers droop as she let loose her wrath upon his head and went away with her nose in the air and her cheeks far more scarlet than when Boreas kissed them, and all in response to a single remark volunteered by the faithful detective. He entered Lamson's store a moment later, singularly abashed and red in the face.

"Doggone," he observed, seeing that an explanation was expected, "she might 'a' knowed I was only foolin'."

A few minutes later he had Alf Reesling, the town sot, in a far corner of the store talking to him in a most peremptory fashion. It may be well to mention that Alf had so far forgotten himself as to laugh at the marshal's temporary discomfiture at the hands of Mrs. Perkins.

"Alf, have you been havin' another baby up to your house without lettin' me know?" demanded Anderson firmly.

"Anderson," replied Alf, maudlin tears starting in his eyes, "it's not kind of you to rake up my feelin's like this.   You know I been a widower fer three years."

"I want you to understand one thing, Alf Reesling. A detective never *knows* anything till he proves it. Let me warn you, sir, you are under suspicion.   An' now, let me tell you one thing more.   Doggone your ornery hide, don't you ever laugh ag'in like you did jest now er I'll——"

Just then the door flew open with a bang and Edna Crow, Anderson's eldest, almost flopped into the store, her cap in her hand, eyes starting from her head.   She had run at top speed all the way from home.

"Pop," she gasped.   "Ma says fer you to hurry home! She says fer you to *run!*"

Anderson covered the distance between Lamson's store and his own home in record time.   Indeed, Edna, flying as fast as her slim legs could twinkle, barely beat her father to the front porch.   It was quite clear to Mr. Crow that something unusual had happened or Mrs. Crow would not have summoned him so peremptorily.

She was in the hallway downstairs awaiting his arrival, visibly agitated.   Before uttering a word she dragged him into the little sitting-room and closed the door.   They were alone.

"Is it dead?" he panted.

"No, but what do you think, Anderson?" she questioned excitedly.

"I ain't had time to think.   You don't mean to say it has begun to talk an' c'n tell who it is," he faltered.

"Heavens no—an' it only six weeks old."

"Well, then, what in thunder *has* happened?"

"A *detective* has been here."

"Good gosh!"

"Yes, a *real* detective. He's out there in the kitchen gettin' his feet warm by the bake-oven. He says he's lookin' for a six-weeks-old baby. Anderson, we're goin' to lose that twenty thousand."

"Don't cry, Eva; mebby we c'n find another baby some day. Has he seen the—the—it?" Anderson was holding to the stair-post for support.

"Not yet, but he says he understands we've got one here that ain't been *tagged*—that's what he said—'tagged.' What does he mean by that?"

"Why—why, don't you see? Just as soon as he tags it, it's *it*. Doggone, I wonder if it would make any legal difference if I tagged it first."

"He's a queer-lookin' feller, Anderson. Says he's in disguise, and he certainly looks like a regular scamp."

"I'll take a look at him an' ast fer his badge." Marshal Crow paraded boldly into the kitchen, where the strange man was regaling the younger Crows with conversation the while he partook comfortably of pie and other things more substantial.

"Are you Mr. Crow?" he asked nonchalantly, as Anderson appeared before him.

"I am. Who are you?"

"I am Hawkshaw, the detective," responded the man, his mouth full of blackberry pie.

"Gee whiz!" gasped Anderson. "Eva, it's the celebrated Hawkshaw."

"Right you are, sir. I'm after the kid."

"You'll have to identify it," something inspired Anderson to say.

"Sure. That's easy. It's the one that was left on your doorstep last night," said the man glibly.

"Well, I guess you're right," began Anderson disconsolately.

"Boy or girl?" demanded Mrs. Crow, shrewdly and very quickly. She had been inspecting the man more

closely than before, and woman's intuition was telling her a truth that Anderson overlooked. Mr. Hawkshaw was not only very seedy, but very drunk.

"Madam," he responded loftily, "it is nothing but a mere child."

"I'll give you jest one minute to get out of this house," said Mrs. Crow sharply, to Anderson's consternation. "If you're not gone, I'll douse you with this kettle of scalding water. Open the back door, Edna. He sha'n't take his dirty self through my parlour again. *Open that door, Edna!*"

Edna, half paralysed with astonishment, opened the kitchen door just in time. Mr. Hawkshaw was not so drunk but he could recognise disaster when it hovered near. As she lifted the steaming kettle from the stove he made a flying leap for the door. The rush of air that followed him as he shot through the aperture almost swept Edna from her feet. In ten seconds the tattered Hawkshaw was scrambling over the garden fence and making lively if inaccurate tracks through last year's cabbage patch.

CHAPTER VII

The Mysterious Visitor

THE entire Crow family watched him in stupefaction until he disappeared down the lane that led to Hapgood's grove. It was then, and not until then, that Anderson Crow took a breath.

"Good Lord, Eva, what do you mean?" he gasped.

"Mean?" she almost shrieked. "Anderson Crow, didn't you recognise that feller? He ain't no more detective than you er me. He's the self-same tramp that you put in the calaboose last week, and the week before, too. I thought I'd seen his ugly face before. He's——"

"Great jumpin' geeswax!" roared the town marshal. "I recollect him now. He's the one that said he'd been exposed to smallpox an' wanted to be kept where it was warm all winter. Well, I'll be—I'll be——"

"Don't say it, pa. He said it fer you when he clumb over that barb-wire fence out there," cried Edna gleefully.

Several days of anxiety and energy followed this interesting episode. In that time two tramps attempted to obtain food and shelter at Crow's home, one on the plea that he was the father of the unfortunate child, the other as an officer for the Foundlings' Home at Boggs City. Three babies were left on the doorstep—two in one night—their fond mothers confessing by letters that they appreciated Anderson's well-known charitable inclinations and implored him to care for their offspring as if they were his own. The harassed marshal experienced some difficulty in forcing the mothers to take back their children.

In each instance he was reviled by the estimable ladies, all of whom accused him of being utterly heartless. Mrs. Crow came to his rescue and told the disappointed mothers that the scalding water was ready for application if they did not take their baskets of babies away on short order. It may be well for the reputation of Tinkletown to mention that one of the donors was Mrs. Raspus, a negro washerwoman who did work for the "dagoes" engaged in building the railroad hard by; another was the wife of Antonio Galli, a member of the grading gang, and the third was Mrs. Pool, the widow of a fisherman who had recently drowned himself in drink.

It is quite possible that Anderson might have had the three infants on his hands permanently had not the mothers been so eager to know their fate. They appeared in person early the next morning to see if the babies had frozen to death on the doorstep. Mrs. Pool even went so far as to fetch some extra baby clothes which she had neglected to drop with her male. Mrs. Raspus came for her basket, claiming it was the only one she had in which to "tote" the washing for the men.

After these annoying but enlivening incidents Anderson was permitted to recover from his daze and to throw off symptoms of nervous prostration.

Tinkletown resumed its tranquil attitude and the checker games began to thrive once more. Little Rosalie was a week older than when she came, but it was five weeks before anything happened to disturb the even tenor of the foster-father's way. He had worked diligently in the effort to discover the parents of the baby, but without result. Two or three exasperated husbands in Tinkletown had threatened to blow his brains out if he persisted in questioning their wives in his insinuating manner, and one of the kitchen girls at the village inn threw a dishpan at him on the occasion of his third visit of inquiry. A colored woman in the employ of the Baptist minister denied that Rosalie was her child, but when he insisted, agreed with fine sarcasm to "go over an' have a look at it," after his assurance that it was perfectly white.

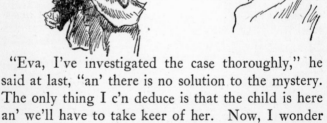

"Eva, I've investigated the case thoroughly," he said at last, "an' there is no solution to the mystery. The only thing I c'n deduce is that the child is here an' we'll have to take keer of her. Now, I wonder if that woman really meant it when she said we'd have a thousand dollars at the end of each year. Doggone, I wish the year was up, jest to see."

"We'll have to wait, Anderson, that's all," said Mrs. Crow. "I love the baby so it can't matter much. I'm glad you're through investigatin'. It's been most tryin' to me. Half the women in town don't speak to me."

It was at the end of Rosalie's fifth week as a member of the family that something happened. Late one night when Anderson opened the front door to put out the cat a heavily veiled woman mounted the steps and accosted him. In some trepidation he drew back and would have closed the door but for her eager remonstrance.

"I must see you, Mr. Crow," she cried in a low, agitated voice.

"Who are you?" he demanded. She was dressed entirely in black.

"I came to see you about the baby."

"That won't do, madam. There's been three tramps here to hornswoggle us an' I———"

"I *must* see her, Mr. Crow," pleaded the stranger, and he was struck by the richness of her voice.

"Mighty queer, it seems to me," he muttered hesitatingly. "Are you any kin to it?"

"I am very much interested."

"By giminy, I believe you're the one who left her here," cried the detective. "Are you a typewriter?"

"I'll answer your questions if you'll allow me to step inside. It is very cold out here."

Anderson Crow stood aside and the tall, black figure

entered the hall. He led her to the warm sitting-room and gave her a chair before the "base-burner."

"Here, Mr. Crow, is an envelope containing two hundred and fifty dollars. That proves my good faith. I cannot tell you who I am nor what relation I bear to the baby. I am quite fully aware that you will not undertake to detain me, for it is not an easy matter to earn a thousand dollars a year in this part of the world. I am going abroad next week and do not expect to return for a long, long time. Try as I would, I could not go without seeing the child. I will not keep you out of bed ten minutes, and you and your wife may be present while I hold Rosalie in my arms. I know that she is in good hands, and I have no intention of taking her away. Please call Mrs. Crow."

Anderson was too amazed to act at once. He began to flounder interrogatively, but the visitor abruptly checked him.

"You are wasting time, Mr. Crow, in attempting to question my authority or identity. No one need know that I have made this visit. You are perfectly secure in the promise to have a thousand dollars a year; why should you hesitate? As long as she lives with you the money is yours. I am advancing the amount you now hold in order that her immediate wants may be provided for. You are not required to keep an account of the money paid to you. There are means of ascertaining at once whether she is being well cared for and educated by you, and if it becomes apparent that you are not doing your duty, she shall be removed from your custody. From time to time you may expect written instructions from—from one who loves her."

"I jest want to ast if you live in Tinkletown?" Anderson managed to say.

"I do not," she replied emphatically.

"Well, then, lift your veil. If you don't live here I sha'n't know you."

"I prefer to keep my face covered, Mr. Crow; believe me and trust me. Please let me see her." The plea was so earnest that Anderson's heart gave a great thump of understanding.

"By ginger, you are her mother!" he gasped. Mrs. Crow came in at this juncture, and she was much quicker at grasping the situation than her husband. It was in her mind to openly denounce the woman for her heartlessness, but her natural thriftiness interposed. She would do nothing that might remove the golden spoon from the family mouth.

The trio stole upstairs and into the warm bedchamber. There, with Anderson Crow and his wife looking on from a remote corner of the room, the tall woman in black knelt beside the crib that had housed a generation of Crows. The sleeping Rosalie did not know of the soft kisses that swept her little cheek. She did not feel the tears that fell when the visitor lifted her veil, nor did she hear the whisperings that rose to the woman's lips.

"That is all," murmured the mysterious stranger at last, dropping her veil as she arose. She staggered as she started for the door, but recovered herself instantly. Without a word she left the room, the

Crows following her down the stairs in silence. At the bottom she paused, and then extended her hands to the old couple. Her voice faltered as she spoke.

"Let me clasp your hands and let me tell you that my love and my prayers are forever for you and for that little one up there. Thank you. I know you will be good to her. She is well born. Her blood is as good as the best. Above all things, Mrs. Crow, she is not illegitimate. You may easily suspect that her parents are wealthy or they could not pay so well for her care. Some day the mystery surrounding her will be cleared. It may not be for many years. I can safely say that she will be left in your care for twenty years at least. Some day you will know why it is that Rosalie is not supposed to exist. God bless you."

She was gone before they could utter a word. They watched her walk swiftly into the darkness; a few minutes later the sound of carriage wheels suddenly broke upon the air. Anderson Crow and his wife stood over the "base-burner," and there were tears in their thoughtful eyes.

"She said twenty years, Eva. Let's see, this is 1883. What would that make it?"

"About 1903 or 1904, Anderson."

"Well, I guess we c'n wait if other people can," mused he. Then they went slowly upstairs and to bed.

CHAPTER VIII

Some Years Go By

TINKLETOWN as a unit supported Anderson in his application for guardianship papers. They were filed immediately after the secret visit of the mysterious woman; the Circuit Court at Boggs City, after hearing the evidence, at once entered the appointment of Mr. Crow. When the court asked in mild surprise why he did not adopt the child, Anderson and Eva looked at each other sheepishly and were silent for a full minute. Then Anderson spoke up, a bit huskily: "Well, you see, judge, her name would have to be Crow, an' while it's a good name an' an honoured one, it don't jest seem to fit the young 'un. She 'pears to be more of a canary than a crow, figuratively speakin', an' Eva an' me jest decided we'd give her a different sort of a last name if we could find one. Seems to me that Rosie Canary would be a good one, but Eva an' the childern are ag'in me. They've decided to call her Rosalie Gray, an' I guess that about settles it. If you don't mind, I reckon that name c'n go in the records. Besides, you must recollect that she's liable to have a lot of property some time, an' it seems more fit fer me to be guardian than foster-father if that time ever comes. It'll be easier to say good-bye if she keers to leave us."

That same day Anderson deposited two hundred and

fifty dollars to his credit in the First National Bank, saying to his wife as he walked away from the teller's window, "I guess Rosalie cain't starve till the bank busts, an' maybe not then."

Of course Tinkletown knew that a sum of money had been paid to Anderson, but no one knew that it had been handed to him in person by an interested party. Had Anderson and his wife even whispered that such a visit had occurred, the town would have gone into a convulsion of wrath; the marshal's pedestal would have been jerked out from under him without compunction or mercy. Eva cautioned him to be more than silent on the subject for the child's sake as well as for their own, and Anderson saw wisdom in her counselling. He even lagged in his avowed intention to unravel the mystery or die in the attempt. A sharp reminder in the shape of an item in the *Banner* restored his energies, and he again took up the case with a vigour that startled even himself. Anything in the shape of vigour startled his wife.

Harry Squires, the reporter, who poked more or less fun at Anderson from time to time because he had the "power of the press behind him," some weeks later wrote the following item about the "baby mystery," as he called it, in large type:

"There is no news in regard to the child found upon the doorstep of our esteemed fellow-citizen, Anderson Crow, last February. The item concerning its discovery first appeared in the columns of the *Banner,* as will be remembered by our many readers.

Detective Crow promised developments some time ago, but they have not showed up. It is rumoured that he has a new clew, but it cannot be substantiated. The general impression is that he does not know whether it is a boy or girl. We advise Mr. Crow to go slow. He should not forget the time when he arrested Mr. John Barnes, two years ago, for the murder of Mr. Grover, and afterward found that the young gent was merely eloping with Judge Brewster's daughter, which was no crime. We saw the girl. Those of our readers who were alive at the time doubtless recall the excitement of that man-hunt two years ago. Mr. Barnes, as innocent as a child un-born, came to our little city engaged in the innocent pastime of getting married. At the same time it was reported that a murder had been committed in this county. Mr. Crow had his suspicions aroused and pursued Mr. Barnes down the river and arrested him. It was a fine piece of detective work. But, unfortu-nately for Mr. Crow, the real murderer had been caught in the meantime. Mr. Barnes was guilty only of stealing Judge Brewster's daughter and getting married to her. The last heard of them they were happy in New York. They even forgave Mr. Crow, it is reported. It is to be hoped that our clever de-tective will soon jump down upon the heartless parents of this innocent child, but it is also to be hoped that he think at least four times before he leaps."

To say that the foregoing editorial disturbed the evenness of Mr. Crow's temper would be saying nothing at all. In the privacy of his barn lot Ander-son did a war dance that shamed Tecumseh. He threatened to annihilate Harry Squires "from head to foot," for publishing the base slander.

"Doggone his hide," roared poor Anderson, "fer two cents I'd tell all I know about him bein' tight up at Boggs City three years ago.   He couldn't walk half an inch that time without staggerin'.   Anyhow, I wouldn't have chased Mr. Barnes that time if it hadn't been fer Harry Squires.   He egged me on, doggone his hide.   If he didn't have that big type-setter from Albany over at the *Banner* office to back him up I'd go over an' bust his snoot fer him.   After all the items I've give him, too.   That's all the thanks

you git fer gittin' up news fer them blamed reporters.
But I'll show him! I wonder what he'd think if I
traced that baby right up to his own—*What's* that,
Eva? Well, now, you don't know anything about it
neither, so keep your mouth shet. Harry Squires is a
purty sly cuss. Mebby it's his'n. You ain't supposed
to know. You jest let me do my own deducin'. I
don't want no blamed woman tellin' me who to
shadder. An' you, too, Edner; get out of the way,
consarn ye! The next thing *you'll* be tellin' me what
to do—an' me your father, too!"

And that is why Anderson Crow resumed his search
for the parents of Rosalie Gray. Not that he hoped
or expected to find them, but to offset the pernicious
influence of Harry's "item." For many days he followed the most highly impossible clews, some of them
intractable, to supply a rather unusual word of description. In other words, they reacted with a vigour
that often found him unprepared but serene. Conse-
quences bothered Anderson but little in those days of
despised activity.

It is not necessary to dwell upon the incidents of the
ensuing years, which saw Rosalie crawl from baby-
hood to childhood and then stride proudly through
the teens with a springiness that boded ill for Father
Time. Regularly each succeeding February there
came to Anderson Crow a package of twenty dollar
bills amounting to one thousand dollars, the mails
being inscrutable. The Crow family prospered cor-
respondingly, but there was a liberal frugality behind
it all that meant well for Rosalie when the time came

for an accounting. Anderson and Eva "laid by" a goodly portion of the money for the child, whom they loved as one of their own flesh and blood. The district school lessons were followed later on by a boarding-school education down State, and then came the finishing touches at Miss Brown's in New York.

Rosalie grew into a rare flower, as dainty as the rose, as piquant as the daisy. The unmistakable mark of the high bred glowed in her face, the fine traces of blue blood graced her every movement, her every tone and look. At the time that she, as well as every one else in Tinkletown, for that matter, was twenty years older than when she first came to Anderson's home, we find her the queen of the village, its one rich human possession, its one truly sophisticated inhabitant. Anderson Crow and his wife were so proud of her that they forgot their duty to their own offspring; but if the Crow children resented this it was not exhibited in the expressions of love and admiration for their foster-sister. Edna Crow, the eldest of the girls—Anderson called her "Edner"—was Rosalie's most devoted slave, while Roscoe, the twelve-year-old boy, who comprised the rear rank of Anderson's little army, knelt so constantly at her shrine that he fell far behind in his studies, and stuck to the third reader for two years.

Anderson had not been idle in all these years. He was fast approaching his seventieth anniversary, but he was not a day older in spirit than when we first made his acquaintance. True, his hair was thinner and whiter, and his whiskers straggled a little more carelessly than in other days, but he was as young and active as a youth of twenty. Hard times did not worry him, nor did domestic troubles. Mrs. Crow often admitted that she tried her best to worry him, but it was like "pouring water on a duck's back." He went blissfully on his way, earning encomiums for himself and honours for Tinkletown. There was no grave crime committed in the land that he did not have a well-defined scheme for apprehending the per-petrators. His "deductions" at Lamson's store never failed to draw out and hold large audiences, and no one disputed his theories in public. The fact that he was responsible for the arrest of various hog, horse, and chicken thieves from time to time, and for the continuous seizure of the two town drunkards, Tom Folly and Alf Reesling, kept his reputation untar-nished, despite the numerous errors of commission and omission that crept in between.

That Rosalie's mysterious friends—or enemies, it might have been—kept close and accurate watch over her was manifested from time to time. Once, when Anderson was very ill with typhoid fever, the package of bills was accompanied by an unsigned, type-written letter. The writer announced that Mr. Crow's state of health was causing some anxiety on Rosalie's account—the child was then six years old—and it was hoped that nothing serious would result. Another time the strange writer, in a letter from Paris, instructed Mr. Crow to send Rosalie to a cer-tain boarding school and to see that she had French, German, and music from competent instructors.

Again, just before the girl went to New York for her two years' stay in Miss Brown's school, there came a package containing $2500 for her own personal use. Rosalie often spoke to Anderson of this mysterious sender as the "fairy godmother"; but the old marshal had a deeper and more significant opinion.

Perhaps the most anxious period in the life of Anderson Crow came when Rosalie was about ten years old. A new sheriff had been elected in Bramble County, and he posed as a reformer. His sister taught school in Tinkletown, and Rosalie was her favourite. She took an interest in the child that was almost the undoing of Mr. Crow's prosperity. Imagining that she was befriending the girl, the teacher appealed to her brother, the sheriff, insisting that he do what he could to solve the mystery of her birth. The sheriff saw a chance to distinguish himself. He enlisted the help of an aggressive prosecuting attorney, also new, and set about to investigate the case.

The two officers of the law descended upon Tinkletown one day and began to ask peremptory questions. They went about it in such a high-handed, lordly manner that Anderson took alarm and his heart sank like lead. He saw in his mind's eye the utter collapse of all his hopes, the dashing away of his cup of leisure and the upsetting of the "fairy godmother's" plans. Pulling his wits together, he set about to frustrate the attack of the meddlers. Whether it was his shrewdness in placing obstacles in their way or whether he coerced the denizens into blocking the sheriff's investigation does not matter.

It is only necessary to say that the officious gentleman from Boggs City finally gave up the quest in disgust and retired into the oblivion usual to county officials who try to be progressive. It was many weeks, however, before Anderson slept soundly. He was once more happy in the consciousness that Rosalie had been saved from disaster and that he had done his duty by her.

"I'd like to know how them doggone jays from Boggs City expected to find out anything about that child when I hain't been able to," growled Mr. Crow in Lamson's store one night. "If they'll jest keep their blamed noses out of this affair I'll find out who her parents are some day. It takes time to trace down things like this. I guess I know what I'm doin', don't I, boys?"

"That's what you do, Anderson," said Mr. Lamson, as Anderson reached over and took a handful of licorice drops from the jar on the counter.

CHAPTER IX

The Village Queen

THE spring of 1903 brought Rosalie back to Tinkletown after her second and last year with Miss Brown in New York City. The sun seemed brighter, the birds sang more blithely, the flowers took on a new fragrance and the village spruced up as if Sunday was the only day in the week. The young men of the town trembled when she passed them by, and not a few of them grew thin and haggard for want of food and sleep, having lost both appetite and repose through a relapse in love. Her smile was the same as of yore, her cheery greetings the same, and yet the village swains stood in awe of this fine young aristocrat for days and days. Gradually it dawned upon them that she was human, after all, despite her New York training, and they slowly resumed the old-time manner of courting, which was with the eyes exclusively.

A few of the more venturesome—but not the more ardent—asked her to go walking, driving, or to the church "sociables," and there was a rivalry in town which threatened to upset commerce. There was no theatre in Tinkletown, but they delighted in her descriptions of the gorgeous play-houses in New York. The town hall seemed smaller than ever to them. The younger merchants and their clerks neglected business with charming impartiality, and trade was going to "rack and ruin" until Rosalie declined to marry George Rawlins, the minister's son. He was looked upon as the favoured one; but she refused him in such a decisive manner that all others lost hope and courage. It is on record that the day after George's *congé* Tinkletown indulged in a complete business somersault. Never before had there been such strict attention to customers; merchants and clerks alike settled down to the inevitable and tried to banish Rosalie's face from the cost tags and trading stamps of their dull, mercantile cloister. Even Tony Brink, the blacksmith's 'prentice, fell into the habits of industry, but with an absent-mindedness that got him kicked through a partition in the smithy when he attempted to shoe the fetlock of Mr. Martin's colt instead of its hoof.

The Crow family took on a new dignity. Anderson gave fifty dollars to the Foreign Missionary Society of the Presbyterian Church, claiming that a foreign education had done so much for his ward; and Mrs. Crow succeeded in holding two big afternoon teas before Rosalie could apply the check rein.

One night Anderson sat up until nearly ten o'clock— an unheard-of proceeding for him. Rosalie, with the elder Crow girls, Edna and Susie, had gone to protracted meeting with a party of young men and women. The younger boys and girls were in bed, and Mrs. Crow was yawning prodigiously. She never retired until Anderson was ready to do likewise. Suddenly it dawned upon her that he was unusually quiet and preoccupied. They were sitting on the moonlit porch.

"What's the matter, Anderson? Ain't you well?" she asked at last.

"No; I'm just thinkin'," he responded, rather dismally. "Doggone, I cain't get it out of my head, Eva."

"Can't get what out?"

"About Rosalie."

"Well, what about her?"

"That's jest like a woman—always fergittin' the most important things in the world. Don't you know that the twenty years is up?"

"Of course I know it, but 'tain't worryin' me any. She's still here, ain't she? Nobody has come to take her away. The thousand dollars came all right last February, didn't it? Well, what's the use worryin'?"

"Mebbe you're right, but I'm skeered to death fer fear some one will turn up an' claim her, er that a big estate will be settled, er somethin' awful like that. I don't mind the money, Eva; I jest hate to think of losin' her, now that she's such a credit to us. Besides, I'm up a stump about next year."

"Well, what happens then?"

"Derned if I know. That's what's worryin' me."

"I don't see why you——"

"Certainly you don't. You never do. I've got to do all the thinkin' fer this fambly. Next year she's twenty-one years old an' her own boss, ain't she? I ain't her guardeen after that, am I? What happens then, I'd like to know."

"You jest have to settle with the court, pay over to her what belongs to her and keep the thousand every spring jest the same. Her people, whoever they be, are payin' you fer keepin' her an' not her fer stayin' here. 'Tain't likely she'll want to leave a good home like this 'un, is it? Don't worry till the time comes, Anderson."

"That's jest the point. She's lived in New York an' she's got used to it. She's got fine idees; even her clothes seem to fit different. Now, do you s'pose that fine-lookin' girl with all her New York trimmin's 's goin' to hang 'round a fool little town like this? Not much! She's goin' to dig out o' here as soon 's she gits a chance; an' she's goin' to live right where her heart tells her she belongs—in the metropolees of New York. She don't belong in no jim-crow town like this. Doggone, Eva, I hate to see 'er go!"

There was such a wail of bitterness in the old constable's remark that Mrs. Crow felt the tears start to her own eyes. It was the girl they both wanted, after all—not the money. Rosalie, coming home with her party some time afterward, found the old couple still seated on the porch. The young people could not conceal their surprise.

"Counting the stars, pop?" asked Edna Crow.

"He's waiting for the eclipse," bawled noisy Ed Higgins, the grocer's clerk. "It's due next winter. H'are you, Anderson?"

"How's that?" was Anderson's rebuke.

"I mean Mr. Crow," corrected Ed, with a nervous

glance at Rosalie, who had been his companion for the evening.

"Oh, I'm jest so-so," remarked Anderson, mollified. "How was the party?"

"It wasn't a party, Daddy Crow," laughed Rosalie, seating herself in front of him on the porch rail. "It was an experience meeting. Alf Reesling has reformed again. He told us all about his last attack of delirium tremens."

"You don't say so! Well, sir, I never thought Alf could find the time to reform ag'in. He's too busy gittin' tight," mused Anderson. "But I guess reformin' c'n git to be as much a habit as anythin' else."

"I think he was a little woozy to-night," ventured 'Rast Little.

"A little what?"

"Drunk," explained 'Rast, without wasting words. 'Rast had acquired the synonym at the business men's carnival in Boggs City the preceding fall. Sometimes he substituted the words "pie-eyed," "skeed," "lit up," etc., just to show his worldliness.

After the young men had departed and the Crow girls had gone upstairs with their mother Rosalie slipped out on the porch and sat herself down upon the knee of her disconsolate guardian.

"You are worried about something, Daddy Crow," she said gently. "Now, speak up, sir. What is it?"

"It's time you were in bed," scolded Anderson, pulling his whiskers nervously.

"Oh, I'm young, daddy. I don't need sleep. But you never have been up as late as this since I've known you."

"I was up later'n this the time you had the whoopin'-cough, all right."

"What's troubling you, daddy?"

"Oh, nothin'—nothin' at all. Doggone, cain't a man set out on his own porch 'thout——"

"Forgive me, daddy. Shall I go away and leave you?"

"Gosh a'mighty, no!" he gasped. "That's what's worryin' me—oh, you didn't mean forever. You jest meant to-night? Geminy crickets, you did give me a skeer!" He sank back with a great sigh of relief.

"Why, I never expect to leave you forever," she cried, caressing his scanty hair. "You couldn't drive me away. This is home, and you've been too good to me all these years. I may want to travel after a while, but I'll always come back to you, Daddy Crow."

"I'm—I'm mighty glad to hear ye say that, Rosie. Ye see—ye see, me an' your ma kinder learned to love you, an'—an'——"

"Why, Daddy Crow, you silly old goose! You're almost crying!"

"What's that? Now, don't talk like that to me, you little whipper-snapper, er you go to bed in a hurry. I never cried in my life," growled Anderson in a great bluster.

"Well, then, let's talk about something else—me, for instance. Do you know, Daddy Crow, that I'm too strong to live an idle life. There is no reason why I shouldn't have an occupation. I want to work —accomplish something."

Anderson was silent a long time collecting his nerves.

"You wouldn't keer to be a female detective, would you?" he asked drily.

CHAPTER X

Rosalie Has Plans of Her Own

"Do be serious, daddy. I want to do something worth while. I could teach school or——"

"Not much! You ain't cut out fer that job. Don't you know that ever'body hates school-teachers when they're growed up? Jerusalem, how I still hate old Rachel Kidwell! An' yet she's bin dead nigh onto thirty years. She was my first teacher. You wasn't born to be hated by all the boys in the district. I don't see what put the idee of work inter your head You got 'bout eight thousand dollars in the bank an'——"

"But I insist that the money is yours, daddy. My fairy godmother paid it to you for keeping, clothing, and educating me. It is not mine."

"You talk like I was a boardin' school instead o' bein' your guardeen. No, siree; it's your money, an' that ends it. You git it when you're twenty-one."

"We'll see, daddy," she replied, a stubborn light in her dark eyes. "But I want to learn to do something worth while. If I had a million it would be just the same."

"You'll have something to do when you git married," observed he sharply.

"Nonsense!"

"I s'pose you're goin' to say you never expect to

git married. They all say it—an' then take the first feller 'at comes along."

"I didn't take the first, or the second, or the third, or the——"

"Hold on! Gosh a'mighty, have you had that many? Well, why don't you go into the matrimonial agent's business? That's an occupation."

"Oh, none of them was serious, daddy," she said naïvely.

"You could have all of the men in the county!" he declared proudly. "Only," he added quickly, "it wouldn't seem jest right an' proper."

"There was a girl at Miss Brown's a year ago who had loads of money, and yet she declared she was going to have an occupation. Nobody knew much about her or why she left school suddenly in the middle of a term. I liked her, for she was very nice to me when I first went there, a stranger. Mr. Reddon—you've heard me speak of him—was devoted to her, and I'm sure she liked him. It was only yesterday I heard from her. She is going to teach school in this township next winter."

"An' she's got money?"

"I am sure she had it in those days. It's the strangest thing in the world that she should be coming here to teach school in No. 5. Congressman Ritchey secured the appointment for her, she says. The township trustee—whatever his name is—for a long time insisted that he must appoint a teacher from Tinkletown and not an outsider. I am glad she is coming here because—well, daddy, because she is like the girls I knew in the city. She has asked me to look up a boarding place for next winter. Do you know of any one, daddy, who could let her have a nice room?"

"I'll bet my ears you'd like to have your ma take her in right here. But I don't see how it c'n be done, Rosie-posie. There's so derned many of us now, an'——"

"Oh, I didn't mean that, daddy. She couldn't come here. But don't you think Mrs. Jim Holabird would take her in for the winter?"

"P'raps. She's a widder. She might let her have Jim's room now that there's a vacancy. You might go over an' ast her about it to-morrer. It's a good thing she's a friend of yourn, Rosalie, because if she wasn't I'd have to fight her app'intment."

"Why, daddy!" reproachfully.

"Well, she's a foreigner, an' I don't think it's right to give her a job when we've got so many home products that want the place an' who look unpopular enough to fill the bill. I'm fer home industry every time, an' 'specially as this girl don't appear to need the place. I don't see what business Congressman Ritchey has foolin' with our school system anyhow. He'd better be reducin' the tariff er increasin' the pensions down to Washington."

"I quite agree with you, Daddy Crow," said Rosalie with a diplomacy that always won for her. She knew precisely how to handle her guardian, and that was why she won where his own daughters failed. "And now, good-night, daddy. Go to bed and don't worry about me. You'll have me on your hands much longer than you think or want. What time is it?"

Anderson patted her head reflectively as he solemnly drew his huge silver time-piece from an unlocated pocket. He held it out into the bright moonlight.

"Geminy crickets!" he exclaimed. "It's forty-nine minutes to twelve!" Anderson Crow's policy was to always look at things through the small end of the telescope.

The slow, hot summer wore away, and to Rosalie it was the longest that she ever had experienced. She was tired of the ceaseless twaddle of Tinkletown, its flow of "missions," "sociables," "buggy-horses," "George Rawlin's new dress-suit," "harvesting," and

"politics"—for even the children talked politics. Nor did the assiduous attentions of the village young men possess the power to shorten the days for her—

and they certainly lengthened the nights. She liked them because they were her friends from the beginning—and Rosalie was not a snob. Not for the world would she have hurt the feelings of one poor, humble, adoring soul in Tinkletown; and while her smile was none the less sweet, her laugh none the less joyous, in her heart there was the hidden longing that smiled only in dreams. She longed for the day that was to bring Elsie Banks to live with Mrs. Holabird, for with her would come a breath of the world she had known for two years, and which she had learned to love so well.

In three months seven men had asked her to marry them. Of the seven, one only had the means or the prospect of means to support her. He was a grass-widower with five grown children. Anderson took occasion to warn her against widowers.

"Why," he said, "they're jest like widders. You know Dave Smith that runs the tavern down street, don't you? Well, doggone ef he didn't turn in an' marry a widder with seven childern an' a husband, an' he's led a dog's life ever sence."

"Seven children and a husband? Daddy Crow!"

"Yep. Her derned husband wouldn't stay divorced when he found out Dave could support a fambly as big as that. He figgered it would be jest as easy to take keer of eight as seven, so he perlitely attached hisself to Dave's kitchen an' started in to eat hisself to death. Dave was goin' to have his wife apply fer another divorce an' leave the name blank, so's he could put in either husband ef it came to a pinch, but

I coaxed him out of it. He finally got rid of the feller by askin' him one day to sweep out the office. He could eat all right, but it wasn't natural fer him to work, so he skipped out. Next I heerd of him he had married a widder who was gittin' a pension because her first husband fit fer his country. The Government shet off the pension jest as soon as she got married ag'in, and then that blamed cuss took in washin' fer her. He stayed away from home on wash-days, but as every day was wash-day with her, he didn't see her by daylight fer three years. She died, an' now he's back at Dave's ag'in. He calls Dave his husband-in-law."

It required all of Anderson's social and official diplomacy to forestall an indignation meeting when it was announced that a stranger, Miss Banks, had been selected to teach school No. 5. There was some talk of mobbing the township trustee and Board of County Commissioners, but Anderson secured the names of the more virulent talkers and threatened to "jail" them for conspiracy.

"Why, Anderson," almost wailed George Ray, "that girl's from the city. What does she know about grammar an' history an' all that? They don't teach anything but French an' Italian in the cities an' you know it."

"Pshaw!" sniffed Anderson. "I hate grammar an' always did. I c'n talk better Italian than grammar right now, an' I hope Miss Banks will teach every child in the district how to talk French. You'd orter hear Rosalie talk it. Besides, Rosie says she's a nice

"SEPTEMBER BROUGHT ELSIE BANKS"

girl an'—an' needs the job." Anderson lied bravely, but he swallowed twice in doing it.

September brought Elsie Banks to make life worth living for Rosalie. The two girls were constantly together, talking over the old days and what the new ones were to bring forth, especially for Miss Gray, who had resumed wood carving as a temporary occupation. Miss Banks was more than ever reluctant to discuss her own affairs, and Rosalie after a few trials was tactful enough to respect her mute appeal. It is doubtful if either of the girls mentioned the name of big, handsome Tom Reddon—Tom, who had rowed in his college crew; but it is safe to say that both of them thought of him more than once those long, soft, autumn nights—nights when Tinkletown's beaux were fairly tumbling over themselves in the effort to make New York life seem like a flimsy shadow in comparison.

CHAPTER XI

Elsie Banks

ANDERSON CROW stood afar off—among the bleak, leafless trees of Badger's Grove—and gazed thoughtfully, even earnestly, upon the little red schoolhouse with its high brick chimney and snow-clad roof. A biting January wind cut through his whiskers and warmed his nose to a half-broiled shade of red. On the lapel of his overcoat glistened his social and official badges, augmented by a new and particularly shiny emblem of respect bestowed by the citizens of Tinkletown.

At first it had been the sense of the town to erect a monument in recognition of his part in the capture of the Bramble County horse-thief gang, but a thrifty and considerate committee of five substituted a fancy gold badge with suitable inscriptions on both sides, extolling him to the skies "long before he went there hisself" (to quote Uncle Gideon Luce, whose bump of perception was a stubborn prophet when it came to picking out the site of Mr. Crow's heaven). For a full half hour the marshal of Tinkletown had been standing among the trees surveying the schoolhouse at the foot of the slope. If his frosted cheeks and watery eyes ached for the warmth that urged the curls of smoke to soar away from the chimney-top, his attitude did not betray the fact. He was watching and thinking, and when Anderson thought of one thing he never thought of another at the same time.

"It'll soon be recess time," he reflected. "Then I'll step down there an' let on to be makin' a social call on the schoolma'am. By gum, I believe she's the one! It'll take some tarnation good work to find out the truth about her, but I guess I c'n do it all right. The only thing I got to guard ag'inst is lettin' anybody else know of the mystery surroundin' her. Gosh! it'll surprise some of the folks 'round here, 'specially Rosalie. An' mebby the township trustee won't be sorry he give the school this year to a strange girl instid o' to Jane Rankin er Effie Dickens! Congressman Ritchey hadn't no business puttin' his nose into our affairs anyhow, no matter if this here teacher is a friend of his fambly. He's got some kind a holt on these here trustees—'y gosh, I'd like to know what 'tis. He c'n jest wrap 'em round his finger an' make 'em app'int anybody he likes. Must be politics. There, it's recess! I'll jest light out an' pay the schoolhouse a little visit."

Inside a capacious and official pocket of Mr. Crow's coat reposed a letter from a law firm in Chicago. It asked if within the last two years a young woman had applied for a position as teacher in the township schools at Tinkletown. A description accompanied the inquiry, but it was admitted she might have applied under a name not her own, which was Marion Lovering. In explanation, the letter said she had left her home in Chicago without the consent of her aunt, imbued with the idea that she would sooner support herself than depend upon the charity of that worthy though wealthy relative. The aunt had recently died, and counsel for the estate was trying to establish proof concerning the actions and whereabouts of Miss Lovering since her departure from Chicago.

The young woman often had said she would become a teacher, a tutor, a governess, or a companion, and it was known that she had made her way to that section of the world presided over by Anderson Crow— although the distinguished lawyers did not put it in those words. A reward of five hundred dollars for positive information concerning the "life of the girl" while in "that or any other community" was promised.

Miss Banks's appointment came through the agency of the district's congressman, in whose home she had acted as governess for a period. Moreover, she answered the description in that she was young, pretty, and refined. Anderson Crow felt that he was on the right track; he was now engaged in as pretty a piece of detective business as had ever fallen to his lot, and he was not going to spoil it by haste and over-confidence.

Just why Anderson Crow should "shadow" the schoolhouse instead of the teacher's temporary place of abode no one could possibly have known but himself—and it is doubtful if *he* knew. He resolved not to answer the Chicago letter until he was quite ready to produce the girl and the proof desired.

"I'd be a gol-swiggled fool to put 'em onter my

s'picions an' then have 'em cheat me out of the reward," he reflected keenly. "You cain't trust them Chicago lawyers an inch an' a half. Doggone it, I'll never fergit that feller who got my pockit-book out to Central Park that time. He tole me positively he was a lawyer from Chicago, an' had an office in the Y. M. C. A. Building. An' the idee of him tellin' me he wanted to see if my pockit-book had better leather in it than hisn!"

The fact that the school children, big and little, loved Miss Banks possessed no point of influence over their elders of the feminine persuasion. They turned up their Tinkletown noses and sniffed at her because she was a "vain creature," who thought more of "attractin' the men than she did of anything else on earth." And all this in spite of the fact that she was the intimate friend of the town goddess, Rosalie Gray.

Everybody in school No. 5 over the age of seven was deeply, jealously in love with Miss Banks. Many a frozen snowball did its deadly work from ambush because of this impotent jealousy.

But the merriest rivalry was that which developed between Ed Higgins, the Beau Brummel of Tinkletown, and 'Rast Little, whose father owned the biggest farm in Bramble County. If she was amused by the frantic efforts of each suitor to outwit the other she was too tactful to display her emotion. Perhaps she was more highly entertained by the manner in which Tinkletown femininity paired its venom with masculine admiration.

"Mornin', Miss Banks," was Anderson's greeting

as he stamped nois-
ily into the room.
He forgot that he
had said good-
morning to her
when she stopped
in to see Rosalie on
her way to the
schoolhouse. The
children c e a s e d
their outdoor game
and peered eagerly
through the win-
d o w s, conscious
that the visit of
this dignitary was
of supreme impor-
tance. Miss Banks
looked up from
the papers she was correcting, the pucker vanishing
from her pretty brow as if by magic.

"Good-morning, Mr. Crow. What are you doing
away out here in the country? Jimmy"—to a small
boy—"please close the door." Anderson had left it
open, and it was a raw January wind which followed
him into the room.

" 'Scuse me," he murmured. "Seems I ain't got sense
enough to shet a door even. My wife says—but you
don't keer to hear about that, do you? Oh, I jest
dropped in," finally answering her question. He took
a bench near the big stove and spread his hands before

the sheet-iron warmth. "Lookin' up a little affair, that's all. Powerful chilly, ain't it?"

"Very." She stood on the opposite side of the stove, puzzled by this unexpected visit, looking at him with undisguised curiosity.

"Ever been to Chicago?" asked Anderson suddenly, hoping to catch her unawares.

"Oh, yes. I have lived there," she answered readily. He shifted his legs twice and took a hasty pull at his whiskers.

"That's what I thought. Why don't you go back there?"

"Because I'm teaching school here, Mr. Crow."

"Well, I reckon that's a good excuse. I thought mebby you had a different one."

"What do you mean?"

"Oh, I dunno. I jest asked."

"You are a detective, are you not?" asked Miss Banks, smiling brightly and with understanding.

"Oh, off an' on I do a little detectin'. See my badge?"

"Am I suspected of a heinous crime?" she asked so abruptly that he gasped. "Won't you take off your cap, Mr. Crow?" He removed it sheepishly.

"Lord, no!" he exclaimed in confusion. "I mean the crime—not the cap. Well, I guess I'll be goin'. School's goin' to take up, I reckon. See you later, Miss Banks." He restored his cap to its accustomed place and was starting toward the door, a trifle dazed and bewildered.

"What is it that you wish to find out, Mr. Crow?" she suddenly called to him. He halted and faced about so quickly that his reply came like a shot out of a gun.

"I'm on the lookout fer a girl—an' she'll be 's rich 's Crowses if I c'n only find 'er. I dassent tell 'er name jest now," he went on, slowly retracing his steps, " 'cause I don't want people—er her either, fer that matter—to git onter my scheme. But you jest wait." He was standing very close to her now and looking her full in the face. "You're sure you don't know anythin' 'bout her?"

"Why, how should I know? You've told me nothing."

"You've got purty good clothes fer a common school-teacher," he flung at her in an aggressive, impertinent tone, but the warm colour that swiftly rose to her cheeks forced him to recall his words, for he quickly tempered them with, "Er, at least, that's what all the women folks say."

"Oh, so some one has been talking about my affairs? Some of your excellent women want to know more about me than——"

"Don't git excited, Miss Banks," he interrupted; "the women ain't got anythin' to do with it—I mean, it's nothin' to them. I——"

"Mr. Crow," she broke in, "if there is anything you or anybody in Tinkletown wants to know about me you will have to deduce it for yourself. I believe that is what you call it—deduce? And now good-bye, Mr. Crow. Recess is over," she said pointedly; and Mr. Crow shuffled out as the children galloped in.

That evening Ed Higgins and 'Rast Little came to call, but she excused herself because of her correspondence. In her little upstairs room she wrote letter after letter, one in particular being voluminous. Mrs. Holabird, as she passed her door, distinctly heard her laugh aloud. It was a point to be recalled afterward with no little consideration. Later she went downstairs, cloaked warmly, for a walk to the post-office.

Ed Higgins was still in the parlour talking to the family. He hastily put in his petition to accompany her, and it was granted absently. Then he surreptitiously and triumphantly glanced through the window, the scene outside pleasing him audibly. 'Rast was standing at the front gate talking to Anderson Crow. Miss Banks noticed as they passed the confused twain at the gate that Anderson carried his dark lantern.

"Any trace of the heiress, Mr. Crow?" she asked merrily.

"Doggone it," muttered Anderson, "she'll give the whole snap away!"

"What's that?" asked 'Rast.

"Nothin' much," said Anderson, repairing the damage. "Ed's got your time beat to-night, 'Rast, that's all!"

"I could 'a' took her out ridin' to-night if I'd wanted to," lied 'Rast promptly. "I'm goin' to take her to the spellin'-bee to-morrow night out to the school-house."

"Did she say she'd go with you?"

"Not yet. I was jest goin' to ast her to-night."

"Mebby Ed's askin' her now."

"Gosh dern it, that's so! Maybe he is," almost wailed 'Rast; and Anderson felt sorry for him as he ambled away from the gate and its love-sick guardian.

CHAPTER XII

The Spelling-Bee

YOUNG Mr. Higgins found his companion bubbling over with vivacity. Her pretty chin was in the air and every word bore the promise of a laugh. He afterward recalled one little incident of their walk through the frosty night, and repeated it to Anderson Crow with more awe than seemed necessary. They were passing the town pump on their way to the post-office. The street was dark and deserted.

"Gosh!" said Ed, "I bet the town pump's froze up!"

"It doesn't seem very cold," she said brightly.

"Gee! it's below zero! I bet 'Rast thinks it's pretty doggone cold up there by your gate."

"Poor 'Rast! His mother should keep him indoors on nights like this." Ed laughed loud and long and a tingle of happiness shot through his erstwhile shivering frame. "I'm not a bit cold," she went on. "See—feel my hand. I'm not even wearing mittens."

Ed Higgins gingerly clasped the little hand, but it was withdrawn at once. He found it as warm as toast. Words of love surged to his humble lips; his knees felt a tendency to lower themselves precipitously to the frozen sidewalk; he was ready to grovel at her feet—and he wondered if they were as warm as toast. But 'Rast Little came up at that instant and the chance was lost.

"Doggone!" slipped unconsciously but bitterly from Ed's lips.

"Can I be your company to the spellin'-bee to-morrow night, Miss Banks?" burst unceremoniously from the lips of the newcomer.

"Thank you, 'Rast. I was just wondering how I should get out to the schoolhouse. You are very kind. We'll go in the bob-sled with the Holabirds."

"Doggone!" came in almost a wail from poor Ed. He could have killed 'Rast for the triumphant laugh that followed.

In the meantime Anderson Crow was preparing to crawl in between the icy sheets at home. Mrs Crow was "sitting up" with old Mrs. Luce, who was ill next door.

"She's a girl with a past," reflected Anderson. "She's

a mystery, that's what she is; but I'll unravel her. She had a mighty good reason fer sawin' me off out there to-day. I was gittin' too close home. She seen I was about to corner her. By gum, I hope she don't suspect nothin'! She's found out that Ed Higgins has a good job down to Lamson's store, an' she's settin' her cap fer him. It shows she'd ruther live in the city than in the country—so it's all up with 'Rast. That proves she's from Chicago er some other big place. Ed's gettin' eight dollars a week down there at Lamson's. By gum, that boy's doin' well! I used to think he wouldn't amount to nothin'. It shows that the best of us git fooled in a feller once in a while. To-morrow night I'll go out to the spellin'-match, an' when the chanct comes I'll sidle up to her an' whisper her real name in her ear. I bet four dollars an' a half that'll fetch her purty prompt. Doggone, these here sheets air cold! It's forty below zero right here in this bed."

Anderson Crow soon slept, but he did not dream of the tragedy the next night was to bring upon Tinkletown, nor of the test his prowess was to endure.

The next night and the "spellin'-bee" at school No. 5 came on apace together. It was bitterly cold and starlight. By eight o'clock the warm schoolhouse was comfortably filled with the "spellers" of the neighbourhood, their numbers increased by competitors from Tinkletown itself. In the crowd were men and women who time after time had "spelled down" whole companies, and who were eager for the conflict. They had "studied up" on their spelling for days in anticipation of a hard battle in the words. Mrs. Borum and Mrs. Cartwill, both famous for their victories and for the rivalry that existed between them, were selected as captains of the opposing sides, and Miss Banks herself was to "give out" the words. The captains selected their forces, choosing alternately from the anxious crowd of grown folks. There were no children there, for it was understood that big words would be given out—words children could not pronounce, much less spell.

The teacher was amazingly pretty on this eventful night. She was dressed as no other woman in Bramble County, except Rosalie Gray, could have attired herself—simply, tastefully, daintily. Her face was flushed and eager and the joy of living glowed in every feature. Ed Higgins and 'Rast Little were struck senseless, nerveless by this vision of health and loveliness. Anderson Crow stealthily admitted to himself that she was a stranger in a strange land; she was not of Tinkletown or any place like it.

Just as the captains were completing their selections of spellers the door opened and three strangers entered the school-room, overcoated and furred to the tips of their noses—two men and a woman. As Miss Banks rushed forward to greet them—she had evidently been expecting them—the startled assemblage caught its breath and stared. To the further amazement of every one, Rosalie hastened to her side and joined in the effusive welcome. Every word of joyous greeting was heard by the amazed listeners and every word from the strangers was as distinct. Surely

"THE TEACHER WAS AMAZINGLY PRETTY ON THIS EVENTFUL NIGHT"

the newcomers were friends of long standing. When their heavy wraps were removed the trio stood forth before as curious an audience as ever sat spellbound. The men were young, well dressed and handsome; the woman a beauty of the most dashing type. Tinkletown's best spellers quivered with excitement.

"Ladies and gentlemen," said Miss Banks, her voice trembling with eagerness, "let me introduce my friends, Mrs. Farnsworth, Mr. Farnsworth, and Mr. Reddon. They have driven over to attend the spelling-match." Ed Higgins and 'Rast Little observed with sinking hearts that it was Mr. Reddon whom she led forward by the hand, and they cursed him inwardly for the look he gave her—because she blushed beneath it.

"You don't live in Boggs City," remarked Mr. Crow, appointing himself spokesman. "I c'n deduce that, 'cause you're carrying satchels an' valises."

"Mr. Crow is a famous detective," explained Miss Banks. Anderson attempted to assume an unconscious pose, but in leaning back he missed the end of the bench, and sat sprawling upon the lap of Mrs. Harbaugh. As Mrs. Harbaugh had little or no lap to speak of, his downward course was diverted but not stayed. He landed on the floor with a grunt that broke simultaneously with the lady's squeak; a fraction of a second later a roar of laughter swept the room. It was many minutes before quiet was restored and the "match" could be opened. Mrs. Cartwill chose Mrs. Farnsworth and her rival selected the husband of the dashing young woman. Mr. Reddon firmly and significantly announced his determination to sit near the teacher "to preserve order," and not enter the contest of words.

Possibly it was the presence of the strangers that rattled and unnerved the famed spellers of both sides,

for it was not long until the lines had dwindled to almost nothing.   Three or four arrogant competitors stood forth and valiantly spelled such words as "Popocatepetl," "Tschaikowsky," "terpsichorean," "Yangtse-Kiang," "Yseult," and scores of words that could scarcely be pronounced by the teacher herself.   But at last, just as the sleepy watchers began to nod and yawn the hardest, Mrs. Cartwill stood alone and victorious, her single opponent having gone down on the word "sassafras." Anderson Crow had "gone down" early in the match by spelling "kerosene" "kerry-seen." Ed Higgins followed with "ceriseen," and 'Rast Little explosively had it "coal-oil."

During the turmoil incident to the dispersing of the gathered hosts Miss Banks made her way to 'Rast Little's side and informed him that the Farnsworths were to take her to Mrs. Holabird's in their big sleigh. 'Rast was floored. When he started to remonstrate, claiming to be her "company," big Tom Reddon interposed and drew Miss Banks away from her lover's wrath.

"But I'm so sorry for him, Tom," she protested contritely. "He *did* bring me here—in a way."

"Well, I'll take you home another way," said good-looking Mr. Reddon. It was also noticed that Rosalie Gray had much of a confidential nature to say to Miss Banks as they parted for the evening, she to go home in Blucher Peabody's new sleigh.

'Rast and Ed Higgins almost came to blows out at the "hitch-rack," where the latter began twitting his discomfited rival. Anderson Crow kept them apart.

"I'll kill that big dude," growled 'Rast. "He's got no business comin' here an' rakin' up trouble between me an' her. You mark my words, I'll fix him before the night's over, doggone his hide!"

At least a dozen men, including Alf Reesling, heard this threat, and not one of them was to forget it soon. Anderson Crow noticed that Mrs. Holabird's bob-sled drove away without either Miss Banks or 'Rast

Little in its capacious depths.' Miss Banks announced that her three friends from the city and she would stay behind and close the schoolhouse, putting everything in order. It was Friday night, and there would be no session until the following Monday. Mr. Crow was very sleepy for a detective. He snored all the way home.

The next morning two farmers drove madly into Tinkletown with the astounding news that some one had been murdered at schoolhouse No. 5. In passing the place soon after daybreak they had noticed blood on the snow at the roadside. The school-room door was half open and they entered. Blood in great quantities smeared the floor near the stove, but there was no sign of humanity, alive or dead. Miss Banks's handkerchief was found on the floor saturated.

Moreover, the school-teacher was missing. She had not returned to the home of Mrs. Holabird the night before. To make the horror all the more ghastly, Anderson Crow, hastening to the schoolhouse, positively identified the blood as that of Miss Banks.

CHAPTER XIII

A Tinkletown Sensation

SENSATIONS came thick and fast in Tinkletown during the next few hours. Investigation proved that
'Rast Little was nowhere to be found. He had not
returned to his home after the spelling-bee, nor had
he been seen since. Mrs. Holabird passed him in the
road on her way home in the "bob-sled." In response
to her command to "climb in" he sullenly said he
was going to walk home by a "short cut" through the
woods. A farmer had seen the stylish Farnsworth
sleigh driving north furiously at half-past eleven, the
occupants huddled in a bunch as if to protect themselves from the biting air. The witness was not able
to tell "which was which" in the sleigh, but he added
interest to the situation by solemnly asserting that one
of the persons in the rear seat was "bundled up" more
than the rest, and evidently was unable to sit erect.

According to his tale, the figure was lying over
against the other occupant of the seat. He was also,
positive that there were three figures in the front seat!
Who was the extra person? was the question that
flashed into the minds of the listeners. A small boy
came to the schoolhouse at nine o'clock in the morning with 'Rast Little's new derby hat. He had picked
it up at the roadside not far from the schoolhouse and
in the direction taken by the Farnsworth party.

Anderson gave orders that no word of the catastrophe be carried to Rosalie, who was reported to be

ill of a fever the next morning after the spelling-bee. She had a cough, and the doctor had said that nothing should be said or done to excite her.

The crowd at the schoolhouse grew larger as the morning passed Everybody talked in whispers; everybody was mystified beyond belief. All eyes were turned to Anderson Crow, who stood aloof, pondering as he had never pondered before. In one hand he held Miss Banks's bloody handkerchief and in the other a common school text-book on physiology. His badges and stars fairly revelled in their own importance.

"Don't pester him with questions," warned Isaac Porter, addressing Alf Reesling, the town drunkard, who had just arrived.

"But I got something I want to say to him," persisted Alf eagerly. Two or three strong men restrained him.

"Thunderation, Alf," whispered Elon Jones, "cain't you see he's figurin' something out? You're liable to throw him clear off the track if you say a word to him."

"Well, this is something he'd oughter know," almost whimpered Alf, rubbing his frozen ears.

"Sh!" muttered the bystanders, and poor Alf subsided. He was unceremoniously hustled into the background as Mr. Crow moved from the window toward the group.

"Gentlemen," said Anderson gravely, "there is somethin' wrong here." It is barely possible that this was not news to the crowd, but with one accord they collectively and severally exchanged looks of appreciation. "I've been readin' up a bit on the human body, an' I've proved one thing sure in my own mind."

"You bet you have, Anderson," said Elon Jones. "It's all settled. Let's go home."

"Settled nothin'!" said the marshal. "It's jest begun. Here's what I deduce: Miss Banks has been foully dealt with. Ain't this her blood, an' ain't she used her own individual handkerchief to stop it up?

It's blood right square from her heart, gentlemen!"

"I don't see how——" began Ed Higgins; but Anderson silenced him with a look.

"Of course *you* don't, but you would if you'd 'a' been a detective as long 's I have. What in thunder do you s'pose I got these badges and these medals fer? Fer *not* seein' how? No, siree! I got 'em fer *seein'* how; that's what!"

"But, Andy——"

"Don't call me 'Andy,'" commanded Mr. Crow.

"Well, then, Anderson, I'd like to know how the dickens she could use her own handkerchief if she was stabbed to the heart," protested Ed. He had been crying half the time. Anderson was stunned for the moment.

"Why—why—now, look here, Ed Higgins, I ain't got time to explain things to a derned idgit like you. Everybody else understands *how,* don't you?" and he turned to the crowd. Everybody said yes. "Well, that shows what a fool you are, Ed. Don't bother me any more. I've got work to do."

"Say, Anderson," began Alf Reesling from the outer circle, "I got something important to tell——"

"Who is that? Alf Reesling?" cried Anderson wrathfully.

"Yes; I want to see you private, Anderson. It's important," begged Alf.

"How many times have I got to set down on you, Alf Reesling?" exploded Anderson. "Doggone, I'd like to know how a man's to solve mysteries if he's got to stand around half the time an' listen to fambly quarrels. Tell yer wife I'll——"

"This ain't no family quarrel. Besides, I ain't got no wife. It's about this here——"

"That'll do, now, Alf! Not another word out of you!" commanded Anderson direfully.

"But, dern you, Anderson," exploded Alf, "I've got to tell you——"

But Anderson held up a hand.

"Don't swear in the presence of the dead," he said solemnly. "You're drunk, Alf; go home!" And Alf, news and all was hustled from the schoolhouse by a self-appointed committee of ten.

"Now, we'll search fer the body," announced Anderson. "Git out of the way, Bud!"

"I ain't standin' on it," protested twelve-year-old Bud Long.

"Well, you're standin' mighty near them blood-stains an'——"

"Yes, 'n ain't blood a part of the body?" rasped Isaac Porter scornfully; whereupon Bud faded into the outer rim.

"First we'll look down cellar," said Mr. Crow. "Where's the cellar at?"

"There ain't none," replied Elon Jones.

"What? No cellar? Well, where in thunder did they hide the body, then?"

"There's an attic," ventured Joe Perkins.

A searching party headed by Anderson Crow shinned up the ladder to the low garret. No trace of a body was to be found, and the searchers came down rather thankfully. Then, under Mr. Crow's direction, they searched the wood piles, the woods, and the fields for many rods in all directions. At noon they congregated at the schoolhouse. Alf Reesling was there.

"Find it?" said he thickly, with a cunning leer. He had been drinking. Anderson was tempted to club him half to death, but instead he sent him home with Joe Perkins, refusing absolutely to hear what the town drunkard had to say.

"Well, you'll wish you'd listened to me," ominously hiccoughed Alf; and then, as a parting shot, "I wouldn't tell you now fer eighteen dollars cash. You c'n go to thunder!" It was *lèse majesté*, but the crowd did nothing worse than stare at the offender.

Before starting off on the trail of the big sleigh, Anderson sent this message by wire to the lawyers in Chicago:

"I have found the girl you want, but the body is lost. Would you just as soon have her dead as alive?

"ANDERSON CROW."

In a big bob-sled the marshal and a picked sextette of men set off at one o'clock on the road over which the sleigh had travelled many hours before. Anderson had failed to report the suspected crime to the sheriff at Boggs City and was working alone on the mystery. He said he did not want anybody from town interfering with his affairs.

"Say, Andy—Anderson," said Harry Squires, now

editor of the *Banner,* "maybe we're hunting the wrong body and the wrong people."

"What do you mean?"

"Well, ain't 'Rast Little missing? Maybe he's been killed, eh? And say, ain't there some chance that he did the killing? Didn't he say he was going to murder that city chap? Well, supposing he did. We're on the wrong track, ain't we?"

"Doggone you, Harry, that don't fit in with my deductions," wailed Anderson. "I wish you'd let me alone. 'Rast may have done the killin', but it's our place to find the body, ain't it? Whoever has been slew was taken away last night in the sleigh. S'posin it was Mr. Reddon! Well, consarn it, ain't he got a body same as anybody else? We've just got to find somebody's body, that's all. We've got to prove the corpus deelicti. Drive up, Bill!"

With a perseverance that spoke well for the detective's endurance, but ill for his intelligence, the "bob" sped along aimlessly. It was ridiculous to think of tracking a sleigh over a well-travelled road, and it was not until they reached the cross-roads that Harry Squires suggested that inquiries be made of the farmers in the neighbourhood. After diligent effort, a farmer was discovered who said he had heard the sleigh bells at midnight, and, peering from his window, had caught a glimpse of the party turning south at the cross-roads.

"Jest as I thought!" exclaimed Anderson. "They went south so 's to skip Boggs City. Boys, they've got her body er 'Rast's body er that other feller's body with 'em, an' they're skootin' down this pike so's to get to the big bridge. My idee is that they allowed to drop the body in the river, which ain't friz plum over."

"Gee! We ain't expected to search all over the bottom of the river, are we, Anderson?" shivered Isaac Porter, the pump repairer.

"*I* ain't," said the leader, "but I can deputise anybody I want to."

And so they hurried on to the six-span bridge that crossed the ice-laden river. As they stood silent, awed and shivering on the middle span, staring down into the black water with its navy of swirling ice-chunks, even the heart of Anderson Crow chilled and grew faint.

"Boys," he said, "we've lost the track! Not even a bloodhound could track 'em in that water."

"Bloodhound?" sniffed Harry Squires. "A hippopotamus, you mean."

They were hungry and cold, and they were ready to turn homeward. Anderson said he "guessed" he'd turn the job over to the sheriff and his men. Plainly, he was much too hungry to do any more trailing. Besides, for more than an hour he had been thinking of the warm wood fire at home. Bill Rubley was putting the "gad" to the horses when a man on horseback rode up from the opposite end of the bridge. He had come far and in a hurry, and he recognised Anderson Crow.

"Say, Anderson!" he called, "somebody broke into Colonel Randall's summer home last night an' they're there yet. Got fires goin' in all the stoves, an' havin' a high old time. They ain't got no business there, becuz the place is closed fer the winter. Aleck Burbank went over to order 'em out; one of the fellers said he'd bust his head if he didn't clear out. I think it's a gang!"

A hurried interview brought out the facts. The invaders had come up in a big sleigh long before dawn, and—but that was sufficient. Anderson and his men returned to the hunt, eager and sure of their prey. Darkness was upon them when they came in sight of Colonel Randall's country place in the hills. There were lights in the windows and people were making merry indoors; while outside the pursuing Nemesis and his men were wondering how and where to assault the stronghold.

"I'll jest walk up an' rap on the door," said Anderson Crow, "lettin' on to be a tramp. I'll ast fer somethin' to eat an' a place to sleep. While I'm out there in the kitchen eatin' you fellers c'n sneak up an' surround us. Then you c'n let on like you're lookin' fer me because I'd robbed a hen-roost er something, an' that'll get 'em off their guard. Once we all git inside the house with these shotguns we've got 'em where we want 'em. Then I'll make 'em purduce the body."

"Don't we git anythin' to eat, too?" demanded Isaac Porter faintly.

"The horses ain't had nothin' to eat, Ike," said Anderson. "Ain't you as good as a horse?"

CHAPTER XIV

A Case of Mistaken Identity

DETECTIVE CROW found little difficulty in gaining admittance to Colonel Randall's summer home. He had secreted his badge, and it was indeed a sorry-looking tramp who asked for a bite to eat at the kitchen door.

Three or four young women were busy with chafing dishes in this department of the house, and some good-looking young men were looking on and bothering them with attentions. In the front part of the house a score of people were laughing and making merry.

"Gosh!" said the new tramp, twisting his chin whiskers, "how many of you are there?"

"Oh, there are many more at home like us," trilled out one of the young women gaily. "You're just in time, you poor old thing, to have some of the bride-to-be's cake."

"I guess I'm in the wrong house," murmured Anderson blankly. "Is it a weddin'?"

"No; but there will be one before many days. It's just a reunion. How I wish Rosalie Gray were here!" cried another girl.

Just then there was a pounding on the door, and an instant later Isaac Porter stalked in at the head of the posse.

"Throw up your hands!" called Anderson, addressing himself to the posse, the members of which stopped in blank amazement. Some of them obligingly stuck their hands on high. "What do you want here?"

"We—we—we're lookin' fer a tramp who said he robbed a hen roost," faltered Isaac Porter.

"What is the meaning of all this?" called a strong voice from the dining-room, and the flabbergasted Tinkletownians turned to face Colonel Randall himself, the owner of the house.

"Derned if I know!" muttered Anderson Crow; and he spoke the truth.

"Why, it's Anderson Crow!" cried a gay young voice.

"Jumpin' Jehosophat!" ejaculated the detective; "it's the body!"

"The school-teacher!" exclaimed the surprised Tinkletownians, as with their eyes they proceeded to search the figure before them for blood stains. But no sooner had the chorused words escaped their lips than they realised how wretchedly commonplace was their blundering expression in comparison with the faultlessly professional phraseology of their leader; and, overwhelmed with mortification, the posse ached to recall them; for that the correct technical term had been applied by one for years trained to the vernacular of his calling was little consolation to these sensitive souls, now consumed with envy.

In the meantime, the quarry, if we may be permitted so to designate her, stood before them as pretty as a picture. At her side was Tom Reddon, and a dozen guests of the house fell in behind them.

"Did Rosalie tell you?" demanded Miss Banks. "The mean thing! She said she wouldn't."

"Ro—Rosalie!" gasped Anderson; "tell me what?" nervously.

"That I was—was coming over here with Tom. Didn't she tell you?"

"I should say not. If she'd told me you don't suppose I'd 'a' driv' clear over here in this kinder weather fer nothin', do you? Thunder! Did she know 'bout it?"

"Certainly, Mr. Crow. She helped with the plans."

"Well, good gosh a'mighty! An' we was a-keepin' from her the awful news fer fear 'twould give her a backset."

"Awful news! What do you mean? Oh, you frighten me terribly!"

"Doggone! I don't believe Rosalie was sick at all," continued Anderson, quite regardless of the impatience of his listeners; "she jest wanted to keep from answerin' questions. She jest regularly let everybody believe you had been slaughtered, an' never opened her mouth."

"Slaughtered!" cried half a dozen people.

"Sure! Hain't you heard 'bout the murder?"

"Murder?" apprehensively from the excited New Yorkers.

"Yes—the teacher of schoolhouse No. 5 was brutally butchered las—las—night—by——"

"Go slow, Anderson! Better hold your horses!"

" ' WHAT IS THE MEANING OF ALL THIS ? ' "

cautioned Harry Squires. "Don't forget the body's alive and kic—" and stopping short, in the hope that his break might escape the school-teacher's attention, he confusedly substituted, "and here."

Anderson's jaw dropped, but the movement was barely perceptible, the discomfiture temporary, for to the analytical mind of the great detective the fact that a murder had been committed was fully established by the discovery of the blood. That a body was obviously necessary for the continuance of further investigations he frankly acknowledged to himself; and not for one instant would any supposition or explanation other than assassination be tolerated. And it was with unshaken conviction that he declared:

"Well, somebody was slew, wasn't they? That's as plain 's the nose on y'r face. Don't you contradict me, Harry Squires. I guess Anderson Crow knows blood when he sees it."

"Do you mean to tell me that you've been trailing us all day in the belief that some one of us had killed somebody?" demanded Tom Reddon.

Harry Squires explained the situation, Anderson being too far gone to step into the breach. It may be of interest to say that the Tinkletown detective was the sensation of the hour. The crowd, merry once more, lauded him to the skies for the manner in which the supposed culprits had been trailed, and the marshal's pomposity grew almost to the bursting point.

"But how about that blood?" he demanded.

"Yes," said Harry Squires with a sly grin, "it was positively identified as yours, Miss Banks."

"Well, it's the first time I was ever fooled," confessed Anderson glibly. "I'll have to admit it. The blood really belonged to 'Rast Little. Boys, the seegars are on me."

"No, they're on me," exclaimed Tom Reddon, producing a box of Perfectos.

"But, Miss Banks, you are wanted in Chicago," insisted Anderson. Reddon interrupted him.

"Right you are, my dear Sherlock, and I'm going to take her there as soon as I can. It's what I came East for."

"Ain't—I mean, wasn't you Miss Lovering?" muttered Anderson Crow.

"Good heavens, no!" cried Miss Banks. "Who is she—a shoplifter?"

"I'll tell you the story, Mr. Crow, if you'll come with me," said Mr. Farnsworth, stepping forward with a wink.

In the library he told the Tinkletown posse that Tom Reddon had met Miss Banks while she was at school in New York. He was a Chicago millionaire's son and she was the daughter of wealthy New York people. Her mother was eager to have the young people marry, but the girl at that time imagined herself to be in love with another man. In a pique she left school and set forth to earn her own living. A year's hardship as governess in the family of Congressman Ritchey and subsequent disillusionment as a country school-teacher brought her to her senses and she realised that she cared for Tom Reddon after all. She and Miss Gray together prepared the letter which told Reddon where she could be found, and that eager young gentleman did the rest. He had been waiting for months for just such a message from her. The night of the spelling-match he induced her to come to Colonel Randall's, and now the whole house-party, including Miss Banks, was to leave on the following day for New York. The marriage would take place in a very few weeks.

"I'll accept your explanation," said Mr. Crow composedly as he took a handful of cigars. "Well, I guess I'll be startin' back. It's gettin' kind o' late-like."

There was a telegram at the livery stable for him when he reached that haven of warmth and rest in Tinkletown about dawn the next day. It was from Chicago and marked "Charges collect."

"What girl and whose body," it said, "do you refer to? Miss Lovering has been dead two years, and we are settling the estate in behalf of the other heirs. We were trying to establish her place of residence. Never mind the body you have lost."

"Doggone," said Anderson, chuckling aloud, "that was an awful good joke on 'Rast, wasn't it?"

The stablemen stood around and looked at him with jaws that were drooping helplessly. The air seemed laden with a sombre uncertainty that had not yet succeeded in penetrating the nature of Marshal Crow.

"Is it from her?" finally asked Ike Smith hoarsely, his lips trembling.

"From what her?"

"Rosalie."

"Thunder, no! It's from my lawyers in Chicago."

"Ain't you—ain't you heerd about it?" half groaned Ike, moving away as if he expected something calamitous.

"What the dickens are you fellers drivin' at?" demanded Anderson. The remainder of his posse deserted the red-hot stove and drew near with the instinctive feeling that something dreadful had happened.

"Ro—Rosalie has been missin' sence early last night. She was grabbed by some feller near Mrs. Luce's, chucked into a big wagon an' rushed out of town before Ros Crow could let out a yell. Clean stole her—look out! Ketch him, Joe!"

Anderson dropped limply into a hostler's arms.

CHAPTER XV

Rosalie Disappears

THINGS had happened in Tinkletown that night. Alf Reesling finally found some one who would listen to his story. He told the minister and the minister alarmed the town. To be brief, Alf admitted that 'Rast Little was at his house in the outskirts of the village, laid up with a broken arm and a bad cut in the top of his head.

"He came crawlin' up to my place about six o'clock in the mornin'," explained Alf, "an' I took the poor cuss in. That's what I wanted to tell Anderson, but the old rip wouldn't listen to me. Seems as though 'Rast waited around the schoolhouse last night to git a crack at that feller from town. Miss Banks and her three friends set around the stove in the school-house for about an hour after the crowd left, an' 'Rast got so cold he liked to died out there in the woodshed.

"Purty soon they all come out, an' 'Rast cut acrost the lot to git inside the house by the fire. He was so derned cold that he didn't feel like crackin' anybody. When they wasn't lookin' he sneaked inside. Jest as he was gittin' ready to hug the stove he heard Miss Banks an' one of the men comin' back. He shinned up the ladder into the garret just in time. In they come an' the feller lit a lamp. 'Rast could hear 'em talkin'. She said good-bye to the schoolhouse forever, an' the feller kissed her a couple of times. 'Rast pretty nigh swore out loud at that. Then she said she'd leave a note in her desk fer the trustees, resignin' her job, er whatever she called it. He heard her read the note to the man, an' it said somethin' about goin' away unexpected to git married. 'Rast says ef Anderson had looked in the desk he'd have found the note.

"Then she packed up some books an' her an' the feller went out. 'Rast was paralysed. He heerd the sleigh-bells jingle an' then he come to. He started down the ladder so quick that he missed his hold and went ker-slam clear to the bottom. Doggone ef he didn't light on his head, too. He don't know how long he laid there, but finally he was resurrected enough to crawl over by the stove.

His arm was broke an' he was bleedin' like a stuck hog. Miss Banks had left her handkerchief on the desk, an' he says he tried to bind up his head with it, but it was too infernal small. Somehow he got outside an' wandered around half crazy fer a long time, finally pullin' up at my house, derned nigh froze to death an' so weak he couldn't walk no more. He'd lost his hat an' his ear muffs an' his way all at the same time. If Anderson had let me talk this mornin' he'd 'a' knowed there wasn't no murder. It was just a match."

Hours passed before Anderson was himself again and able to comprehend the details of the story which involved the disappearance of his ward. It slowly filtered through his mind as he sat stark-eyed and numb before the kitchen fire that this was the means her mysterious people had taken to remove her from his custody. The twenty years had expired, and they had come to claim their own. There was gloom in the home of Anderson Crow—gloom so dense that death would have seemed bright in comparison. Mrs. Crow was prostrated, Anderson in a state of mental and physical collapse, the children hysterical.

All Tinkletown stood close and ministered dumbly to the misery of the bereaved ones, but made no effort to follow or frustrate the abductors. The town seemed as helpless as the marshal, not willingly or wittingly, but because it had so long known him as leader that no one possessed the temerity to step into his place, even in an hour of emergency.

A dull state of paralysis fell upon the citizens, big

and little. It was as if universal palsy had been or-
dained to pinch the limbs and brains of Tinkletown
until the hour came for the rehabilitation of Anderson Crow himself. No one suggested a move in any
direction—in fact, no one felt like moving at all.
Everything stood stockstill while Anderson slowly
pulled himself together; everything waited dumbly
for its own comatose condition to be dispelled by the
man who had been hit the hardest.

It was not until late in the afternoon that Blucher
Peabody, the druggist, awoke from his lethargy and
moved as though he intended to take the initiative.
"Blootch" was Rosalie's most persistent admirer. He
had fallen heir to his father's apothecary shop and
notion store, and he was regarded as one of the best
catches in town. He approached the half-frozen
crowd that huddled near old Mrs. Luce's front gate.
In this crowd were some of the prominent men of
the town, young and old; they left their places of
business every half hour or so and wandered aimlessly to the now historic spot, as if drawn by a magnet. Just why they congregated there no one could
explain and no one attempted to do so. Presumably
it was because the whole town centred its mind on one
of two places—the spot where Rosalie was seized or
the home of Anderson Crow. When they were not
at Mrs. Luce's gate they were tramping through
Anderson's front yard and into his house.

"Say," said "Blootch" so loudly that the crowd felt
like remonstrating with him, "what's the *use* of all
this?"

No one responded. No one was equal to it on such short notice.

"We've got to do something besides stand around and whisper," he said. "We've got to find Rosalie Gray."

"But good gosh!" ejaculated Isaac Porter, "they've got purty nigh a day's start of us."

"Well, that don't matter. Anderson would do as much for us. Let's get a move on."

"But where in thunder will we hunt?" murmured George Ray.

"To the end of the earth," announced Blootch, inflating his chest and slapping it violently, a strangely personal proceeding, which went unnoticed. He had reached the conclusion that his chance to be a hero was at hand and not to be despised. Here was the opportunity to outstrip all of his competitors in the race for Rosalie's favour. It might be confessed that, with all his good intentions, his plans were hopelessly vague. The group braced up a little at the sound of his heroic words.

"But the derned thing's round," was the only thing Ed Higgins could find to say. Ed, as fickle as the wind, was once more deeply in love with Rosalie, having switched from Miss Banks immediately after the visit to Colonel Randall's.

"Aw, you go to Guinea!" was Blootch's insulting reply. Nothing could be more disparaging than that, but Ed failed to retaliate. "Let's appoint a committee to wait on Anderson and find out what he thinks we'd better do."

"But Anderson ain't—" began some one. Blootch calmly waived him into silence.

"What he wants is encouragement, and not a lot of soup and broth and lemonade. He ain't sick. He's as able-bodied as I am. Every woman in town took soup to him this noon. He needs a good stiff drink of whiskey and a committee to cheer him up. I took a bottle up to 'Rast Little last night and he acted like another man."

At last it was decided that a committee should first wait on Anderson, ascertaining his wishes in the premises, and then proceed to get at the bottom of the mystery. In forming this committee the wise men of the town ignored Mr. Peabody, and he might have been left off completely had he not stepped in and appointed himself chairman.

The five good men and true descended upon the marshal late in the afternoon, half fearful of the result, but resolute. They found him slowly emerging from his spell of lassitude. He greeted them with a solemn nod of the head. Since early morning he had been conscious of a long stream of sympathisers passing through the house, but it was not until now that he felt equal to the task of recognising any of them.

His son Roscoe had just finished telling him the story of the abduction. Roscoe's awestruck tones and reddened eyes carried great weight with them, and for the tenth time that day he had his sisters in tears. With each succeeding repetition the details grew until at last there was but little of the original event remaining, a fact which his own family properly overlooked.

"Gentlemen," said Anderson, as if suddenly coming from a trance, "this wasn't the work of Tinkletown desperadoes." Whereupon the committee felt mightily relieved. The marshal displayed signs of a returning energy that augured well for the enterprise. After the chairman had impressively announced that something must be done, and that he was willing to lead his little band to death's door—and beyond, if necessary—Mr. Crow pathetically upset all their hopes by saying that he had long been expecting such a calamity, and that nothing could be done.

"They took the very night when I was not here to pertect her," he lamented. "It shows that they been a-watchin' me all along. The job was did by persons who was in the employ of her family, an' she has been carried off secretly to keep me from findin' out who and what her parents were. Don't ye see? Her mother—er father, fer that matter—couldn't afford to come right out plain an' say they wanted their child after all these years. The only way was to take her away without givin' themselves away. It's

been the plan all along. There ain't no use huntin'
fer her, gentlemen. She's in New York by this time,
an' maybe she's ready fer a trip to Europe."

"But I should think she'd telegraph to you," said
Blootch.

"Telegraph yer granny! Do you s'pose they'd 'a'
stole her if they intended to let her telegraph to anybody? Not much. They're spiritin' her away until
her estate's settled. After a while it will all come
out, an' you'll see if I ain't right. But she's gone.
They've got her away from me an'—an' we got to
stand it, that's all. I—I—cain't bear to think about
it. It's broke my heart mighty ne—near. Don't
mind me if—I—cry, boys. You would, too, if you
was me."

As the committee departed soon after without any
plan of action arising from the interview with the
dejected marshal, it may be well to acquaint the
reader with the history of the abduction, as told by
Roscoe Crow and his bosom friend, Bud Long, thoroughly expurgated.

According to instructions, no one in the Crow family mentioned the strange disappearance of Elsie
Banks to Rosalie. Nor was she told of the pursuit by
the marshal and his posse. The girl, far from being
afflicted with a fever, really now kept in her room by
grief over the departure of her friend and companion.
She was in tears all that night and the next day,
suffering intensely in her loss. Rosalie did not know
that the teacher was to leave Tinkletown surreptitiously until after the spelling-bee. The sly, blush-

ing announcement came as a shock, but she was loyal
to her friend, and not a word in exposure escaped
from her lips. Of course, she knew nothing of the
sensational developments that followed the uncalled-
for flight of Elsie Banks.

Shortly after the supper dishes had been cleared
away Rosalie came downstairs and announced that she
was going over to read to old Mrs. Luce, who was
bedridden. Her guardian's absence was not explained
to her, and she did not in the least suspect that he
had been away all day on a fool's errand. Roscoe
and Bud accompanied her to Mrs. Luce's front door,
heavily bound by promises to hold their tongues regarding Miss Banks.

"We left her there at old Mis' Luce's," related
Roscoe, "an' then went over to Robertson's Pond to
skate. She tole us to stop in fer her about nine

o'clock, didn't she, Bud? Er was it eight?" He saw the necessity for accuracy.

"Ten," corrected Bud deliberately.

"Well, pop, we stopped fer her, an'—an'——"

"Stop yer blubberin', Roscoe," commanded Anderson as harshly as he could.

"An' got her," concluded Roscoe. "She put on her shawl an' mittens an' said she'd run us a race all the way home. We all got ready to start right in front of old Mis' Luce's gate. Bud he stopped an' said, 'Here comes Tony Brink.' We all looked around, an' sure enough, a heavy-set feller was comin' to'rds us. It looked like Tony, but when he got up to us I see it wasn't him. He ast us if we could tell him where Mr. Crow lived——"

"He must 'a' been a stranger," deduced Anderson mechanically.

"—an' Bud said you lived right on ahead where the street lamps was. Jest then a big sleigh turned out of the lane back of Mis' Luce's an' drove up to where we was standin'. Bud was standin' jest like this— me here an' Rosalie a little off to one side. S'posin' this chair was her an'——"

"Yes—yes, go on," from Anderson.

"The sleigh stopped, and there was two fellers in it. There was two seats, too."

"Front and back?"

"Yes, sir."

"I understand. It was a double-seated one," again deduced the marshal.

"An' nen, by gum, 'fore we could say Jack Robinson, one of the fellers jumped out an' grabbed Rosalie. The feller on the groun', he up an' hit me a clip in the ear. I fell down, an' so did Bud——"

"He hit me on top of the head," corrected Bud sourly.

"I heerd Rosalie start to scream, but the next minute they had a blanket over her head an' she was chucked into the back seat. It was all over in a second. I got up, but 'fore I could run a feller yelled, 'Ketch him!' An' another feller did. 'Don't let 'em get away,' said the driver in low, hissin' tones——"

"Regular villains," vowed Anderson.

"Yes, sir. 'Don't let 'em git away er they'll rouse the town.' 'What'll we do with 'em?' asked the feller who held both of us. 'Kill 'em?' Gosh, I was skeered. Neither one of us could yell, 'cause he had us by the neck, an' he was powerful strong. 'Chuck 'em in here an' I'll tend to 'em,' said the driver. Next thing we knowed we was in the front of the sleigh, an' the whole outfit was off like a runaway. They said they'd kill us if we made a noise, an' we didn't. I wish I'd 'a' had my rifle, doggone it! I'd 'a' showed 'em."

"They drove like thunder out to'rds Boggs City fer about two mile," said Bud, who had been silent as long as human nature would permit. " 'Nen they stopped an' throwed us out in the road. 'Go home, you devils, an' don't you tell anybody about us er I'll come back here some day an' give you a kick in the slats.' "

"Slats?" murmured Anderson.

"That's short fer ribs," explained Bud loftily.

"Well, why couldn't he have said short ribs an' been done with it?" complained Anderson.

"Then they whipped up an' turned off west in the pike," resumed Bud. "We run all the way home an' tole Mr. Lamson, an' he——"

"Where was Rosalie all this time?" asked Anderson.

"Layin' in the back seat covered with a blanket, jest the same as if she was dead. I heerd 'em say somethin' about chloroformin' her. What does chloroform smell like, Mr. Crow?"

"Jest like any medicine. It has drugs in it. They use it to pull teeth. Well, what then?"

"Well," interposed Roscoe, "Mr. Lamson gave the alarm, an' nearly ever'body in town got out o' bed. They telegraphed to Boggs City an' all around, but it didn't seem to do no good. Them horses went faster'n telegraphs."

"Did you ever see them fellers before?"

"No, sir; but I think I'd know 'em with their masks off."

"Was they masked?"

"Their faces were."

"Oh, my poor little Rosalie!" sobbed old Anderson hopelessly.

CHAPTER XVI

The Haunted House

DAYS passed without word or sign from the missing girl. The marshal haunted the post-office and the railroad station, hoping with all his poor old heart that word would come from her; but the letter was not there, nor was there a telegram at the station when he strolled over to that place. The county officials at Boggs City came down and began a cursory investigation, but Anderson's emphatic though doleful opinions set them quite straight, and they gave up the quest. There was nothing to do but to sit back and wait.

In those three days Anderson Crow turned greyer and older, although he maintained a splendid show of resignation. He had made a perfunctory offer of reward for Rosalie, dead or alive, but he knew all the time that it would be fruitless. Mark Riley, the billposter, stuck up the glaring reward notices as far away as the telegraph poles in Clay County. The world was given to understand that $1000 reward would be paid for Rosalie's return or for information leading to the apprehension and capture of her abductors.

There was one very mysterious point in connection with the affair—something so strange that it bordered on the supernatural. No human being in Bramble

County except the two boys had seen the double-seated sleigh. It had disappeared as if swallowed by the earth itself.

"Well, it don't do any good to cry over spilt milk," said Anderson bravely. "She's gone, an' I only hope she ain't bein' mistreated. I don't see why they should harm her. She's never done nobody a wrong. Like as not she's been taken to a comfortable place in New York, an' we'll hear from her as soon as she recovers from the shock. There ain't no use huntin' fer her, I know, but I jest can't help nosin' around a little. Mebby I can git some track of her. I'd give all I got in this world to know that she's safe an' sound, no matter if I never see her ag'in."

The hungry look in his eyes deepened, and no one bandied jests with him as was the custom in days gone by.

*   *   *   *   *

There were not many tramps practising in that section of the State. Anderson Crow proudly announced that they gave Tinkletown a wide berth because of his prowess; but the vagabond gentry took an entirely different view of the question. They did not infest the upper part of the State for the simple but eloquent reason that it meant starvation to them. The farmers compelled the weary wayfarer to work all day like a borrowed horse for a single meal at the "second table." There was no such thing as a "hand-out," as it is known in the tramp's vocabulary. It is not extraordinary, therefore, that tramps found the community so unattractive that they cheerfully walked miles to avoid it. A peculiarly well-informed vagrant once characterised the up-State farmer as being so "close that he never shaved because it was a waste of hair."

It is hardly necessary to state, in view of the attitude of both farmer and tramp, that the misguided vagrant who wandered that way was the object of distinct, if not distinguished, curiosity. In the country roads he was stared at with a malevolence that chilled his appetite, no matter how long he had been cultivating it on barren soil. In the streets of Tinkletown, and even at the county seat, he was an object of such amazing concern that he slunk away in pure distress. It was indeed an unsophisticated tramp who thought to thrive in Bramble County even for a day and a night. In front of the general store and post-office at Tinkletown there was a sign-post, on which Anderson Crow had painted these words:

"No tramps or Live Stock Allowed on these Streets.
"By order of
"A. CROW, Marshal."

The live stock disregarded the command, but the tramp took warning. On rare occasions he may have gone through some of the houses in Tinkletown, but if he went through the streets no one was the wiser. Anderson Crow solemnly but studiously headed him off in the outskirts, and he took another direction. Twice in his career he drove out tramps who had burglarised the houses of prominent citizens in broad daylight, but what did it matter so long as the "hoboes" were kept from desecrating the main street of the town? Mr. Crow's official star, together with his badge from the New York detective agency, his Sons of the Revolution pin, and his G. A. R. insignia, made him a person to be feared. If the weather became too hot for coat and vest the proud dignitary fastened the badges to his suspenders, and their presence glorified the otherwise humble "galluses."

On the fourth day after the abduction Marshal Crow was suddenly aroused from his lethargy by the news that the peace and security of the neighbourhood was being imposed upon.

"The dickens you say!" he observed, abandoning the perpetual grip upon his straggling chin whiskers.

"Yes, sir," responded the excited small boy, who, with two companions, had run himself quite out of breath all over town before he found the officer at Harkin's blacksmith shop.

"Well, dang 'em!" said Mr. Crow impressively.

"We was skatin' in the marsh when we heerd 'em plain as day," said the other boy. "You bet I'm nuvver goin' nigh that house ag'in."

"Sho! Bud, they ain't no sech thing as ghosts," said Mr. Crow; "it's tramps."

"You know that house is ha'nted," protested Bud. "Wasn't ole Mrs. Rank slew there by her son-in-law? Wasn't she chopped to pieces and buried there right in her own cellar?"

"Thunderation, boy, that was thirty year ago!"

"Well, nobody's lived in the ha'nted house sence then, has they? Didn't Jim Smith try to sleep there

The haunted house

oncet on a bet, an' didn't he hear sech awful noises 'at he liked to went crazy?" insisted Bud.

"I *do* recollect that Jim run two mile past his own house before he could stop, he was in sech a hurry to git away from the place. But Jim didn't *see* anything. Besides, that was twenty year ago. Ghosts don't hang aroun' a place when there ain't nothin' to ha'nt. Her son-in-law was hung, an' she ain't got no one else to pester. I tell you it's tramps."

"Well, we just thought we'd tell you, Mr. Crow," said the first boy.

In a few minutes it was known throughout the business centre of Tinkletown that tramps were making their home in the haunted house down the river, and that Anderson Crow was to ride forth on his bicycle to rout them out. The haunted house was three miles from town and in the most desolate section of the bottomland. It was approachable only through the treacherous swamp on one side or by means of the river on the other. Not until after the murder of its owner and builder, old Johanna Rank, was there an explanation offered for the existence of a home in such an unwholesome locality.

Federal authorities discovered that she and her son-in-law, Dave Wolfe, were at the head of a great counterfeiting gang, and that they had been working up there in security for years, turning out spurious coins by the hundred. One night Dave up and killed his mother-in-law, and was hanged for his good deed before he could be punished for his bad ones. For thirty years the weather-beaten, ramshackle old cabin in the swamp had been unoccupied except by birds, lizards, and other denizens of the solitude—always, of course, including the ghost of old Mrs. Rank.

Inasmuch as Dave chopped her into small bits and buried them in the cellar, while her own daughter held the lantern, it was not beyond the range of possibility that certain atoms of the unlamented Johanna were never unearthed by the searchers. It was generally believed in the community that Mrs. Rank's spirit came back every little while to nose around in the dirt of the cellar in quest of such portions of her person as had not been respectably interred in the village graveyard.

Mysterious noises had been heard about the place at the dead hour of night, and ghostly lights had flitted past the cellar windows. All Tinkletown agreed that the place was haunted and kept at a most respectful distance. The three small boys who startled Marshal Crow from his moping had gone down the river to skate instead of going to school. They swore that the sound of muffled voices came from the interior of the cabin, near which they had inadvertently wan-

dered. Although Dave Wolfe had been dead thirty years, one of the youngest of the lads was positive that he recognised the voice of the desperado. And at once the trio fled the 'cursed spot and brought the horrifying news to Anderson Crow. The detective was immediately called upon to solve the ghostly mystery.

Marshal Crow first went to his home and donned his blue coat, transferring the stars and badges to the greasy lapel of the garment. He also secured his dark lantern and the official cane of the village, but why he should carry a cane on a bicycle expedition was known only to himself. Followed by a horde of small boys and a few representative citizens of Tinkletown on antiquated wheels, Mr. Crow pedalled majestically off to the south. Skirting the swamp, the party approached the haunted house over the narrow path which ran along the river bank. Once in sight of the dilapidated cabin, which seemed to slink farther and farther back into the dense shadows of the late afternoon, with all the diffidence of the supernatural, the marshal called a halt and announced his plans.

"You kids go up an' tell them fellers I want to see 'em," he commanded. The boys fell back and prepared to whimper.

"I don't want to," protested Bud.

"Why don't you go an' tell 'em yourself, Anderson?" demanded Isaac Porter, the pump repairer.

"Thunderation, Ike, who's runnin' this thing?" retorted Anderson Crow. "I got a right to deputise anybody to do anything at any time. Don't you s'pose I know how to handle a job like this? I got my own idees how to waylay them raskils, an' I reckon I been in the detectin' business long enough to know how to manage a gol-derned tramp, ain't I? How's that? Who says I ain't?"

"Nobody said a word, Anderson," meekly observed Jim Borum.

"Well, I *thought* somebody did. An' I don't want nobody interferin' with an officer, either. Bud, you an' them two Heffner boys go up an' tell them loafers to step down here right spry er I'll come up there an' see about it."

"Gosh, Mr. Crow, I'm a-skeered to!" whimpered Bud. The Heffner boys started for home on a dead run.

"Askeered to?" sniffed Anderson. "An' your great-grand-dad was in the Revolution, too. Geminy crickets, ef you was my boy I'd give you somethin' to be askeered of! Now, Bud, nothin' kin happen to you. Ain't I here?"

"But suppose they won't come when I tell 'em?"

"Yes, 'n' supposin' 'tain't tramps, but ghosts?" volunteered Mr. Porter, edging away with his bicycle. It was now quite dark and menacing in there where the cabin stood. As the outcome of half an hour's discussion, the whole party advanced slowly upon the house, Anderson Crow in the lead, his dark lantern in one hand, his cane in the other. Half way to the house he stopped short and turned to Bud.

"Gosh dern you, Bud! I don't believe you heerd any noise in there at all! There ain't no use goin' any further with this, gentlemen. The dern boys was lyin'. We might jest as well go home." And he would have started for home had not Isaac Porter uttered a fearful groan and staggered back against a swamp reed for support, his horrified eyes glued upon a window in the log house. The reed was inadequate, and Isaac tumbled over backward.

For a full minute the company stared dumbly at the indistinct little window, paralysis attacking every sense but that of sight. At the expiration of another minute the place was deserted, and Anderson Crow was the first to reach the bicycles far up the river bank. Every face was as white as chalk, and every voice trembled. Mr. Crow's dignity asserted itself just as the valiant posse prepared to "straddle" the wheels in mad flight.

"Hold on!" he panted. "I lost my dark lantern down there. Go back an' git it, Bud."

"Land o' mighty! Did y'ever see anythin' like it?" gasped Jim Borum, trying to mount a ten-year-old boy's wheel instead of his own.

"I'd like to have anybody tell me there ain't no sech things as ghosts," faltered Uncle Jimmy Borton, who had always said there wasn't. "Let go, there! Ouch!" The command and subsequent exclamation were the inevitable results of his unsuccessful attempt to mount with Elon Jones the same wheel.

"What 'd I tell you, Anderson?" exclaimed Isaac Porter. "Didn't I say it was ghosts? Tramps nothin'! A tramp wouldn't last a second up in that house. It's been ha'nted fer thirty years an' it gits worse all the time. What air we goin' to do next?"

Even the valiant Mr. Crow approved of an immediate return to Tinkletown, and the posse was trying to disentangle its collection of bicycles when an interruption came from an unsuspected quarter——a deep, masculine voice arose from the ice-covered river hard by, almost directly below that section of the bank on which Anderson and his friends were herded. The result was startling. Every man leaped a foot in the air and every hair stood on end; bicycles rattled and clashed together, and Ed Higgins, hopelessly bewildered, started to run in the direction of the haunted house.

CHAPTER XVII

Wicker Bonner, Harvard

"HELLO, up there!" was what the deep, masculine voice shouted from the river. Anderson Crow was the first to distinguish the form of the speaker, and he was not long in deciding that it was far from ghost-like. With a word of command he brought his disorganised forces out of chaos and huddled them together as if to resist attack.

"What's the matter with you?" he demanded, addressing his men in a loud tone. "Don't get rattled!"

"Are you speaking to me?" called the fresh voice from below.

"Who are you?" demanded Mr. Crow in return.

"Nobody in particular. What's going on up there? What's the fuss?"

"Come up an' find out." Then Mr. Crow, observing that the man below was preparing to comply, turned and addressed his squad in low, earnest tones. "This feller will bear watchin'. He's mixed up in this thing somehow. Else why is he wanderin' around here close to the house? I'll question him."

"By gosh, he ain't no ghost!" murmured Ed Higgins, eyeing the newcomer as he crawled up the bank. "Say, did y' see me a minute ago? If you fellers had come on, I was goin' right up to search that house from top to bottom. Was you all askeered to come?"

"Aw, you!" said Anderson Crow in deep scorn.

The next instant a stalwart young fellow stood before the marshal, who was eyeing him keenly, even imperiously. The newcomer's good-looking, strong-featured face was lighted up by a smile of surpassing friendliness.

"It's lonesome as thunder down here, isn't it? Glad to see you, gentlemen. What's up—a bicycle race?"

"No, sir; we got a little business up here, that's all," responded Anderson Crow diplomatically. "What air you doin' here?"

"Skating. My name is Wicker Bonner, and I'm visiting my uncle, Congressman Bonner, across the river. You know him, I dare say. I've been hanging around here for a week's hunting, and haven't had an ounce of luck in all that time. It's rotten! Aha, I see that you are an officer, sir—a detective, too. By George, can it be possible that you are searching for some one? If you are, let me in on it. I'm dying for excitement."

The young man's face was eager and his voice rang true. Besides, he was a tall, athletic chap, with brawny arms and a broad back. Altogether, he would make a splendid recruit, thought Anderson Crow. He was dressed in rough corduroy knickerbockers, the thick coat buttoned up close to his muffled neck. A woollen cap came down over his ears and a pair of skates dangled from his arm.

"Yes, sir; I'm a detective, and we are up here doin'

a little investigatin'. You are from Chicago, I see."

"What makes you think so?"

"Can't fool me. I c'n always tell. You said, 'I've *bean* hangin',' instead of 'I've *ben* hangin'.' See? They say *bean* in Chicago. Ha! ha! You didn't think I could deduce that, did you?"

"I'll confess that I didn't," said Mr. Bonner with a dry smile. "I'm from Boston, however."

"Sure," interposed Isaac Porter; "that's where the beans come from, Anderson."

"Well, that's neither here nor there," said Mr. Crow, hastily changing the subject. "We're wastin' time."

"Stayin' here, you mean?" asked Ed Higgins, quite ready to start. Involuntarily the eyes of the posse turned toward the house among the willows. The stranger saw the concerted glance and made inquiry. Whereupon Mr. Crow, assisted by seven men and five small boys, told Mr. Wicker Bonner, late of Harvard, what had brought them from Tinkletown to the haunted house, and what they had seen upon their arrival. Young Bonner's face glowed with the joy of excitement.

"Great!" he cried, fastening his happy eyes upon the hated thing among the trees. "Let's search the place. By George, this is glorious!"

"Not on your life!" said Ed Higgins. "You can't get me inside that house. Like as not a feller'd never come out alive."

"Well, better men than we have died," said Mr.

WICKER BONNER

Bonner tranquilly. "Come on; I'll go in first. It's all tommy-rot about the place being haunted. In any event, ghosts don't monkey around at this time of day. It's hardly dusk."

"But, gosh dern it," exploded Anderson Crow, "we seen it!"

"I seen it first," said Isaac Porter proudly.

"But I heerd it first," peeped up Master Bud.

"You've all been drinking hard cider or pop or something like that," said the brawny scoffer.

"Now, see here, you're gittin' fresh, an—" began the marshal, swelling up like a pigeon.

"Look out behind!" sang out Mr. Bonner, and Anderson jumped almost out of his shoes, besides ripping his shirt in the back, he turned so suddenly.

"Jeemses River!" he gasped.

"Never turn your back on an unknown danger," cautioned the young man serenely. "Be ready to meet it."

"If you're turned t'other way you c'n git a quicker start if you want to run," suggested Jim Borum, bracing himself with a fresh chew of tobacco.

"What time is it?" asked Wicker Bonner.

Anderson Crow squinted up through the leafless tree-tops toward the setting sun; then he looked at the shadow of a sapling down on the bank.

"It's about seven minutes past five—in the evenin'," he said conclusively. Bonner was impolite enough to pull out his watch for verification.

"You're a minute fast," he observed; but he looked at Anderson with a new and respectful admiration.

"He c'n detect anything under the sun," said Porter with a feeble laugh at his own joke.

"Well, let's go up and ransack that old cabin," announced Bonner, starting toward the willows. The crowd held back. "I'll go alone if you're afraid to come," he went on. "It's my firm belief that you didn't see anything and the noise you boys heard was the wind whistling through the trees. Now, tell the truth, how many of you saw it?"

"I did," came from every throat so unanimously that Jim Borum's supplemental oath stood out alone and forceful as a climax.

"Then it's worth investigating," announced the Boston man. "It is certainly a very mysterious affair, and you, at least, Mr. Town Marshal, should back me up in the effort to unravel it. Tell me again just what it was you saw and what it looked like."

"I won't let no man tell me what my duties are," snorted Anderson, his stars trembling with injured pride. "Of course I'm going to solve the mystery. We've got to see what's inside that house. I thought it was tramps at first."

"Well, lead on, then; I'll follow!" said Bonner with a grin.

"I thought you was so anxious to go first!" exclaimed Anderson with fine tact. "Go ahead yourself, ef you're so derned brave. I dare you to."

Bonner laughed loud enough to awaken every ghost in Bramble County and then strode rapidly toward the house. Anderson Crow followed slowly and the rest straggled after, all alert for the first sign of resistance.

"I wish I could find that derned lantern," said Anderson, searching diligently in the deep grass as he walked along, in the meantime permitting Bonner to reach the grim old doorway far in advance of him.

"Come on!" called back the intrepid leader, seeing that all save the marshal had halted. "You don't need the lantern. It's still daylight, old chap. We'll find out what it was you all saw in the window."

"That's the last of him," muttered Isaac Porter, as the broad back disappeared through the low aperture that was called a doorway. There were no window sashes or panes in the house, and the door had long since rotted from the hinges.

"He'll never come out. Let's go home," added Ed Higgins conclusively.

"Are you coming?" sang out Bonner from the interior of the house. His voice sounded prophetically sepulchral.

"Consarn it, cain't you wait a minute?" replied Anderson Crow, still bravely but consistently looking for the much-needed dark lantern.

"It's all right in here. There hasn't been a human being in the house for years. Come on in; it's fine!"

Anderson Crow finally ventured up to the doorway and peeped in. Bonner was standing near the tumble-down fireplace, placidly lighting a cigarette.

"This is a fine job you've put up on me," he growled. "I thought there would be something doing. There isn't a soul here, and there hasn't been, either."

"Thunderation, man, you cain't see ghosts when they don't want you to!" said Anderson Crow. "It was a ghost, that's settled. I knowed it all the time. Nothin' human ever looked like it, and nothin' alive ever moaned like it did."

By this time the rest of the party had reached the cabin door. The less timorous ventured inside, while others contented themselves by looking through the small windows.

"Well, if you're sure you really saw something, we'd better make a thorough search of the house and the grounds," said Bonner, and forthwith began nosing about the two rooms.

The floors were shaky and the place had the odour of decayed wood. Mould clung to the half-plastered walls, cobwebs matted the ceilings, and rotted fungi covered the filth in the corners. Altogether it was a most uninviting hole, in which no self-respecting ghost would have made its home. When the time came to climb up to the little garret Bonner's followers rebelled. He was compelled to go alone, carrying the lantern, which one of the small boys had found. This part of the house was even more loathsome than below, and it would be impossible to describe its condition. He saw no sign of life, and retired in utter disgust. Then came the trip to the cellar. Again he had no followers, the Tinkletown men emphatically refusing to go down where old Mrs. Rank's body had been buried. Bonner laughed at them and went down alone. It was nauseous with age and the smell of damp earth, but it was cleaner there than above stairs. The cellar was smaller than either of the living rooms, and was to be reached only through the kitchen.

There was no exit leading directly to the exterior of the house, but there was one small window at the south end. Bonner examined the room carefully and then rejoined the party. For some reason the posse had retired to the open air as soon as he left them to go below. No one knew exactly why, but when one started to go forth the others followed with more or less alacrity.

"Did you see anything?" demanded the marshal.

"What did old Mrs. Rank look like when she was alive?" asked Bonner with a beautifully mysterious air. No one answered; but there was a sudden shifting of feet backward, while an expression of alarmed inquiry came into every face. "Don't back into that open well," warned the amused young man in the doorway. Anderson Crow looked sharply behind, and flushed indignantly when he saw that the well was at least fifty feet away. "I saw something down there that looked like a woman's toe," went on Bonner very soberly.

"Good Lord! What did I tell you?" cried the marshal, turning to his friends. To the best of their ability they could not remember that Anderson had told them anything, but with one accord the whole party nodded approval.

"I fancy it was the ghost of a toe, however, for when I tried to pick it up it wriggled away, and I think it chuckled. It disappear—what's the matter? Where are you going?"

It is only necessary to state that the marshal and his posse retreated in good order to a distant spot where it was not quite so dark, there to await the approach of Wicker Bonner, who leisurely but laughingly inspected the exterior of the house and the grounds adjoining. Finding nothing out of the ordinary, except as to dilapidation, he rejoined the party with palpable displeasure in his face.

"Well, I think I'll go back to the ice," he said; "that place is as quiet as the grave. You are a fine lot of jokers, and I'll admit that the laugh is on me."

But Bonner was mystified, uncertain. He had searched the house thoroughly from top to bottom, and he had seen nothing unusual, but these men and boys were so positive that he could not believe the eyes of all had been deceived.

"This interests me," he said at last. "I'll tell you what we'll do, Mr. Crow. You and I will come down here to-night, rig up a tent of some sort and divide watch until morning. If there is anything to be seen we'll find out what it is. I'll get a couple of straw mattresses from our boathouse and——"

"I've got rheumatiz, Mr. Bonner, an' it would be the death o' me to sleep in this swamp," objected Anderson hastily.

"Well, I'll come alone, then. I'm not afraid. I don't mean to say I'll sleep in that old shack, but I'll bunk out here in the woods. No human being could sleep in that place. Will any one volunteer to keep me company?"

Silence.

"I don't blame you. It does take nerve, I'll confess. My only stipulation is that you shall come down here from the village early to-morrow morning. I may have something of importance to tell you, Mr. Crow."

"We'll find his dead body," groaned old Mr. Borton.

"Say, mister," piped up a shrill voice, "I'll stay with you." It was Bud who spoke, and all Tinkletown was afterward to resound with stories of his bravery. The boy had been silently admiring the bold sportsman from Boston town, and he was ready to cast his lot with him in this adventure. He thrilled with pleasure when the big hero slapped him on the back and called him the only man in the crowd.

At eight o'clock that night Bonner and the determined but trembling Bud came up the bank from the

river and pitched a tent among the trees near the
haunted house. From the sledge on the river below
they trundled up their bedding and their stores. Bud
had an old single-barrel shotgun, a knife and a pipe,
which he was just learning to smoke; Bonner brought
a Navajo blanket, a revolver and a heavy walking
stick. He also had a large flask of whiskey and the
pipe that had graduated from Harvard with him.

At nine o'clock he put to bed in one of the chilly
nests a very sick boy, who hated to admit that the
pipe was too strong for him, but who felt very much
relieved when he found himself wrapped snugly in
the blankets with his head tucked entirely out of sight.
Bud had spent the hour in regaling Bonner with the
story of Rosalie Gray's abduction and his own heroic
conduct in connection with the case. He confessed
that he had knocked one of the villains down, but they
were too many for him. Bonner listened politely and
then—put the hero to bed.

Bonner dozed off at midnight. An hour or so later
he suddenly sat bolt upright, wide awake and alert.
He had the vague impression that he was deathly
cold and that his hair was standing on end.

CHAPTER XVIII

The Men in the Sleigh

LET us go back to the night on which Rosalie was seized and carried away from Mrs. Luce's front gate, despite the valiant resistance of her youthful defenders.

Rosalie had drooned Thackeray to the old lady until both of them were dozing, and it was indeed a welcome relief that came with Roscoe's resounding thumps on the front door. Mrs. Luce was too old to be frightened out of a year's growth, but it is perfectly safe to agree with her that the noise cost her at least three months.

Desperately blue over the defection of Elsie Banks, Rosalie had found little to make her evening cheerful indoors, but the fresh, crisp air set her spirits bounding the instant she closed Mrs. Luce's door from the outside. We have only to refer to Roscoe's lively narrative for proof of what followed almost instantly. She was seized, her head tightly wrapped in a thick cloak or blanket; then she was thrown into a sleigh, and knew nothing more except a smothering sensation and the odour of chloroform.

When she regained consciousness she was lying on the ground in the open air, dark night about her. Three men were standing nearby, but there was no

vehicle in sight. She tried to rise, but on account of
her bonds was powerless to do so. Speech was prevented by the cloth which closed her lips tightly.
After a time she began to grasp the meaning of the
muttered words that passed between the men.

"You got the rig in all right, Bill—you're sure that
no one heard or saw you?" were the first questions
she could make out, evidently arising from a previous
report or explanation.

"Sure. Everybody in these parts goes to bed at sun-
down. They ain't got nothing to do but sleep up
'ere."

"Nobody knows we had that feller's sleigh an' horses
out—nobody ever will know," said the big man, evidently the leader. She noticed they called him Sam.
"Next thing is to git her across the river without
leavin' any tracks. We ain't on a travelled road now,
pals; we got to be careful. I'll carry her down to the
bank; but be sure to step squarely in my footprints—
it'll look like they were made by one man. See?"

"The river's froze over an' we can't be tracked on
the ice. It's too dark, too, for any one to see us. Go
ahead, Sammy; it's d—— cold here."

The big man lifted her from the ground as if she
were a feather, and she was conscious of being borne
swiftly through a stretch of sloping woodland down
to the river bank, a journey of two or three hundred
yards, it seemed. Here the party paused for many
minutes before venturing out upon the wide expanse
of frozen river, evidently making sure that the way
was clear. Rosalie, her senses quite fully restored by

this time, began to analyse the situation with a clearness and calmness that afterward was the object of considerable surprise to her. Instead of being hysterical with fear, she was actually experiencing the thrill of a real emotion. She had no doubt but that her abductors were persons hired by those connected with her early history, and, strange as it may seem, she could not believe that bodily harm was to be her fate after all these years of secret attention on the part of those so deeply, though remotely, interested.

Somehow there raced through her brain the exhilarating conviction that at last the mystery of her origin was to be cleared away, and with it all that had been as a closed book. No thought of death entered her mind at that time. Afterward she was to feel that death would be most welcome, no matter how it came.

Her captors made the trip across the river in dead silence. There was no moon and the night was inky black. The exposed portions of her face tingled with cold, but she was so heavily wrapped in the blanket that her body did not feel the effects of the zero weather.

At length the icy stretch was passed, and after resting a few minutes, Sam proceeded to ascend the steep bank with her in his arms. Why she was not permitted to walk she did not know then or afterward. It is possible, even likely, that the men thought their charge was unconscious. She did nothing to cause them to think otherwise. Again they passed among trees, Sam's companions following in his footprints as before. Another halt and a brief command for

Davy to go ahead and see that the coast was clear came after a long and tortuous struggle through the underbrush. Twice they seemed to have lost their bearings in the darkness, but eventually they came into the open.

"Here we are!" grunted Sam as they hurried across the clearing. "A hard night's work, pals, but I guess we're in Easy Street now. Go ahead, Davy, an' open the trap!"

Davy swore a mighty but sibilant oath and urged his thick, ugly figure ahead of the others.

A moment later the desperadoes and their victim passed through a door and into a darkness even blacker than that outside. Davy was pounding carefully upon the floor of the room in which they stood. Suddenly a faint light spread throughout the room and a hoarse, raucous voice whispered:

"Have you got her?"

"Get out of the way—we're near froze," responded Davy gruffly.

"Get down there, Bill, and take her; I'm tired carryin' this hundred and twenty pounder," growled Sam.

The next instant Rosalie was conscious of being lowered through a trap door in the floor, and then of being borne rapidly through a long, narrow passage, lighted fitfully by the rays of a lantern in the hands of a fourth and as yet unseen member of the band.

"There!" said Bill, impolitely dropping his burden upon a pile of straw in the corner of the rather extensive cave at the end of the passage; "wonder if the little fool is dead. She ought to be coming to by this time."

"She's got her eyes wide open," uttered the raucous voice on the opposite side; and Rosalie turned her eyes in that direction. She looked for a full minute as if spellbound with terror, her gaze centred at the most repulsive human face she ever had seen—the face of Davy's mother.

The woman was a giantess, a huge, hideous creature with the face of a man, hairy and bloated. Her unkempt hair was grey almost to whiteness, her teeth were snags, and her eyes were almost hidden beneath the shaggy brow. There was a glare of brutal satisfaction in them that appalled the girl.

For the first time since the adventure began her heart
failed her, and she shuddered perceptibly as her lids fell.

"What the h—— are you skeering her fer like that,
ma," growled Davy. "Don't look at her like that,
or——"

"See here, my boy, don't talk like that to me if you
don't want me to kick your head off right where you
stand. I'm your mother, Davy, an'——"

"That'll do. This ain't no time to chew the rag,"
muttered Sam. "We're done fer. Get us something
to eat an' something to drink, old woman; give the
girl a nifter, too. She's fainted, I reckon. Hurry
up; I want to turn in."

"Better untie her hands—see if she's froze," added
Bill savagely.

Roughly the old woman slashed the bonds from the
girl's hands and feet and then looked askance at Sam,
who stood warming his hands over a kerosene stove
not far away. He nodded his head, and she instantly
untied the cloth that covered Rosalie's mouth.

"It won't do no good to scream, girl. Nobody'll
hear ye but us—and we're your friends," snarled the
old woman.

"Let her yell if she wants to, Maude. It may relieve
her a bit," said Sam, meaning to be kind. Instinctively Rosalie looked about for the person addressed as
Maude. There was but one woman in the gang.
Maude! That was the creature's name. Instead of
crying or shrieking, Rosalie laughed outright.

At the sound of the laugh the woman drew back
hastily.

"By gor!" she gasped; "the—she's gone daffy!"

The men turned toward them with wonder in their faces. Bill was the first to comprehend. He saw the girl's face grow sober with an effort, and realised that she was checking her amusement because it was sure to offend.

"Aw," he grinned, "I don't blame her fer laughin'! Say what ye will, Maude, your name don't fit you."

"It's as good as any name—" began the old hag, glaring at him; but Sam interposed with a command to her to get them some hot coffee while he had a talk with the girl. "Set up!" he said roughly, addressing Rosalie. "We ain't goin' to hurt you."

Rosalie struggled to a sitting posture, her limbs and back stiff from the cold and inaction. "Don't ask questions, because they won't be answered. I jest want to give you some advice as to how you must act while you are our guest. You must be like one of the family. Maybe we'll be here a day, maybe a week, but it won't be any longer than that."

"Would you mind telling me where I am and what this all means? Why have you committed this outrage? What have I done—" she found voice to say. He held up his hand.

"You forget what I said about askin' questions. There ain't nothin' to tell you, that's all. You're here and that's enough."

"Well, who is it that has the power to answer questions, sir? I have some right to ask them. You have——"

"That'll do, now!" he growled. "I'll put the gag

back on you if you keep it up. So's you won't worry, I want to say this to you: Your friends don't know where you are, and they couldn't find you if they tried. You are to stay right here in this cave until we get orders to move you. When the time comes we'll take you to wherever we're ordered, and then we're through with you. Somebody else will have the say. You won't be hurt here unless you try to escape—it won't do you any good to yell. It ain't a palace, but it's better than the grave. So be wise. All we got to do is to turn you over to the proper parties at the proper time. That's all."

"Is the person you speak of my—my mother or my father?" Rosalie asked with bated breath.

CHAPTER XIX

With the Kidnapers

SAM stared at her, and there was something like real amazement in his eyes.

"Yer mother or father?" he repeated interrogatively. "Wha—what the devil can they have to do with this affair? I guess they're askin' a lot of questions themselves about this time."

"Mr. and Mrs. Crow are not my parents," she said; and then shrewdly added, "and you know it, sir."

"I've heard that sayin' 'bout a child never knowin' its own father, but this business of both the father and mother is a new one on me. I guess it's the chloroform. Give us that booze, Bill. She's dippy yet."

He tried to induce her to swallow some of the whiskey, but steadfastly she refused, until finally, with an evil snarl, Sam commanded the giantess to hold her while he forced the burning liquor down her throat. There was a brief struggle, but Rosalie was no match for the huge woman, whose enormous arms encircled her; and as the liquid trickled in upon her tongue she heard above the brutal laughter of the would-be doctors the hoarse voice of Bill crying:

"Don't hurt her, Sam! Let 'er alone!"

"Close yer face! Don't you monkey in this thing, Bill Briggs. I'll—well, you know. Drink this, damn you!"

Sputtering and choking, her heart beating wildly with fear and rage, Rosalie was thrown back upon the straw by the woman. Her throat was burning from the effects of the whiskey and her eyes were blinded by the tears of anger and helplessness.

"Don't come any of your highfalutin' airs with me, you little cat," shrieked the old woman, rubbing a knee that Rosalie had kicked in her struggles.

"Lay still there," added Sam. "We don't want to hurt you, but you got to do as I tell you. Understand? Not a word, now! Gimme that coffee-pot, Davy. Go an' see that everything's locked up an' we'll turn in fer the night. Maude, you set up an' keep watch. If she makes a crack, soak her one."

"You bet I will. She'll find she ain't attendin' no Sunday-school picnic."

"No boozin'!" was Sam's order as he told out small portions of whiskey. Then the gang ate ravenously of the bacon and beans and drank cup after cup of coffee. Later the men threw themselves upon the piles of straw and soon all were snoring. The big woman refilled the lantern and hung it on a peg in the wall of the cave; then she took up her post near the square door leading to the underground passage, her throne an upturned whiskey barrel, her back against the wall of the cave. She glared at Rosalie through the semi-darkness, frequently addressing her with the vilest invectives cautiously uttered—and all because her victim had beautiful eyes and was unable to close them in sleep.

Rosalie's heart sank as she surveyed the surround-

"Rosalie was no match for the huge woman"

ings with her mind once more clear and composed. After her recovery from the shock of contact with the old woman and Sam she shrank into a state of mental lassitude that foretold the despair which was to come later on. She did not sleep that night. Her brain was full of whirling thoughts of escape, speculations as to what was to become of her, miserable fears that the end would not be what the first impressions had made it, and, over all, a most intense horror of the old woman, who dozed, but guarded her as no dragon ever watched in the days of long ago.

The cave in which they were housed was thirty or forty feet from side to side, almost circular in shape, a low roof slanting to the rocky floor. Here and there were niches in the walls, and in the side opposite to the entrance to the passageway there was a small, black opening, lead-ing without doubt to the outer world. The fact that it was not used at any time during her stay in the cave led her to believe it was not of practical use. Two or three coal-oil stoves were used to heat the cave and for cooking pur-poses. There were several lanterns, a

number of implements (such as spades, axes, crow-
bars, sledges, and so forth), stool-kegs, a rough
table, which was used for all purposes known
to the dining-room, kitchen, scullery and even
bedchamber. Sam slept on the table. Horse
blankets were thrown about the floor in confusion.
They served as bedclothes when the gang slept.
At other times they might as well have been
called doormats. One of the niches in the wall was
used as the resting place for such bones or remnants
as might strike it when hurled in that direction by
the occupants. No one took the trouble to carefully
bestow anything in the garbage hole, and no one pre-
tended to clean up after the other. The place was
foul smelling, hot and almost suffocating with the
fumes from the stoves, for which there seemed no
avenue of escape.

Hours afterward, although they seemed drawn out
into years, the men began to breathe naturally, and
a weird silence reigned in the cave. They were
awake. The venerable Maude emerged from her
doze, looked apprehensively at Sam, prodded the
corner to see that the prize had not faded away, and
then began ponderously to make preparations for a
meal, supposedly breakfast. Meagre ablutions, such
as they were, were performed in the "living room,"
a bucket of water serving as a general wash-basin.
No one had removed his clothing during the night,
not even his shoes. It seemed to her that the gang
was in an ever-ready condition to evacuate the place
at a moment's notice.

Rosalie would not eat, nor would she bathe her face in the water that had been used by the quartette before her. Bill Briggs, with some sense of delicacy in his nature, brought some fresh water from the far end of the passageway. For this act he was reviled by his companions.

"It's no easy job to get water here, Briggs," roared Sam. "We got to be savin' with it."

"Well, don't let it hurt you," retorted Bill. "I'll carry it up from the river to-night. You won't have to do it."

"She ain't any better'n I am," snorted Maude, "and nobody goes out to bring me a private bath, I take notice. Get up here and eat something, you rat! Do you want us to force it down you——"

"If she don't want to eat don't coax her," said Sam. "She'll soon get over that. We was only hired to get her here and get her away again, and not to make her eat or even wash. That's nothing to us."

"Well, she's got to eat or she'll die, and you know, Sam Welch, that ain't to be," retorted the old woman.

"She'll eat before she'll die, Maudie; don't worry."

"I'll never eat a mouthful!" cried Rosalie, a brave, stubborn light in her eyes. She was standing in the far corner drying her face with her handkerchief.

"Oho, you can talk again, eh? Hooray! Now we'll hear the story of her life," laughed big Sam, his mouth full of bacon and bread. Rosalie flushed and the tears welled to her eyes.

All day long she suffered taunts and gibes from the gang. She grew to fear Davy's ugly leers more than the brutal words of the others. When he came near she shrank back against the wall; when he spoke she cringed; when he attempted to touch her person she

screamed. It was this act that brought Sam's wrath upon Davy's head. He won something like gratitude from the girl by profanely commanding Davy to confine his love to looks and not to acts.

"She ain't to be harmed," was Sam's edict. "That goes, too."

"Aw, you go to—" began Davy belligerently.

"What's that?" snarled Sam, whirling upon him with a glare. Davy slunk behind his mother and glared back. Bill moved over to Sam's side. For a moment the air was heavy with signs of an affray. Rosalie crouched in her corner, her hand over her ears, her eyes closed. There was murder in Davy's face. "I'll break every bone in your body!" added Sam; but Bill laconically stayed him with a word.

"Rats!" It was brief, but it brought the irate Sam to his senses. Trouble was averted for the time being.

"Davy ain't afraid of him," cried that worthy's mother shrilly.

"You bet I ain't!" added Davy after a long string of oaths. Sam grinned viciously.

"There ain't nothin' to fight about, I guess," he said, although he did not look it. "We'd be fools to scrap. Everything to lose and nothin' to gain. All I got to say, Davy, is that you ain't to touch that girl."

"Who's goin' to touch her?" roared Davy, bristling bravely. "An' you ain't to touch her nuther," he added.

The day wore away, although it was always night in the windowless cave, and again the trio of men slept, with Maude as guard. Exhausted and faint, Rosalie fell into a sound sleep. The next morning she ate sparingly of the bacon and bread and drank some steaming coffee, much to the derisive delight of the hag.

"You had to come to it, eh?" she croaked. "Had to feed that purty face, after all. I guess we're all alike. We're all flesh and blood, my lady."

The old woman never openly offered personal vio-

lence to the girl. She stood in some fear of the leader
—not physical fear, but the strange homage that a
brute pays to its master. Secretly she took savage

delight in treading on
the girl's toes or in
pinching her arms and
legs, twisting her hair,
spilling hot coffee on
her hands, cursing her
softly and perpetrating
all sorts of little indig-
nities that could not be
r e s e n t e d, for the
simple reason that they
could not be proved
a g a i n s t her. Her
word was as good as
Rosalie's.

Hourly the strain
grew worse and worse.
The girl became ill and feverish with fear, loathing
and uncertainty. Her ears rang with the horrors of
their lewdness, her eyes came to see but little, for she
kept them closed for the very pain of what they were
likely to witness. In her heart there grew a constant
prayer for deliverance from their clutches. She was
much too strong-minded and healthy to pray for
death, but her mind fairly reeled with the thoughts
of the vengeance she would exact.

The third day found the gang morose and ugly.
The confinement was as irksome to them as it was

to her. They fretted and worried, swore and growled. At nightfall of each day Sam ventured forth through the passage and out into the night. Each time he was gone for two or three hours, and each succeeding return to the vile cave threw the gang into deeper wrath. The word they were expecting was not forthcoming, the command from the real master was not given. They played cards all day, and at last began to drink more deeply than was wise. Two desperate fights occurred between Davy and Sam on the third day. Bill and the old woman pulled them apart after both had been battered savagely.

"She's sick, Sam," growled Bill, standing over the cowering, white-faced prisoner near the close of the fourth day. Sam had been away nearly all of the previous night, returning gloomily without news from headquarters. "She'll die in this d—— place and so will we if we don't get out soon. Look at her! Why, she's as white as a sheet. Let's give her some fresh air, Sammy. It's safe. Take her up in the cabin for a while. To-night we can take her outside the place. Good Lord, Sammy, I've got a bit of heart! I can't see her die in this hole. Look at her! Can't you see she's nearly done for?"

After considerable argument, pro and con, it was decided that it would be safe and certainly wise to let the girl breathe the fresh air once in a while. That morning Sam took her into the cabin through the passage. The half hour in the cold, fresh air revived her, strengthened her perceptibly. Her spirits took an upward bound. She began to ask questions, and for some reason he began to take notice of them. It may have been the irksomeness of the situation, his own longing to be away, his anger toward the person who had failed to keep the promise made before the abduction, that led him to talk quite freely.

CHAPTER XX

In the Cave

"IT's not my fault that we're still here," he growled in answer to her pathetic appeal. "I've heard you prayin' for Daddy Crow to come and take you away. Well, it's lucky for him that he don't know where you are. We'd make mincemeat of that old jay in three minutes. Don't do any more prayin'. Prayers are like dreams—you have 'em at night and wonder why the next day. Now, look 'ere, Miss Gray, we didn't do this rotten job for the love of excitement. We're just as anxious to get out of it as you are."

"I only ask why I am held here and what is to become of me?" said Rosalie resignedly. She was standing across the table from where he sat smoking his great, black pipe. The other members of the gang were lounging about, surly and black-browed, chafing inwardly over the delay in getting away from the cave.

"I don't know why you've been held here. I only know it's d—— slow. I'd chuck the job, if there wasn't so much dust in it for me."

"But what is to become of me? I cannot endure this much longer. It is killing me. Look! I am black and blue from pinches. The old woman never misses an opportunity to hurt me."

"She's jealous of you because you're purty, that's all. Women are all alike, hang 'em! I wouldn't be in this sort of work if it hadn't been for a jealous wife."

He puffed at his pipe moodily for a long time, evidently turning some problem over and over in his mind. At last, heaving a deep sigh, and prefacing his remarks with an oath, he let light in upon the mystery. "I'll put you next to the job. Can't give any names; it wouldn't be square. You see, it's this way: you ain't wanted in this country. I don't know why, but you ain't."

"Not wanted in this country?" she cried blankly. "I don't stand in any one's way. My life and my love are for the peaceful home that you have taken me from. I don't ask for anything else. Won't you tell your employer as much for me? If I am released, I shall never interfere with the plans of——"

" 'Tain't that, I reckon. You must be mighty important to somebody, or all this trouble wouldn't be gone through with. The funny part of it is that we ain't to hurt you. You ain't to be killed, you know. That's the queer part of it, ain't it?"

"I'll admit it has an agreeable sound to me," said Rosalie with a shadow of a smile on her trembling lips. "It seems ghastly, though."

"Well, anyhow, it's part of somebody's scheme to get you out of this country altogether. You are to be taken away on a ship, across the ocean, I think. Paris or London, mebby, and you are never to come

"SHE SHRANK BACK FROM ANOTHER BLOW WHICH SEEMED
IMPENDING"

back to the United States. Never, that's what I'm told."

Rosalie was speechless, stunned. Her eyes grew wide with the misery of doubt and horror, her lips moved as if forming the words which would not come. Before she could bring a sound from the contracted throat the raucous voice of old Maude broke in:

"What are you tellin' her, Sam Welch? Can't you keep your face closed?" she called, advancing upon him with a menacing look.

"Aw, it's nothin' to you," he retorted, but an uncomfortable expression suddenly crept into his face. A loud, angry discussion ensued, the whole gang engaging. Three to one was the way it stood against the leader, who was forced to admit, secretly if not publicly, that he had no right to talk freely of the matter to the girl. In vain she pleaded and promised. Her tears were of no avail, once Sam had concluded to hold his tongue. Angry with himself for having to submit to the demands of the others, furious because she saw his surrender, Sam, without a word of warning, suddenly struck her on the side of the head with the flat of his broad hand, sending her reeling into the corner. Dazed, hurt and half stunned, she dropped to her knees, unable to stand. With a piteous look in her eyes she shrank back from another blow which seemed impending. Bill Briggs grasped his leader's arm and drew him away, cursing and snarling.

Late in the afternoon, Bill was permitted to conduct her into the cabin above, for a few minutes in the air,

and for a glimpse of the failing sunlight. She had scarcely taken her stand before t h e little window when s h e w a s hastily jerked away, but not b e f o r e s h e thought she had perceived a crowd of men, huddling among the trees not far away. A scream for help started to her lips; but Bill's heavy hand checked it effectually. His burly arm sent her scuttling toward the trap-door; and a second later she was below, bruised from the fall and half fainting with disappointment and despair.

Brief as the glimpse had been, she was positive she recognised two faces in the crowd of men—Anderson Crow's and Ed Higgins's. It meant, if her eyes did not deceive her, that the searchers were near at hand, and that dear, old Daddy Crow was leading them. Her hopes flew upward and she could not subdue the triumphant glance that swept the startled crowd when Bill breathlessly broke the news.

Absolute quiet reigned in the cave after that. Maude cowed the prisoner into silence with the threat to cut out her tongue if she uttered a cry. Later, the tramp of feet could be heard on the floor of the cabin.

There was a sound of voices, loud peals of laughter, and then the noise made by some one in the cellar that served as a blind at one end of the cabin. After that, dead silence. At nightfall, Sam stealthily ventured forth to reconnoitre. He came back with the report that the woods and swamps were clear and that the searchers, if such they were, had gone away.

"The house, since Davy's grandma's bones were stored away in that cellar for several moons, has always been thought to be haunted. The fools probably thought they saw a ghost—an' they're runnin' yet."

Then for the first time Rosalie realised that she was in the haunted cabin in the swamp, the most fearsome of all places in the world to Tinkletown, large and small. Not more than three miles from her own fireside! Not more than half an hour's walk from Daddy Crow and others in the warmth of whose love she had lived so long!

"It's gettin' too hot here for us," growled Sam at supper. "We've just got to do something. I'm going out to-night to see if there's any word from the—from the party. These guys ain't all fools. Somebody is liable to nose out the trap-door before long and there'll be hell to pay. They won't come back before to-morrow, I reckon. By thunder, there ought to be word from the—the boss by this time. Lay low, everybody; I'll be back before daybreak. This time I'm a-goin' to find out something sure or know the reason why. I'm gettin' tired of this business. Never know what minute the jig's up, nor when the balloon busts."

Again he stole forth into the night, leaving his companions more or less uneasy as to the result, after the startling events of the afternoon. Hour after hour passed, and with every minute therein, Rosalie's ears strained themselves to catch the first sound of approaching rescuers. Her spirits fell, but her hopes were high. She felt sure that the men outside had

seen her face and that at last they had discovered the place in which she was kept. It would only be a question of time until they learned the baffling secret of the trap-door. Her only fear lay in the possibility that she might be removed by her captors before the rescuers could accomplish her delivery. Her bright, feverish, eager eyes, gleaming from the sunken white cheeks, appealed to Bill Briggs more than he cared to admit. The ruffian, less hardened than his fellows, began to feel sorry for her.

Eleven o'clock found the trio anxious and ugly in their restlessness. There was no sleep for them. Davy visited the trap over a hundred times that night. His mother, breaking over the traces of restraint, hugged the jug of whiskey, taking swig after swig as the vigil wore on. At last Davy, driven to it, insisted upon having his share. Bill drank but little, and it was not long before Rosalie observed the shifty, nervous look in his eyes. From time to time he slyly appropriated certain articles, dropping them into his coat pocket. His ear muffs, muffler, gloves, matches, tobacco and many chunks of bread and bacon were stowed stealthily in the pockets of his coat. At last it dawned upon her that Bill was preparing to desert. Hope lay with him, then. If he could only be induced to give her an equal chance to escape!

Mother and son became maudlin in their—not cups, but jug; but Davy had the sense to imbibe more cautiously, a fact which seemed to annoy the nervous Bill.

"I must have air—fresh air," suddenly moaned Rosalie from her corner, the strain proving too great for her nerves. Bill strode over and looked down upon the trembling form for a full minute. "Take me outside for just a minute—just a minute, please. I am dying in here."

"Lemme take her out," cackled old Maude. "I'll

give her all the air she wants. Want so—some air myself. Lemme give her air, Bill. Have some air on me, pardner. Lemme———"

"Shut up, Maude!" growled Bill, glancing uneasily about the cave. "I'll take her up in the cabin fer a couple of minutes. There ain't no danger."

Davy protested, but Bill carried his point, simply because he was sober and knew his power over the half-stupefied pair. Davy let them out through the trap, promising to wait below until they were ready to return.

"Are you going away?" whispered Rosalie, as they passed out into the cold, black night.

"Sh! Don't talk, damn you!" he hissed.

"Let me go too. I know the way home and you need have no fear of me. I like you, but I hate the others. Please, please! For God's sake, let me go! They can't catch me if I have a little start."

"I'd like to, but I—I dassent. Sam would hunt me down and kill me—he would sure. I am goin' my-self—I can't stand it no longer."

"Have pity! Don't leave me alone with them. Oh, God, if you———"

Moaning piteously, she pleaded with him; but he was obdurate, chiefly through fear of the conse-quences. In his heart he might have been willing to give her the chance, but his head saw the danger to itself and it was firm.

"I'll tell you what I'll do," he whispered in the end. "I'll take you back there and then I'll go and tell your friends where you are and how to help you. Honest! Honest, I will. I know it's as broad as it is long, but I'd rather do it that way. They'll be here in a couple of hours and you'll be free. Nobody will be the wiser. Curse your whining! Shut up! Damn you, get back in there! Don't give me away to Davy, and I'll swear to help you out of this."

A minute of two later, he dragged her back into the cabin, moaning, pleading, and crying from the pain of a sudden blow. Ten minutes afterward he went forth again, this time ostensibly to meet Sam; but Rosalie knew that he was gone forever.

CHAPTER XXI

The Trap-Door

A SICKLY new moon threw vague ghostly beams across the willow-lined swamp, out beyond the little cabin that stood on its border. Through the dense undergrowth and high among the skeleton treetops ugly shadows played with each other, while a sepulchral orchestra of wind and bough shrieked a dirge that flattened in Bonner's ears; but it was not the weird music of the swamp that sent the shudder of actual terror through the frame of the big athlete. A series of muffled, heartbreaking moans, like those of a woman in dire pain, came to his ears. He felt the cold perspiration start over his body. His nerves grew tense with trepidation, his eyes wide with horror. Instinctively, his fingers clutched the revolver at his side and his gaze went toward the black, square thing which marked the presence of the haunted house. The orchestra of the night seemed to bring its dirge to a close; a chill interlude of silence ensued. The moans died away into choking sobs, and Bonner's ears could hear nothing else. A sudden thought striking him, he rolled out of his bed and made his way to Bud's pile of blankets. But the solution was not there. The lad was sound asleep and no sound issued from his lips. The moans came from another source, human or otherwise, out there in the crinkling night.

Carefully making his way from the tent, his courage once more restored but his flesh still quivering, Bonner looked intently for manifestations in the black home of Johanna Rank. He half expected to see a ghostly light flit past a window. It was intensely dark in the thicket, but the shadowy marsh beyond silhouetted the house into a black relief. He was on all fours behind a thick pile of brush, nervously drawing his pipe from his pocket, conscious that he needed it to steady his nerves, when a fresh sound, rising above the faint sobs, reached his ears. Then the low voice of a man came from some place in the darkness, and these words rang out distinctly:

"Damn you!"

He drew back involuntarily, for the voice seemed to be at his elbow. The sobs ceased suddenly, as if choked by a mighty hand.

The listener's inclination was to follow the example of Anderson Crow and run madly off into the night. But beneath this natural panic was the soul of chivalry. Something told him that a woman out there in the solitude needed the arms of a man; and his blood began to grow hot again. Presently the silence was broken by a sharp cry of despair :

"Have pity! Oh, God—" moaned the voice that sent thrills through his body—the voice of a woman, tender, refined, crushed. His fingers gripped the revolver with fresh vigor, but almost instantly the rustling of dead leaves reached his ears: the man and his victim were making their way toward the house.

Bonner crouched among the bushes as if paralysed. He began to comprehend the situation. In a vague sort of way he remembered hearing of Tinkletown's sensation over at his uncle's house, where he was living with a couple of servants for a month's shooting. The atmosphere had been full of the sensational abduction story for several days—the abduction of a beautiful young woman and the helpless attitude of the relatives and friends. Like a whirlwind the whole situation spread itself before him; it left him weak. He had come upon the gang and their victim in this out-of-the-way corner of the world, far from the city toward which they were supposed to have fled. He had the solution in his hands and he was filled with the fire of the ancients.

A light appeared in the low doorway and the squat figure of a man held a lantern on high. An instant later, another man dragged the helpless girl across the threshold and into the house. Even as Bonner squared himself to rush down upon them the light disappeared and darkness fell over the cabin. There was a sound of footsteps on the floor, a creaking of hinges and the stealthy closing of a door. Then there was absolute quiet.

Bonner was wise as well as brave. He saw that to rush down upon the house now might prove his own as well as her undoing. In the darkness, the bandits would have every advantage. For a moment he glared at the black shadow ahead, his brain working like lightning.

"That poor girl!" he muttered vaguely. "Damn

beasts! But I'll fix 'em, by heaven! It won't be long, my boys."

His pondering brought quick results. Crawling to Bud's cot, he aroused him from a deep sleep. Inside of two minutes the lad was streaking off through the woods toward town, with instructions to bring Anderson Crow and a large force of men to the spot as quickly as possible.

"I'll stand guard," said Wicker Bonner.

As the minutes went by Bonner's thoughts dwelt more and more intently upon the poor, imprisoned girl in the cabin. His blood charged his reason and he could scarce control the impulse to dash in upon the wretches. Then he brought himself up with a jerk. Where was he to find them? Had he not searched the house that morning and was there a sign of life to be found? He was stunned by this memory. For many minutes he stood with his perplexed eyes upon the house before a solution came to him.

He now knew that there was a secret apartment in the old house and a secret means of entrance and exit. With this explanation firmly impressed upon his mind, Wicker Bonner decided to begin his own campaign for the liberation of Rosalie Gray. It would be hours before the sluggish Anderson Crow appeared; and Bonner was not the sort to leave a woman in jeopardy if it was in his power to help her. Besides, the country people had filled him with stories of Miss Gray's beauty, and they found him at an impressionable and heart-free age. The thrill of romance seized him and he was ready to dare.

He crept up to the doorway and listened. Reason told him that the coast was clear; the necessity for a sentinel did not exist, so cleverly were the desperadoes under cover. After a few moments, he crawled into the room, holding his breath, as he made his way toward the cellar staircase. He had gone but a few feet when the sound of voices came to him. Slinking into a corner, he awaited developments. The sounds came from below, but not from the cellar room, as he had located it. A moment later, a man crawled into the room, coming through a hole in the floor, just as he had suspected. A faint light from below revealed the sinister figure plainly, but Bonner felt himself to be quite thoroughly hidden. The man in the room spoke to some one below.

"I'll be back in half an hour, Davy. I'll wait fer Sam out there on the Point. He ought to have some news from headquarters by this time. I don't see why we have to hang around this place forever. She ought to be half way to Paris by now."

"They don't want to take chances, Bill, till the excitement blows over."

"Well, you an' your mother just keep your hands off of her while I'm out, that's all," warned Bill Briggs.

The trap-door was closed, and Bonner heard the other occupant of the room shuffle out into the night. He was not long in deciding what to do. Here was the chance to dispose of one of the bandits, and he was not slow to seize it. There was a meeting in the thicket a few minutes later, and Bill was "out of the way" for the time being. Wicker Bonner dropped him with a sledge-hammer blow, and when he returned to the cabin Bill was lying bound and gagged in the tent, a helpless captive.

His conqueror, immensely satisfied, supplied himself with the surplus ends of "guy ropes" from the tent and calmly sat down to await the approach of the one called Sam, he who had doubtless gone to a rendezvous "for news." He could well afford to bide his time. With two of the desperadoes disposed of in ambuscade, he could have a fairly even chance with the man called Davy.

It seemed hours before he heard the stealthy approach of some one moving through the bushes. He was stiff with cold, and chafing at the interminable delay, but the approach of real danger quickened his blood once more. There was another short, sharp, silent struggle near the doorway, and once more Wicker Bonner stood victorious over an unsuspecting and now unconscious bandit. Sam, a big, powerful man, was soon bound and gagged and his bulk dragged off to the tent among the bushes.

"Now for Davy," muttered Bonner, stretching his great arms in the pure relish of power. "There will be something doing around your heart, Miss Babe-in-the-Woods, in a very few minutes."

He chuckled as he crept into the cabin, first having listened intently for sounds. For some minutes he lay quietly with his ear to the floor. In that time he solved one of the problems confronting him. The man Davy was a son of old Mrs. Rank's murderer,

and the "old woman" who kept watch with him was
his mother, wife of the historic David. It was she who
had held the lantern, no doubt, while David Wolfe
chopped her own mother to mincemeat. This accounted for the presence of the gang in the haunted
house and for their knowledge of the underground
room.

Bonner's inspiration began to wear off. Pure luck
had aided him up to this stage, but the bearding of
David in his lair was another proposition altogether.
His only hope was that he might find the man asleep.
He was not taking the old woman into consideration
at all. Had he but known it, she was the most
dangerous of all.

His chance, he thought, lay in strategy. It was
impossible to open the trap-door from above, he had
found by investigation. There was but one way to
get to Miss Gray, and that was by means of a daring
ruse. Trusting to luck, he tapped gently on the
floor at the spot where memory told him the trap-
door was situated. His heart was thumping violently.

There was a movement below him, and then the
sound of some one handling the bolts in the door.
Bonner drew back, hoping against hope that a light
would not be shown. In one hand he held his revolver ready for use; in the other his heavy walking
stick. His plans were fully developed. After a
moment the trap was lifted partially and a draft of
warm air came out upon him.

CHAPTER XXII

Jack, the Giant Killer

"THAT you, Sam?" half whispered a man's voice. There was no light.

"Sh!" hissed Bonner, muffling his voice. "Is everybody in?"

"Bill's waitin' fer you outside. Ma an' me are here. Come on down. What's up?"

"How's the girl?"

"Bellerin' like a baby. Ma's with her in the cave. Hurry up! This thing's heavy."

For reply Bonner seized the edge of the door with his left hand, first pushing his revolver in his trousers' pocket. Then he silently swung the heavy cane through the air and downward, a very faint light from below revealing the shock head of Davy in the aperture. It was a mighty blow and true. Davy's body fell away from the trap, and a second later Bonner's dropped through the hole. He left the trap wide open in case retreat were necessary. Pausing long enough to assure himself that the man was unconscious and bleeding profusely, and to snatch the big revolver from Davy's person, Bonner turned his attention to the surroundings.

Perhaps a hundred feet away, at the end of a long, low passage, he saw the glimmer of a light. Without a second's hesitation he started toward it, feeling that the worst of the adventure was past. A shadow coming between him and the light, he paused in his approach. This shadow resolved itself into the form of a woman, a gigantic creature, who peered intently up the passage.

"What's the matter, Davy?" she called in raucous tones. "You damn fool, can't you do anything without breaking your neck? I reckon you fell down the steps? That you, Sam?"

Receiving no answer, the woman clutched the lantern and advanced boldly upon Bonner, who stood far down the passage, amazed and irresolute. She looked more formidable to him than any of the men, so he prepared for a struggle.

"Halt!" he cried, when she was within ten feet of him. "Don't resist; you are surrounded!"

The woman stopped like one shot, glared ahead as if she saw him for the first time, and then uttered a frightful shriek of rage. Dashing the lantern to the ground, she raised her arm and fired a revolver point blank at Bonner, despite the fact that his pistol was covering her. He heard the bullet crash into the rotten timbers near his ear. Contrary to her design, the lantern was not extinguished. Instead, it lay sputtering but effective upon the floor.

Before Bonner could make up his mind to shoot at the woman she was upon him, firing again as she came. He did not have time to retaliate. The huge frame crushed down upon him and his pistol flew from his hand. As luck would have it, his free hand clutched her revolver, and she was prevented from

blowing his brains out with the succeeding shots, all
of which went wild.

Then came a desperate struggle. Bonner, a trained
athlete, realised that she was even stronger than he,
more desperate in her frenzy, and with murder in her
heart. As they lunged to and fro, her curses and

shrieks in his ear, he began to feel the despair of
defeat. She was beating him down with one mighty
arm, crushing blows, every one of them. Then came
the sound which turned the tide of battle, for it filled
him with a frenzy equal to her own. The scream of
a woman came down through the passage, piteous,
terror-stricken.

He knew the fate of that poor girl if his adversary
overcame him. The thought sent his blood hot and
cold at once. Infuriatedly, he exerted his fine
strength, and the tide turned. Panting and snarling,
the big woman was battered down. He flung her
heavily to the ground and then leaped back to pick
up his revolver, expecting a renewal of the attack.
For the first time he was conscious of intense pain in
his left leg. The woman made a violent effort to
rise, and then fell back, groaning and cursing.

"You've done it! You've got me!" she yelled.
"My leg's broke!" Then she shrieked for Davy and
Bill and Sam, raining curses upon the law and upon
the traitor who had been their undoing.

Bonner, his own leg wobbling and covered with
blood, tried to quiet her, but without success. He
saw that she was utterly helpless, her leg twisted
under her heavy body. Her screams of pain as he
turned her over proved conclusively that she was not
shamming. Her hip was dislocated. The young
man had sense enough left to return to Davy before
venturing into the cave where Miss Gray was doubtless in a dead faint. The man was breathing, but
still unconscious from the blow on the head. Bonner

quickly tied his hands and feet, guarding against emergencies in case of his own incapacitation as the result of the bullet wound in his leg; then he hobbled off with the lantern past the groaning Amazon in quest of Rosalie Gray. It did not occur to him until afterward that single handed he had overcome a most desperate band of criminals, so simply had it all worked out up to the time of the encounter with the woman.

A few yards beyond where the old woman lay moaning he came upon the cave in which the bandits made their home. Holding the lantern above his head, Bonner peered eagerly into the cavern. In the farthest corner crouched a girl, her terror-struck eyes fastened upon the stranger.

"How do you do, Miss Gray," came the cheery greeting from his lips. She gasped, swept her hand over her eyes, and tried piteously to speak. The words would not come. "The long-prayed-for rescue has come. You are free—that is, as soon as we find our way out of this place. Let me introduce myself as Jack, the Giant Killer—hello! Don't do that! Oh, the devil!" She had toppled over in a dead faint.

How Wicker Bonner, with his wounded leg, weak from loss of blood, and faint from the reaction, carried her from the cave through the passage and the trap-door and into the tent can only be imagined, not described. He only knew that it was necessary to remove her from the place, and that his strength would soon be gone. The sun was tinting the east before she opened her eyes and shuddered. In the meantime he had stanched the flow of blood in the fleshy part of his leg, binding the limb tightly with a piece of rope. It was an ugly, glancing cut made by a bullet of large calibre, and it was sure to put him on crutches for some time to come. Even now he was scarcely able to move the member. For an hour he had been venting his wrath upon the sluggish Anderson Crow, who should have been on the scene long before this. Two of his captives, now fully conscious, were glaring at their companions in the tent with hate in their eyes.

Rosalie Gray, wan, dishevelled, but more beautiful than the reports had foretold, could not at first believe herself to be free from the clutches of the bandits. It took him many minutes—many painful minutes—to convince her that it was not a dream, and that in truth he was Wicker Bonner, gentleman. Sitting with his back against a tent pole, facing the cabin through the flap, with a revolver in his trembling hand, he told her of the night's adventures, and was repaid tenfold by the gratitude which shone from her eyes and trembled in her voice. In return she told him of her capture, of the awful experiences in the cave, and of the threats which had driven her almost to the end of endurance.

"Oh, oh, I could love you forever for this!" she cried in the fulness of her joy. A rapturous smile flew to Bonner's eyes.

"Forever begins with this instant, Miss Gray," he said; and without any apparent reason the two shook hands. Afterward they were to think of this trivial act and vow that it was truly the beginning. They were young, heart-free, and full of the romance of life.

"And those awful men are really captured—and the woman?" she cried, after another exciting recital from him. Sam and Bill fairly snarled. "Suppose they should get loose?" Her eyes grew wide with the thought of it.

"They can't," he said laconically. "I wish the marshal and his bicycle army would hurry along. That woman and Davy need attention. I'd hate like the mischief to have either of them die. One doesn't want to kill people, you know, Miss Gray."

"But they were killing me by inches," she protested.

"Ouch!" he groaned, his leg giving him a mighty twinge.

"What is it?" she cried in alarm. "Why should we wait for those men? Come, Mr. Bonner, take me to the village—please do. I am crazy, absolutely crazy, to see Daddy Crow and mother. I can walk there—how far is it?—please come." She was running on eagerly in this strain until she saw the look of pain in his face—the look he tried so hard to conceal. She was standing straight and strong and eager before him, and he was very pale under the tan.

"I can't, Miss Gray. I'm sorry, you know. See! Where there's smoke there's fire—I mean, where there's blood there's a wound. I'm done for, in other words."

"Done for? Oh, you're not—not going to die!

Are you hurt? Why didn't you tell me?" Whereupon she dropped to her knees at his side, her dark eyes searching his intently, despair in them until the winning smile struggled back into his. The captives chuckled audibly. "What can I—what shall I do? Oh, why don't those men come! It must be noon or——"

"It's barely six A.M., Miss Gray. Don't worry. I'm all right. A cut in my leg; the old woman plugged me. I can't walk, you know—but——"

"And you carried me out here and did all that and never said a word about—oh, how good and brave and noble you are!"

When Anderson Crow and half of Tinkletown, routed out *en masse* by Bud, appeared on the scene an hour or two later, they found Wicker Bonner stretched out on a mattress, his head in Rosalie's lap. The young woman held his revolver in her hand, and there was a look in her face which said that she would shoot any one who came to molest her charge. Two helpless desperadoes lay cursing in the corner of the tent.

Anderson Crow, after an hour of deliberation and explanation, fell upon the bound and helpless bandits and bravely carted the whole lot to the town "calaboose." Wicker Bonner and his nurse were taken into town, and the news of the rescue went flying over the county, and eventually to the four corners of the land, for Congressman Bonner's nephew was a person of prominence.

Bonner, as he passed up the main street in Peabody's

sleigh on the way to Anderson Crow's home, was the centre of attraction. He was the hero of the hour, for was not Rosalie Gray herself, pale and ill with torture, his most devoted slave? What else could Tinkletown do but pay homage when it saw Bonner's head against her shoulder and Anderson Crow shouting approval from the bob-sled that carried the kidnapers. The four bandits, two of them much the worse for the night's contact with Wicker Bonner, were bundled into the lock-up, a sadly morose gang of ghosts.

"I owe you a thousand dollars," said Anderson to Bonner as they drew up in front of the marshal's home. All Tinkletown was there to see how Mrs. Crow and the family would act when Rosalie was restored to them. The yard was full of gaping villagers, and there was a diffident cheer when Mrs. Crow rushed forth and fairly dragged Rosalie from the sleigh. "Blootch" Peabody gallantly interposed and undertook to hand the girl forth with the grace of a Chesterfield. But Mrs. Crow had her way.

"I'll take it out in board and lodging," grinned Wicker Bonner to Anderson as two strong men lifted him from the sleigh.

"Where's Bud?" demanded Anderson after the others had entered the house.

"He stayed down to the 'calaboose' to guard the prisoners," said "Blootch." "Nobody could find the key to the door and nobody else would stay. They ain't locked in, but Bud's got two revolvers, and he says they can only escape over his dead body."

CHAPTER XXIII

Tinkletown's Convulsion

ANDERSON CROW was himself once more. He was twenty years younger than when he went to bed the night before. His joy and pride had reached the bursting point—dignity alone prevented the catastrophe.

"What do you expect to do with the gang, Mr. Crow?" asked Bonner, reclining with amiable ease in the marshal's Morris chair. He was feeling very comfortable, despite "Doc" Smith's stitches; and he could not help acknowledging, with more or less of a glow in his heart, that it was nice to play hero to such a heroine.

"Well, I'll protect 'em, of course. Nobody c'n lynch 'em while I'm marshal of this town," Anderson said, forgetful of the fact that he had not been near the jail, where Master Bud still had full charge of affairs, keyless but determined. "I'll have to turn them over to the county sheriff to-day er to-morrow, I reckon. This derned old calaboose of ourn ain't any too safe. That's a mighty desperit gang we've captured. I cain't remember havin' took sech a mob before."

"Has it occurred to you, Mr. Crow, that we have captured only the hirelings? Their employer, whoever he or she may be, is at large and probably laugh-

ing at us. Isn't there some way in which we can follow the case up and land the leader?"

"'y Gosh, you're right," said Anderson. "I thought
of that this mornin', but it clean skipped my mind since
then. There's where the mistake was made, Mr.
Bonner. It's probably too late now. You'd oughter
thought about the leader. Seems to me——"

"Why, Daddy Crow," cried Rosalie, a warm flush
in her cheeks once more, "hasn't Mr. Bonner done
his part? Hasn't he taken them single-handed and
hasn't he saved me from worse than death?"

"I ain't castin' any insinyations at him, Rosalie,"
retorted Anderson, very sternly for him. "How *can*
you talk like that?"

"I'm not offended, Miss Gray," laughed Bonner.
"We all make mistakes. It has just occurred to me,
however, that Mr. Crow may still be able to find
out who the leader is. The prisoners can be pumped,
I dare say."

"You're right ag'in, Mr. Bonner. It's funny how
you c'n read my thoughts. I was jest goin' down to
the jail to put 'em through the sweat cell."

"Sweat cell? You mean sweat box, Mr. Crow,"
said Bonner, laughing in spite of himself.

"No, sir; it's a cell. We couldn't find a box big
enough. I use the cell reserved fer women prisoners.
Mebby some day the town board will put in a reg'lar
box, but, so far, the cell has done all right. I'll be
back 'bout supper-time, Eva. You take keer o'
Rosalie. Make her sleep a while an' I guess you'd
better dose her up a bit with quinine an'——"

"I guess I know what to give her, Anderson Crow," resented his wife. "Go 'long with you. You'd oughter been lookin' after them kidnapers three hours ago. I bet Bud's purty nigh wore out guardin' them. He's been there ever sence nine o'clock, an' it's half-past two now."

"Roscoe's helpin' him," muttered Anderson, abashed.

At that instant there came a rush of footsteps across the front porch and in burst Ed Higgins and "Blootch" Peabody, fairly gasping with excitement.

"Hurry up, Anderson—down to the jail," sputtered the former; and then he was gone like the wind. "Blootch," determined to miss nothing, whirled to follow, or pass him if possible. He had time to shout over his shoulder as he went forth without closing the door:

"The old woman has lynched herself!"

It would now be superfluous to remark, after all the convulsions Tinkletown had experienced inside of twenty-four hours, that the populace went completely to pieces in face of this last trying experiment of Fate. With one accord the village toppled over as if struck by a broadside and lay, figuratively speaking, writhing in its own gore. Stupefaction assailed the town. Then one by one the minds of the people scrambled up from the ashes, slowly but surely, only to wonder where lightning would strike next. Not since the days of the American Revolution had the town experienced such an incessant rush of incident. The Judgment Day itself, with Gabriel's clarion

blasts, could not be expected to surpass this product-
ive hour in thrills.

It was true that old Maude had committed suicide
in the calaboose. She had been placed on a cot in
the office of the prison and Dr. Smith had been sent
for, immediately after her arrival; but he was making a call in the country. Bud Long, supported by
half a dozen boys armed with Revolutionary muskets,
which would not go off unless carried, stood in front
of the little jail with its wooden walls and iron bars,
guarding the prisoners zealously. The calaboose was
built to hold tramps and drunken men, but not for the
purpose of housing desperadoes. Even as the heroic
Bud watched with persevering faithfulness, his
charges were planning to knock their prison to
smithereens and at the proper moment escape to the
woods and hills. They knew the grated door was
unlocked, but they imagined the place to be completely surrounded by vengeful villagers, who would
cut them down like rats if they ventured forth. Had
they but known that Bud was alone, it is quite likely
they would have sallied forth and relieved him of his
guns, spanked him soundly and then ambled off un-
molested to the country.

All the morning old Maude had been groaning and
swearing in the office, where she lay unattended. Bud
was telling his friends how he had knocked her down
twice in the cave, after she had shot six times and
slashed at him with her dagger, when a sudden cessa-
tion of groans from the interior attracted the attention of all. "Doc" Smith arrived at that juncture

and found the boys listening intently for a resumption of the picturesque profanity. It was some time before the crowd became large enough to inspire a visit to the interior of the calaboose. As became his dignity, Bud led the way.

The old woman, unable to endure the pain any longer, and knowing full well that her days were bound to end in prison, had managed, in some way, to hang herself from a window bar beside her bed, using a twisted bed sheet. She was quite dead when "Doc" made the examination. A committee of the whole started at once to notify Anderson Crow. For a minute it looked as though the jail would be left entirely unguarded, but Bud loyally returned to his post, reinforced by Roscoe and the doctor.

Upon Mr. Crow's arrival at the jail, affairs assumed some aspect of order. He first locked the grate doors, thereby keeping the fiery David from coming out to see his mother before they cut her down. A messenger was sent for the coroner at Boggs City, and then the big body was released from its last hanging place.

"Doggone, but this is a busy day fer me!" said Anderson. "I won't have time to pump them fellers till this evenin'. But I guess they'll keep. What's that, Blootch?"

"I was just goin' to ask Bud if they're still in there," said Blootch.

"Are they, Bud?" asked Anderson in quick alarm.

"Sure," replied Bud with a mighty swelling of the chest. Even Blootch envied him.

"She's been dead jest an hour an' seven minutes," observed Anderson, gingerly touching the dead woman's wrist. "Doggone, I'm glad o' one thing!"

"What's that, Anderson?"

"We won't have to set her hip. Saved expense."

"But we'll have to bury her, like as not," said Isaac Porter.

"Yes," said Anderson reflectively. "She'll have to be buried. But—but—" and here his face lightened up in relief—"not fer a day er two; so what's the use worryin'."

When the coroner arrived, soon after six o'clock, a jury was empanelled and witnesses sworn. In ten minutes a verdict of suicide was returned and the coroner was on his way back to Boggs City. He did not even know that a hip had been dislocated. Anderson insisted upon a post-mortem examination, but was laughed out of countenance by the officious M.D.

"I voted fer that fool last November," said Anderson wrathfully, as the coroner drove off, "but you c'n kick the daylights out of me if I ever do it ag'in. Look out there, Bud! What in thunder are you doin' with them pistols? Doggone, ain't you got no sense? Pointin' 'em around that way. Why, you're liable to shoot somebody——"

"Aw, them ain't pistols," scoffed Bud, his mouth full of something. "They're bologny sausages. I ain't had nothin' to eat sence last night and I'm hungry."

"Well, it's dark out here," explained Anderson, suddenly shuffling into the jail. "I guess I'll put them fellers through the sweat box."

"The *what?*" demanded George Ray.

"The sweat-box— b-o-x, box. Cain't you hear?"

"I thought you used a cell."

"Thunderation, no! Nobody but country jakes call it a cell," said Anderson in fine scorn.

The three prisoners scowled at him so fiercely and snarled so vindictively when they asked him if they were to be starved to death, that poor Anderson hurried home and commanded his wife to pack "a baskit of bread and butter an' things fer the prisoners." It was nine o'clock before he could make up his mind to venture back to the calaboose with his basket. He spent the intervening hours in telling Rosalie and Bonner about the shocking incident at the jail and in absorbing advice from the clear-headed young man from Boston.

"I'd like to go with you to see those fellows, Mr. Crow," was Bonner's rueful lament. "But the doctor says I must be quiet until this confounded thing heals a bit. Together, I think we could bluff the whole story out of those scoundrels."

"Oh, never you fear," said the marshal; "I'll learn all there is to be learnt. You jest ask Alf Reesling what kind of a pumper I am."

"Who is Alf Reesling?"

"Ain't you heerd of him in Boston? Why, every temperance lecturer that comes here says he's the biggest drunkard in the world. I supposed his reputation had got to Boston by this time. He's been sober only once in twenty-five years."

"Is it possible?"

"That was when his wife died. He said he felt so good it wasn't necessary to get drunk. Well, I'll tell you all about it when I come back. Don't worry no more, Rosalie. I'll find out who's back of this business an' then we'll know all about you. It's a long lane that has no turn."

"Them prisoners must be mighty near starved to death by this time, Anderson," warned Mrs. Crow.

"Doggone, that's so!" he cried, and hustled out into the night.

The calaboose was almost totally dark—quite so, had it not been for the single lamp that burned in the office where the body of the old woman was lying. Two or three timid citizens stood afar off, in front of Thompson's feed yard, looking with awe upon the dungeon keep. Anderson's footsteps grew slower and more halting as they approached the entrance to the forbidding square of black. The snow creaked resoundingly under his heels and the chill wind nipped his muffless ears with a spitefulness that annoyed. In fact, he became so incensed, that he set his basket down and slapped his ears vigorously for some minutes before resuming his slow progress. He hated the thought of going in where the dead woman lay.

Suddenly he made up his mind that a confession from the men would be worthless unless he had ear witnesses to substantiate it in court. Without further deliberation, he retraced his steps hurriedly to Lamson's store, where, after half an hour's conversation on the topics of the day, he deputised the entire crowd to accompany him to the jail.

"Where's Bud?" he demanded sharply.

"Home in bed, poor child," said old Mr. Borton.

"Well, doggone his ornery hide, why ain't he here to—" began Anderson, but checked himself in time to prevent the crowd from seeing that he expected Bud to act as leader in the expedition. "I wanted him to jot down notes," he substituted. Editor Squires volunteered to act as secretary, prompter, interpreter, and everything else that his scoffing tongue could utter.

"Well, go ahead, then," said Anderson, pushing him forward. Harry led the party down the dark street with more rapidity than seemed necessary; few in the crowd could keep pace with him. A majority fell hopelessly behind, in fact.

Straight into the office walked Harry, closely followed by Blootch and the marshal. Maude, looking like a monument of sheets, still occupied the centre of the floor. Without a word, the party filed past the gruesome, silent thing and into the jail corridor. It was as dark as Erebus in the barred section of the prison; a cold draft of air flew into the faces of the visitors.

"Come here, you fellers!" called Anderson bravely into the darkness; but there was no response from the prisoners.

For the very good reason that some hours earlier they had calmly removed a window from its moorings and by this time were much too far away to answer questions.

CHAPTER XXIV

The Flight of the Kidnapers

SEARCHING parties were organised and sent out to scour the country, late as it was. Swift riders gave the alarm along every roadway, and the station agent telegraphed the news into every section of the land. At Boggs City, the sheriff, berating Anderson Crow for a fool and Tinkletown for an open-air lunatic asylum, sent his deputies down to assist in the pursuit. The marshal himself undertook to lead each separate and distinct posse. He was so overwhelmed by the magnitude of his misfortune that it is no wonder his brain whirled widely enough to encompass the whole enterprise.

Be it said to the credit of Tinkletown, her citizens made every reasonable effort to recapture the men. The few hundred able-bodied men of the town rallied to the support of their marshal and the law, and there was not one who refused to turn out in the cold night air for a sweeping search of the woods and fields.

Rosalie, who had been awakened early in the evening by Mr. Crow's noisy preparations for the pursuit, came downstairs, and instantly lost all desire to sleep. Bonner was lying on a couch in the "sitting-room," which now served as a temporary bedchamber.

"If you'll just hand me those revolvers, Mr. Crow," said he, indicating the two big automatics he had taken from Davy and Bill, "I'll stand guard over the house as best I can while you're away."

"Stand guard? What fer? Nobody's goin' to steal the house."

"We should not forget that these same rascals may take it into their heads to double on their tracks and try to carry Miss Gray away again. With her in their possession they'll receive their pay; without her their work will have been for nothing. It is a desperate crowd, and they may think the plan at least worth trying."

Rosalie's grateful, beaming glance sent a quiver that was not of pain through Bonner's frame.

"Don't worry about that," said the marshal. "We'll have 'em shot to pieces inside of an hour an' a half."

"Anderson, I want you to be very careful with that horse pistol," said his wife nervously. "It ain't been shot off sence the war, an' like as not it'll kill you from behind."

"Gosh blast it, Eva!" roared Anderson, "don't you suppose I know which end to shoot with?" And away he rushed in great dudgeon.

Edna Crow sat at the front window, keeping watch for hours. She reported to the other members of the household as each scurrying band of searchers passed the place. Bonner commanded Rosalie to keep away from the windows, fearing a shot from the outside. From time to time Roscoe replenished the big blaze in the fireplace. It was cosey in the old-fashioned sitting-room, even though the strain upon its occupants was trying in the extreme.

Great excitement came to them when the figure of a man was seen to drop to the walk near the front gate. At first it was feared that one of the bandits, injured by pursuers, had fallen to die, but the mournful calls for help that soon came from the sidewalk were more or less reassuring. The prostrate figure had a queer habit from time to time of raising itself high enough to peer between the pickets of the fence, and each succeeding shout seemed more vigorous than the others. Finally they became impatient, and then full of wrath. It was evident that the stranger resented the inhospitality of the house.

"Who are you?" called Edna, opening the window ever so slightly. Whereupon the man at the gate sank to the ground and groaned with splendid misery.

"It's me," he replied.

"Who's me?"

" 'Rast—'Rast Little. I think I'm dyin'."

There was a hurried consultation indoors, and then Roscoe bravely ventured out to the sidewalk.

"Are you shot, 'Rast?" he asked in trembling tones.

"No; I'm just wounded. Is Rosalie in there?"

"Yep. She's——"

"I guess I'll go in, then. Dern it! It's a long walk from our house over here. I guess I'll stay all night. If I don't get better to-morrow I'll have to stay longer. I ought to be nursed, too."

"Rosalie's playin' nurse fer Mr. Bonner," volun-

teered Roscoe, still blocking the gate through which
'Rast was trying to wedge himself.

"Mr. who?"

"Bonner."

"Well," said 'Rast after a moment's consideration,
"he ought to be moved to a hospital. Lemme lean
on you, Roscoe. I can't hardly walk, my arm hurts
so."

Mr. Little, with his bandages and his hobble, had
joined in the expedition, and was not to be deterred
until faintness overcame him and he dropped by the
wayside. He was taken in and given a warm chair
before the fire. One long look at Bonner and the
newcomer lapsed into a stubborn pout. He groaned
occasionally and made much ado over his condition,
but sourly resented any approach at sympathy.
Finally he fell asleep in the chair, his last speech
being to the effect that he was going home early in the
morning if he had to drag himself every foot of the
way. Plainly, 'Rast had forgotten Miss Banks in the
sudden revival of affection for Rosalie Gray. The course
of true love did not run smoothly in Tinkletown.

The searchers straggled in empty handed. Early
morning found most of them asleep at their homes,
tucked away by thankful wives, and with the promises
of late breakfasts. The next day business was slow
in asserting its claim upon public attention. Masculine Tinkletown dozed while femininity chattered to
its heart's content. There was much to talk about
and more to anticipate. The officials in all counties
contiguous had out their dragnets, and word was ex-

pected at any time that the fugitives had fallen into their hands.

But not that day, nor the next, nor any day, in fact, did news come of their capture, so Tinkletown was obliged to settle back into a state of tranquility. Some little interest was aroused when the town board ordered the calaboose repaired, and there was a ripple of excitement attached to the funeral of the only kidnaper in captivity. It was necessary to postpone the oyster supper at the Methodist Church, but there was some consolation in the knowledge that it would soon be summer-time and the benighted Africans would not need the money for winter clothes. The reception at the minister's house was a fizzle. He was warned in time, however, and it was his own fault that he received no more than a jug of vinegar, two loaves of bread and a pound of honey as the result of his expectations. It was the first time that a "pound" party had proven a losing enterprise.

Anderson Crow maintained a relentless search for the desperadoes. He refused to accept Wicker Bonner's theory that they were safe in the city of New York. It was his own opinion that they were still in the neighbourhood, waiting for a chance to exhume the body of Davy's mother and make off with it.

"Don't try to tell me, Mr. Bonner, that even a raskil like him hasn't any love fer his mother," he contended. "Davy may not be much of a model, but he had a feelin' fer the woman who bore him, an' don't you fergit it."

"Why, Daddy Crow, he was the most heartless brute in the world!" cried Rosalie. "I've seen him knock her down more than once—and kick her, too."

"A slip of the memory, that's all. He was probably thinkin' of his wife, if he has one."

At a public meeting the town board was condemned for its failure to strengthen the jail at the time Anderson made his demand three years before.

"What's the use in me catchin' thieves, and so forth, if the jail won't hold 'em?" Anderson declared. "I cain't afford to waste time in runnin' desperite characters down if the town board ain't goin' to obstruct 'em from gittin' away as soon as the sun sits. What's the use, I'd like to know? Where's the justice? I don't want it to git noised aroun' that the on'y way we c'n hold a prisoner is to have him commit suicide as soon as he's arrested. Fer two cents I'd resign right now."

Of course no one would hear to that. As a result, nearly five hundred dollars was voted from the corporation funds to strengthen and modernise the "calaboose." It was the sense of the meeting that a "sweat box" should be installed under Mr. Crow's supervision, and that the marshal's salary should be increased fifty dollars a year. After the adoption of this popular resolution Mr. Crow arose and solemnly informed the people that their faith in him was not misplaced. He threw the meeting into a state of great excitement by announcing that the kidnapers would soon be in the toils once more. In response to eager queries he merely stated that he had a valuable

"LEFT THE YOUNG MAN TO THE CARE OF AN EXCELLENT
NURSE"

clew, which could not be divulged without detriment to the cause. Everybody went home that night with the assurance that the fugitives would soon be taken. Anderson promised the town board that he would not take them until the jail was repaired.

It was almost a fortnight before Wicker Bonner was able to walk about with crutches. The wound in his leg was an ugly one and healed slowly. His uncle, the Congressman, sent up a surgeon from New York, but that worthy approved of "Doc" Smith's methods, and abruptly left the young man to the care of an excellent nurse, Rosalie Gray. Congressman Bonner's servants came over every day or two with books, newspapers, sweetmeats, and fresh supplies from the city, but it was impossible for them to get any satisfaction from the young man in reply to their inquiries as to when he expected to return to the big house across the river. Bonner was beginning to hate the thought of giving up Rosalie's readings, her ministrations, and the no uncertain development of his own opinions as to her personal attractiveness.

"I don't know when I'll be able to walk, Watkins," he said to the caretaker. "I'm afraid my heart is affected."

Bonner's enforced presence at Anderson Crow's home was the source of extreme annoyance to the young men of the town. "Blootch" Peabody created a frightful scandal by getting boiling drunk toward the end of the week, so great was his dejection. As it was his first real spree, he did not recover from the effect for three days. He then took the pledge,

and talked about the evils of strong d r i n k with so much feeling at prayer meeting that the women of the town inaugurated a movement to stop the sale of liquor in the town. As Peabody's drug store was the only place where whiskey could be obtained, "Blootch" soon saw the error of his ways and came down from his pedestal to mend them.

Bonner was a friend in need to Anderson Crow. The two were in consultation half of the time, and the young man's opinions were not to be disregarded. He advanced a theory concerning the motives of the leader in the plot to send Rosalie into an exile from which she was not expected to return. It was his belief that the person who abandoned her as a babe was actuated by the desire to possess a fortune which should have been the child's. The conditions attending the final disposition of this fortune doubtless were such as to make it unwise to destroy the girl's life. The plotter, whatever his or her relation to the child may have been, must have felt that a time might come when the existence of the real heiress would be necessary. Either such a fear was the inspiration or the relationship was so dear that the heart of the archplotter was full of love for the innocent victim.

"Who is to say, Miss Gray," said Bonner one night as they sat before the fire, "that the woman who left you with Mr. Crow was not your own mother? Suppose that a vast estate was to be yours in trust after the death of some rich relative, say grandparent. It would naturally mean that some one else resented this bequest, and probably with some justice. The property was to become your own when you attained a certain age, let us say. Don't you see that the day would rob the disinherited person of every hope to retain the fortune? Even a mother might be tempted, for ambitious reasons, to go to extreme measures to secure the fortune for herself. Or she might have been influenced by a will stronger than her own—the will of an unscrupulous man. There are many contingencies, all probable, as you choose to analyse them."

"But why should this person wish to banish me from the country altogether? I am no more dangerous here than I would be anywhere in Europe. And then think of the means they would have employed to get me away from Tinkletown. Have I not been lost to the world for years? Why——"

"True; but I am quite convinced, and I think Mr. Crow agrees with me, that the recent move was made necessary by the demands of one whose heart is not interested, but whose hand wields the sceptre of power over the love which tries to shield you. Any other would have cut off your life at the beginning."

"That's my idee," agreed Anderson solemnly.

"I don't want the fortune!" cried Rosalie. "I am happy here! Why can't they let me alone?"

"I tell you, Miss Gray, unless something happens to prevent it, that woman will some day give you back your own—your fortune and your name."

"I can't believe it, Mr. Bonner. "It is too much like a dream to me."

"Well, doggone it, Rosalie, dreams don't last forever!" broke in Anderson Crow. "You've got to wake up some time, don't you see?"

CHAPTER XXV

As the Heart Grows Older

BONNER'S eagerness to begin probing into the mystery grew as his strength came back to him. He volunteered to interest his uncle in the matter, and through him to begin a systematic effort to unravel the tangled ends of Rosalie's life. Money was not to be spared; time and intelligence were to be devoted to the cause. He knew that Rosalie was in reality a creature of good birth and worthy of the name that any man might seek to bestow upon her—a name given in love by a man to the woman who would share it with him forever.

The days and nights were teaching him the sacredness of a growing attachment. He was not closing his eyes to the truth. It was quite as impossible for big, worldly Wick Bonner to be near her and not fall a victim, as it was for the crude, humble youth of Tinkletown. His heart was just as fragile as theirs when it bared itself to her attack. Her beauty attracted him, her natural refinement of character appealed to him; her pureness, her tenderness, her goodness, wrought havoc with his impressions. Fresh, bright, as clear-headed as the June sunshine, she was a revelation to him—to Bonner, who had known her sex in all its environments. His heart was full of her, day and night; for day and night he was wonder-

ing whether she could care for him as he knew he
was coming to care for her.

One day he received a telegram. It was from his
mother and his sister, who had just reached Boston
from Bermuda, and it carried the brief though emphatic information that they were starting to Tinkletown to nurse and care for him. Bonner was thrown
into a panic. He realised in the instant that it would
be impossible for them to come to Mr. Crow's home,
and he knew they could not be deceived as to his
real condition. His mother would naturally insist
upon his going at once to Bonner Place, across the
river, and on to Boston as soon as he was able; his
clever sister would see through his motives like a flash
of lightning. Young Mr. Bonner loved them, but he
was distinctly bored by the prospect of their coming.
In some haste and confusion, he sent for "Doc"
Smith.

"Doctor, how soon will I be able to navigate?" he
asked anxiously.

"Right now."

"You don't say so! I don't feel strong, you know."

"Well, your leg's doing well and all danger is past.
Of course, you won't be as spry as usual for some
time, and you can't walk without crutches, but I don't
see any sense in your loafing around here on that account. You'd be safe to go at any time, Mr. Bonner."

"Look here, doctor, I'm afraid to change doctors.
You've handled this case mighty well, and if I went
to some other chap, he might undo it all. I've made
up my mind to have you look out for me until this

wound is completely healed. That's all right, now.
I know what I'm talking about. I'll take no chances.
How long will it be until it is completely healed?"

"A couple of weeks, I suppose."

"Well, I'll stay right here and have you look at it
every day. It's too serious a matter for me to trifle
with. By the way, my mother is coming up, and I
dare say she'll want me to go to Boston. Our family
doctor is an old fossil and I don't like to trust him
with this thing. You'll be doing me a favour, doctor, if you keep me here until I'm thoroughly well.
I intend to tell my mother that it will not be wise to
move me until all danger of blood poisoning is past."

"Blood poisoning? There's no danger now, sir."

"You never can tell," said Bonner sagely.

"But I'd be a perfect fool, Mr. Bonner, if
there were still danger of that," complained the
doctor. "What sort of a doctor would they consider
me?"

"They'd certainly give you credit for being careful,
and that's what appeals to a mother, you know," said
Bonner still more sagely. "Besides, it's *my* leg, doctor, and I'll have it treated my way. I think a couple
of weeks more under your care will put me straight.
Mother has to consider me, that's all. I wish you'd
stop in to-morrow and change these bandages,
doctor; if you don't mind——"

"Doc" Smith was not slow. He saw more than
Bonner thought, so he winked to himself as he
crossed over to his office. At the corner he met
Anderson Crow.

"Say, Anderson," he said, half chuckling, "that young Bonner has had a relapse."

"Thunderation!"

"He can't be moved for a week or two."

"Will you have to cut it off?"

"The leg?"

"Certainly. That's the only thing that pains him, ain't it?"

"I think not. I'm going to put his heart in a sling," said Smith, laughing heartily at what he thought would be taken as a brilliant piece of jesting. But he erred. Anderson went home in a great flurry and privately cautioned every member of the household, including Rosalie, to treat Bonner with every consideration, as his heart was weak and liable to give him great trouble. Above all, he cautioned them to keep the distressing news from Bonner. It would discourage him mightily. For a full week Anderson watched Bonner with anxious eyes, writhing every time the big fellow exerted himself, groaning when he gave vent to his hearty laugh.

"Have you heard anything?" asked Bonner with faithful regularity when Anderson came home each night. He referred to the chase for the fugitives.

"Nothin' worth while," replied Anderson dismally. "Uncle Jiminy Borton had a letter from Albany to-day, an' his son-in-law said three strange men had been seen in the Albany depot the other day. I had Uncle Jiminy write an' ast him if he had seen any-body answerin' the description, you know. But the three men he spoke of took a train for New York, so I suppose they're lost by this time. It's the most bafflin' case I ever worked on."

"Has it occurred to you that the real leader was in this neighbourhood at the time? In Boggs City, let us say. According to Rosa—Miss Gray's story, the man Sam went out nightly for instructions. Well, he either went to Boggs City or to a meeting place agreed upon between him and his superior. It is possible that he saw this person on the very night of my own adventure. Now, the thing for us to do is to find out if a stranger was seen in these parts on that night. The hotel registers in Boggs City may give us a clew. If you don't mind, Mr. Crow, I'll have this New York detective, who is coming up to-morrow, take a look into this phase of the case. It won't interfere with your plans, will it?" asked Bonner, always considerate of the feelings of the good-hearted, simple-minded old marshal.

"Not at all, an' I'll help him all I can, sir," responded Anderson magnanimously. "Here, Eva, here's a letter fer Rosalie. It's the second she's had from New York in three days."

"It's from Miss Banks. They correspond, Anderson," said Mrs. Crow.

"And say, Eva, I've decided on one thing. We've got to calculate on gittin' along without that thousand dollars after this."

"Why, An—der—son Crow!"

"Yep. We're goin' to find her folks, no matter if we do have to give up the thousand. It's no more'n right. She'll be twenty-one in March, an' I'll have to settle the guardeenship business anyhow. But, doggone it, Mr. Bonner, she says she won't take the money we've saved fer her."

"She has told me as much, Mr. Crow. I think she's partly right. If she takes my advice she will divide it with you. You are entitled to all of it, you know —it was to be your pay—and she will not listen to your plan to give all of it to her. Still, I feel that she should not be penniless at this time. She may never need it—she certainly will not as long as you are alive—but it seems a wise thing for her to be protected against emergencies. But I dare say you can arrange that between yourselves. I have no right to interfere. Was there any mail for me?"

"Yep. I almost fergot to fork it over. Here's one from your mother, I figger. This is from your sister, an' here's one from your—your sweetheart, I reckon. I deduce all this by sizin' up the—" and he went on to tell how he reached his conclusions, all of which were wrong. They were invitations to social affairs in Boston. "But I got somethin' important to tell you, Mr. Bonner. I think a trap is bein' set fer me by the desperadoes we're after. I guess I'm gittin' too hot on their trail. I had an ananymous letter to-day."

"A what?"

"Ananymous letter. Didn't you ever hear of one? This one was writ fer the express purpose of lurin' me into a trap. They want to git me out of the way.

But I'll fool 'em. I'll not pay any attention to it."

"Goodness, Anderson, I bet you'll be assassinated yet!" cried his poor wife. "I wish you'd give up chasin' people down."

"May I have a look at the letter, Mr. Crow?" asked Bonner. Anderson stealthily drew the square envelope from his inside pocket and passed it over.

"They've got to git up purty early to ketch me asleep," he said proudly. Bonner drew the enclosure from the envelope. As he read, his eyes twinkled and the corners of his mouth twitched, but his face was politely sober as he handed the missive back to the marshal. "Looks like a trap, don't it?" said Anderson. "You see there ain't no signature. The raskils were afraid to sign a name."

"I wouldn't say anything to Miss Gray about this if I were you, Mr. Crow. It might disturb her, you know," said Bonner.

"That means you, too, Eva," commanded Anderson in turn. "Don't worry the girl. She mustn't know anything about this."

"I don't think it's a trap," remarked Eva as she finished reading the missive. Bonner took this opportunity to laugh heartily. He had held it back as long as possible. What Anderson described as an "ananymous" letter was nothing more than a polite, formal invitation to attend a "house warming" at Colonel Randall's on the opposite side of the river. It read:

"Mr. and Mrs. D. F. Randall request the honour of your presence at a house warming, Friday evening, January 30, 190—, at eight o'clock. Rockden-of-the-Hills."

"It is addressed to me, too, Anderson," said his wife, pointing to the envelope. "It's the new house they finished last fall. Anonymous letter! Fiddlesticks! I bet there's one at the post-office fer each one of the girls."

"Roscoe got some of the mail," murmured the marshal sheepishly. "Where is that infernal boy? He'd oughter be strapped good and hard fer holdin' back letters like this," growled he, eager to run the subject into another channel. After pondering all evening, he screwed up the courage and asked Bonner not to tell any one of his error in regard to the invitation. Roscoe produced invitations for his sister and Rosalie. He furthermore announced that half the people in town had received them.

"There's a telegram comin' up fer you after a while, Mr. Bonner," he said. "Bud's out delivering one to Mr. Grimes, and he's going to stop here on the way back. I was at the station when it come in. It's from your ma, and it says she'll be over from Boggs City early in the morning."

"Thanks, Roscoe," said Bonner with an amused glance at Rosalie; "you've saved me the trouble of reading it."

"They are coming to-morrow," said Rosalie long afterward, as the last of the Crows straggled off to bed. "You will have to go away with them, won't you?"

"I'm an awful nuisance about here, I fancy, and you'll be glad to be rid of me," he said softly, his gaze on the blazing "back-log."

"No more so than you will be to go," she said so coolly that his pride suffered a distinct shock. He stole a shy glance at the face of the girl opposite. It was as calm and serene as a May morning. Her eyes likewise were gazing into the blaze, and her fingers were idly toying with the fringe on the arm of the chair.

"By George!" he thought, a weakness assailing his heart suddenly; "I don't believe she cares a rap!"

CHAPTER XXVI

The Left Ventricle

THE next day Mrs. Bonner and Miss Bonner descended upon Tinkletown. They were driven over from Boggs City in an automobile, and their advent caused a new thrill of excitement in town. Half of the women in Tinkletown found excuse to walk past Mr. Crow's home some time during the day, and not a few of them called to pay their respects to Mrs. Crow, whether they owed them or not, much to that estimable lady's discomfiture.

Wicker's mother was a handsome, aristocratic woman with a pedigree reaching back to Babylon or some other historic starting place. Her ancestors were Tories at the time of the American Revolution, and she was proud of it. Her husband's forefathers had shot a few British in those days, it is true, and had successfully chased some of her own ancestors over to Long Island, but that did not matter in these twentieth century days. Mr. Bonner long since had gone to the tomb; and his widow at fifty was quite the queen of all she surveyed, which was not inconsiderable. The Bonners were rich in worldly possessions, rich in social position, rich in traditions. The daughter, just out in society, was a pretty girl, several years younger than Wicker. She was the idol of his heart. This slip of a girl had been to him the brightest, wittiest and prettiest girl in all the world. Now, he was wondering how the other girl, who was not his sister, would compare with her when they stood together before him.

Naturally, Mrs. Crow and her daughters sank into a nervous panic as soon as these fashionable women from Boston set foot inside the humble home. They lost what little self-possession they had managed to acquire and floundered miserably through the preliminaries.

But calm, sweet and composed as the most fastidious would require, Rosalie greeted the visitors without a shadow of confusion or a sign of gaucherie. Bonner felt a thrill of joy and pride as he took note of the look of surprise that crept into his mother's face—a surprise that did not diminish as the girl went through her unconscious test.

"By George!" he cried jubilantly to himself, "she's something to be proud of—she's a queen!"

Later in the day, after the humble though imposing lunch (the paradox was permissible in Tinkletown), Mrs. Bonner found time and opportunity to express her surprise and her approval to him. With the insight of the real aristocrat, she was not blind to the charms of the girl, who blossomed like a rose in this out-of-the-way patch of nature. The tact which impelled Rosalie to withdraw herself and all of the Crows from the house, giving the Bonners an opportunity to be together undisturbed, did not escape the clever woman of the world.

"She is remarkable, Wicker. Tell me about her.

Why does she happen to be living in this wretched town and among such people?"

Whereupon Bonner rushed into a detailed and somewhat lengthy history of the mysterious Miss Gray, repeating it as it had come to him from her own frank lips, but with embellishments of his own that would have brought the red to her cheeks, could she have heard them. His mother's interest was not assumed; his sister was fascinated by the recital.

"Who knows," she cried, her dark eyes sparkling, "she may be an heiress to millions!"

"Or a princess of the royal blood!" amended her mother with an enthusiasm that was uncommon. "Blood alone has made this girl what she is. Heaven knows that billions or trillions could not have overcome the influences of a lifetime spent in—in Winkletown—or is that the name? It doesn't matter, Wicker—any name will satisfy. Frankly, I am interested in the girl. It is a crime to permit her to vegetate and die in a place like this."

"But, mother, she loves these people," protested Bonner lifelessly. "They have been kind to her all these years. They have been parents, protectors——"

"And they have been well paid for it, my son. Please do not misunderstand me, I am not planning to take her off their hands. I am not going to reconstruct her sphere in life. Not by any means. I am merely saying that it is a crime for her to be penned up for life in this—this desert. I doubt very much whether her parentage will ever be known, and perhaps it is just as well that it isn't to be. Still, I am interested."

"Mamma, I think it would be very nice to ask her to come to Boston for a week or two, don't you?" suggested Edith Bonner, warmly but doubtfully.

"Bully!" exclaimed Wicker, forgetting in his excitement that he was a cripple. "Have her come on to stop a while with you, Ede. It will be a great treat for her and, by George, I'm inclined to think it maybe somewhat beneficial to us."

"Your enthusiasm is beautiful, Wicker," said his mother, perfectly unruffled. "I have no doubt you think Boston would be benefited, too."

"Now, you know, mother, it's not just like you to be snippish," said he easily. "Besides, after living a while in other parts of the world, I'm beginning to feel that population is not the only thing about Boston that can be enlarged. It's all very nice to pave our streets with intellect so that we can't stray from our own footsteps, but I rather like the idea of losing my way, once in a while, even if I have to look at the same common, old sky up there that the rest of the world looks at, don't you know. I've learned recently that the same sun that shines on Boston also radiates for the rest of the world."

"Yes, it shines in Tinkletown," agreed his mother serenely. "But, my dear—" turning to her daughter—"I think you would better wait a while before extending the invitation. There is no excuse for rushing into the unknown. Let time have a chance."

"By Jove, mother, you talk sometimes like Anderson Crow. He often says things like that," cried Wicker delightedly.

"Dear me! How can you say such a thing, Wicker?"

"Well, you'd like old Anderson. He's a jewel!"

"I dare say—an emerald. No, no—that was not fair or kind, Wicker. I unsay it. Mr. Crow and all of them have been good to you. Forgive me the sarcasm. Mr. Crow is perfectly impossible, but I like him. He has a heart, and that is more than most of us can say. And now let us return to earth once more. When will you be ready to start for Boston? To-morrow?"

"Heavens, no! I'm not to be moved for quite a long time—danger of gangrene or something of the sort. It's astonishing, mother, what capable men these country doctors are. Dr. Smith is something of a marvel. He—he—saved my leg."

"My boy—you don't mean that—" his mother was saying, her voice trembling.

"Yes; that's what I mean. I'm all right now, but, of course, I shall be very careful for a couple of weeks. One can't tell, you know. Blood poisoning and all that sort of thing. But let's not talk of it—it's gruesome."

"Indeed it is. You must be extremely careful, Wicker. Promise me that you will do nothing foolish. Don't use your leg until the doctor—but I have something better. We will send for Dr. J——. He can run up from Boston two or three times——"

"Nothing of the sort, mother! Nonsense! Smith

knows more in a minute than J—— does in a month. He's handling the case exactly as I want him to. Let well enough alone, say I. You know J—— always wants to amputate everything that can be cut or sawed off. For heaven's sake, don't let him try it on me. I need my legs."

It is not necessary to say that Mrs. Bonner was completely won over by this argument. She commanded him to stay where he was until it was perfectly safe to be moved across the river, where he could recuperate before venturing into the city of his birth. Moreover, she announced that Edith and she would remain in Boggs City until he was quite out of danger, driving over every day in their chartered automobile. It suddenly struck Bonner that it would be necessary to bribe "Doc" Smith and the entire Crow family, if he was to maintain his position as an invalid.

"Doc" Smith when put to the test lied ably in behalf of his client (he refused to call him his patient), and Mrs. Bonner was convinced. Mr. Crow and Eva vigorously protested that the young man would not be a "mite of trouble," and that he could stay as long as he liked.

"He's a gentleman, Mrs. Bonner," announced the marshal, as if the mother was being made aware of the fact for the first time. "Mrs. Crow an' me have talked it over, an' I know what I'm talkin' about. He's a perfect gentleman."

"Thank you, Mr. Crow. I am happy to hear you say that," said Mrs. Bonner, with fine tact. "You

will not mind if he stops here a while longer
then?"

"I should say not. If he'll take the job, I'll app'int
him deputy marshal."

"I'd like a picture of you with the badge and uni-
form, Wick," said Edith with good-natured banter.

Just before the two ladies left for Boggs City
that evening Bonner managed to say something to
Edith.

"Say, Ede, I think it would be uncommonly decent
of you to ask Miss Gray down to Boston this spring.
You'll like her."

"Wicker, if it were not so awfully common, I'd
laugh in my sleeve," said she, surveying him with a
calm scrutiny that disconcerted. "I wasn't born yesterday, you know. Mother was, perhaps, but not
your dear little sister. Cheer up, brother. You'll
get over it, just like all the rest. I'll ask her to
come, but— Please don't frown like that. I'll
suspect something."

During the many little automobile excursions that
the two girls enjoyed during those few days in Tinkletown, Miss Bonner found much to love in Rosalie,
much to esteem and a great deal to anticipate. Purposely, she set about to learn by "deduction" just
what Rosalie's feelings were for the big brother.
She would not have been surprised to discover the
telltale signs of a real but secret affection on Rosalie's
part, but she was, on the contrary, amazed and not
a little chagrined to have the young girl meet every
advance with a joyous candour, that definitely set

aside any possibility of love for the supposedly irresistible brother. Miss Edith's mind was quite at rest, but with the arrogant pride of a sister, she resented the fact that any one could know this cherished brother and not fall a victim. Perversely, she would have hated Rosalie had she caught her, in a single moment of unguardedness, revealing a feeling more tender than friendly interest for him.

Sophisticated and world-wise, the gay, careless Miss Bonner read her pages quickly—she skimmed them—but she saw a great deal between the lines. If her mother had been equally discerning, that very estimable lady might have found herself immensely relieved along certain lines.

Bonner was having a hard time of it these days. It was worse than misery to stay indoors, and it was utterly out of the question for him to venture out. His leg was healing with disgusting rashness, but his heart was going into an illness that was to scoff at the cures of man. And if his parting with his mother and the rosy-faced young woman savoured of relief, he must be forgiven. A sore breast is no respecter of persons.

They were returning to the Hub by the early morning train from Boggs City, and it was understood that Rosalie was to come to them in June. Let it be said in good truth that both Mrs. Bonner and her daughter were delighted to have her promise. If they felt any uneasiness as to the possibility of unwholesome revelations in connection with her birth, they purposely blindfolded themselves and indulged in the game of consequences.

Mrs. Bonner was waiting in the automobile, having said good-bye to Wicker.

"I'll keep close watch on him, Mrs. Bonner," promised Anderson, "and telegraph you if his condition changes a mite. I ast 'Doc' Smith to-day to tell me the real truth 'bout him, an'——"

"The real truth? What do you mean?" she cried, in fresh alarm.

"Don't worry, ma'am. He's improvin' fine, 'doc' says. He told me he'd be out o' danger when he got back to Boston. His heart's worryin' 'doc' a little. I ast 'im to speak plain an' tell me jest how bad it's affected. He said: 'At present, only the left ventricle —whatever that be—only the left one is punctured, but the right one seems to need a change of air.'"

CHAPTER XXVII

The Grin Derisive

"I LIKE your ma," said Anderson to Wicker, later in the evening. "She's a perfect lady. Doggone, it's a relief to see a rich woman that knows how to be a lady. She ain't a bit stuck up an' yet she's a reg'lar aristocrat. Did I ever tell you about what happened to Judge Courtwright's wife? No? Well, it was a long time ago, right here in Tinkletown. The judge concluded this would be a good place fer a summer home—so him an' her put up a grand residence down there on the river bluff. It was the only summer place on this side of the river. Well, of course Mrs. Courtwright had to turn in an' be the leader of the women in this place. She lorded it over 'em an' she give 'em to understand that she was a queen er some-thin' like that an' they was nothin' but peasants. An' the derned fool women 'lowed her to do it, too. Seems as though her great-grandfather was a 'squire over in England, an' she had a right to be swell. Well, she ruled the roost fer two summers an' no-body could get near her without a special dispensa-tion from the Almighty. She wouldn't look at any-body with her eyes; her chin was so high in the air that she had to look through her nose.

"Her husband was as old as Methoosalum—that is, he was as old as Methoosalum was when he was a

boy, so to speak—an' she had him skeered of his
life. But I fixed her. At the end of the second summer she was ready to git up an' git, duke er no duke.
Lemme me give you a tip, Wick. If you want to
fetch a queen down to your level, jest let her know
you're laughin' at her. Well, sir, the judge's wife
used to turn up her nose at me until I got to feelin'
too small to be seen. My pride was wallerin' in the
dust. Finally, I thought of a scheme to fix her.
Every time I saw her, I'd grin at her—not sayin' a
word, mind you, but jest lookin' at her as if she
struck me as bein' funny. Well, sir, I kept it up good
an' strong. First thing I knowed, she was beginnin' to
look as though a bee had stung her an' she couldn't find
the place. I'd ketch her stealin' sly glances at me an'
she allus found me with a grin on my face—a good,
healthy grin, too.

"There wasn't anything to laugh at, mind you, but
she didn't know that. She got to fixin' her back hair
and lookin' worried about her clothes. 'Nen she'd
wipe her face to see if the powder was on straight,
all the time wonderin' what in thunder I was laughin'
at. If she passed in her kerridge she'd peep back to
see if I was laughin'; and I allus was. I never failed.
All this time I wasn't sayin' a word—jest grinnin'
as though she tickled me half to death. Gradually
I begin to be scientific about it. I got so that when
she caught me laughin', I'd try my best to hide the
grin. Course that made it all the worse. She fid-
geted an' squirmed an' got red in the face till it
looked like she was pickled. Doggone, ef she didn't

begin to neglect her business as a great-grand-daughter! She didn't have time to lord it over her peasants. She was too blame busy wonderin' what I was laughin' at.

"'Nen she begin to look peaked an' thin. She looked like she was seein' ghosts all the time. That blamed grin of mine pursued her every minute. Course, she couldn't kick about it. That wouldn't do at all. She jest had to bear it without grinnin'. There wasn't anything to say. Finally, she got to stayin' away from the meetin's an' almost quit drivin' through the town. Everybody noticed the change in her. People said she was goin' crazy about her back hair. She lost thirty pounds worryin' before August, and when September come, the judge had to take her to a rest cure. They never come back to Tinkletown, an' the judge had to sell the place fer half what it cost him. Fer two years she almost went into hysterics when anybody laughed. But it done her good. It changed her idees. She got over her high an' mighty ways, they say, an' I hear she's one of the nicest, sweetest old ladies in Boggs City nowadays. But Blootch Peabody says that to this day she looks flustered when anybody notices her back hair. The Lord knows I wa'n't laughin' at her hair. I don't see why she thought so, do you?"

Bonner laughed long and heartily over the experiment; but Rosalie vigorously expressed her disapproval of the marshal's methods.

"It's the only real mean thing I ever heard of you doing, daddy Crow!" she cried. "It was cruel!"

"Course you'd take her part, bein' a woman," said he serenely. "Mrs. Crow did, too, when I told her about it twenty years ago. Women ain't got much sense of humour, have they, Wick?" He was calling him Wick nowadays; and the young man enjoyed the familiarity.

The days came when Bonner could walk about with his cane, and he was not slow to avail himself of the privilege this afforded. It meant enjoyable strolls with Rosalie, and it meant the elevation of his spirits to such heights that the skies formed no bounds for them. The town was not slow to draw conclusions. Every one said it would be a "match." It was certain that the interesting Boston man had acquired a clear field. Tinkletown's beaux gave up in despair and dropped out of the contest with the hope that complete recovery from his injuries might not only banish Bonner from the village, but also from the thoughts of Rosalie Gray. Most of the young men took their medicine philosophically. They had known from the first that their chances were small. Blootch Peabody and Ed Higgins, because of the personal rivalry between themselves, hoped on and on and grew more bitter between themselves, instead of toward Bonner.

Anderson Crow and Eva were delighted and the Misses Crow, after futile efforts to interest the young man in their own wares, fell in with the old folks and exuberantly whispered to the world that "it would be perfectly glorious." Roscoe was not so charitable. He was soundly disgusted with the thought of losing his friend Bonner in the hated bonds of matrimony. From his juvenile point of view, it was a fate that a good fellow like Bonner did not deserve. Even Rosalie was not good enough for him, so he told Bud Long; but Bud, who had worshipped Rosalie with a hopeless devotion through most of his short life, took strong though sheepish exceptions to the remark. It seemed quite settled in the minds of every one but Bonner and Rosalie themselves. They went along evenly, happily, perhaps dreamily, letting the present and the future take care of themselves as best they could, making mountains of the past—mountains so high and sheer that they could not be surmounted in retreat.

Bonner was helplessly in love—so much so, indeed, that in the face of it, he lost the courage that had carried him through trivial affairs of the past, and left him floundering vaguely in seas that looked old and yet were new. Hourly, he sought for the first sign of love in her eyes, for the first touch of sentiment; but if there was a point of weakness in her defence, it was not revealed to the hungry perception of the would-be conqueror. And so they drifted on through the February chill, that seemed warm to them, through the light hours and the dark ones, quickly and surely to the day which was to call him cured of one ill and yet sorely afflicted by another.

Through it all he was saying to himself that it did not matter what her birth may have been, so long as she lived at this hour in his life, and yet a still, cool voice was whispering procrastination with ding-dong persistency through every avenue of his brain.

"Wait!" said the cool voice of prejudice. His heart did not hear, but his brain did. One look of submission from her tender eyes and his brain would have turned deaf to the small, cool voice—but her eyes stood their ground and the voice survived.

The day was fast approaching when it would be necessary for him to leave the home of Mr. Crow. He could no longer encroach upon the hospitality and good nature of the marshal—especially as he had declined the proffered appointment to become deputy town marshal. Together they had discussed every possible side to the abduction mystery and had laid the groundwork for a systematic attempt at a solution. There was nothing more for them to do. True to his promise, Bonner had put the case in the hands of one of the greatest detectives in the land, together with every known point in the girl's history. Tinkletown was not to provide the solution, although it contained the mystery. On that point there could be no doubt; so, Mr. Bonner was reluctantly compelled to admit to himself that he had no plausible excuse for staying on. The great detective from New York had come to town, gathered all of the facts under cover of strictest secrecy, run down every possible shadow of a clew in Boggs City, and had returned to the metropolis, there to begin the search twenty-one years back.

"Four weeks," Bonner was saying to her reflectively, as they came homeward from their last visit to the abandoned mill on Turnip Creek. It was a bright, warm February morning, suggestive of spring and fraught with the fragrance of something far sweeter. "Four weeks of idleness and joy to me— almost a lifetime in the waste of years. Does it seem long to you, Miss Gray—oh, I remember, I am to call you Rosalie."

"It seems that I have known you always instead of for four weeks," she said gently. "They have been happy weeks, haven't they? My—our only fear is that you haven't been comfortable in our poor little home. It's not what you are accustomed——"

"Home is what the home folks make it," he said, striving to quote a vague old saying. He was dimly conscious of a subdued smile on her part and he felt the fool. "At any rate, I was more than comfortable. I was happy—never so happy. All my life shall be built about this single month—my past ends with it, my future begins. You, Rosalie," he went on swiftly, his eyes gleaming with the love that would not be denied, "are the spirit of life as I shall know it from this day forth. It is you who have made Tinkletown a kingdom, one of its homes a palace. Don't turn your face away, Rosalie."

But she turned her face toward him and her dark eyes did not flinch as they met his, out there in the bleak old wood.

"Don't, please don't, Wicker," she said softly, firmly. Her hand touched his arm for an instant. "You will understand, won't you? Please don't!" There was a world of meaning in it.

His heart turned cold as ice, the blood left his face. He understood. She did not love him.

"Yes," he said, his voice dead and hoarse, "I think I understand, Rosalie. I have taken too much for granted, fool that I am. Bah! The egotism of a fool!"

"You must not speak like that," she said, her face contracted by pain and pity. "You are the most wonderful man I've ever known—the best and the truest. But—" and she paused, with a wan, drear smile on her lips.

"I understand," he interrupted. "Don't say it. I want to think that some day you will feel like saying something else, and I want to hope, Rosalie, that it won't always be like this. Let us talk about something else." But neither cared to speak for what seemed an hour. They were in sight of home before the stony silence was broken. "I may come over from Bonner Place to see you?" he asked at last. He was to cross the river the next day for a stay of a week or two at his uncle's place.

"Yes—often, Wicker. I shall want to see you every day. Yes, every day; I'm sure of it," she said wistfully, a hungry look in her eyes that he did not see, for he was staring straight ahead. Had he seen that look or caught the true tone in her voice, the world might not have looked so dark to him. When he did look at her again, her face was calm almost to sereneness.

"And you will come to Boston in June just the same?"

"If your sister and—and your mother still want me to come."

"'I think I understand, Rosalie'"

She was thinking of herself, the nameless one, in the house of his people; she was thinking of the doubts, the speculations—even the fears that would form the background of her welcome in that proud house. No longer was Rosalie Gray regarding herself as the happy, careless foster-child of Anderson Crow; she was seeing herself only as the castaway, the unwanted, and the world was growing bitter for her. But Bonner was blind to all this; he could not, should not know.

"You know they want you to come. Why do you say that?" he asked quickly, a strange, dim perspective rising before him for an instant, only to fade away before it could be analysed.

"One always says that," she replied with a smile. "It is the penalty of being invited. Your sister has written the dearest letter to me, and I have answered it. We love one another, she and I."

"Rosalie, I am going to write to you," said he suddenly; "you will answer?"

"Yes," she told him simply. His heart quickened, but faltered, and was lost. "I had a long letter from Elsie Banks to-day," she went on with an indifference that chilled.

"Oh," he said; "she is your friend who was or is to marry Tom Reddon, I believe. I knew him at Harvard. Tell me, are they married?"

"No. It was not to take place until March, but now she writes that her mother is ill and must go to California for several months. Mr. Reddon wants to be married at once, or before they go West, at least; but she says she cannot consent while her mother requires so much of her. I don't know how it will end, but I presume they will be married and all go to California. That seems the simple and just way, doesn't it?"

"Any way seems just, I'd say," he said. "They love one another, so what's the odds? Do you know Reddon well?"

"I have seen him many times," she replied with apparent evasiveness.

"He is a——" but here he stopped as if paralysis had seized him suddenly. The truth shot into his brain like a deadly bolt. Everything was as plain as day to him now. She stooped to pick up a slim, broken reed that crossed her path, and her face was averted. "God!" was the cry that almost escaped his lips. "She loves Reddon, and he is going to marry her best friend!" Cold perspiration started from every pore in his body. He had met the doom of love—the end of hope.

"He has always loved her," said Rosalie so calmly that he was shocked by her courage. "I hope she will not ask him to wait."

Rosalie never understood why Bonner looked at her in amazement and said:

"By Jove, you are a——a marvel, Rosalie!"

CHAPTER XXVIII

The Blind Man's Eyes

Bonner went away without another word of love to her. He saw the futility of hoping, and he was noble enough to respect her plea for silence on the subject that seemed distasteful to her. He went as one conquered and subdued; he went with the iron in his heart for the first time—deeply imbedded and racking.

Bonner came twice from the place across the river. Anderson observed that he looked "peaked," and Rosalie mistook the hungry, wan look in his face for the emaciation natural to confinement indoors. He was whiter than was his wont, and there was a dogged, stubborn look growing about his eyes and mouth that would have been understood by the sophisticated. It was the first indication of the battle his love was to wage in days to come. He saw no sign of weakening in Rosalie. She would not let him look into her brave little heart, and so he turned his back upon the field and fled to Boston, half beaten, but unconsciously collecting his forces for the strife of another day. He did not know it then, nor did she, but his love was not vanquished; it had met its first rebuff, that was all.

Tinkletown was sorry to see him depart, but it thrived on his promise to return. Every one winked slyly behind his back, for, of course, Tinkletown understood it all. He would come back often and then not at all—for the magnet would go away with him in the end. The busybodies, good-natured but garrulous, did not have to rehearse the story to its end; it would have been superfluous. Be it said here, however, that Rosalie was not long in settling many of the speculators straight in their minds. It seemed improbable that it should not be as they had thought and hoped. The news soon reached Blootch Peabody and Ed Higgins, and, both eager to revive a blighted hope, in high spirits, called to see Rosalie on the same night. It is on record that neither of them uttered two dozen words between eight o'clock and ten, so bitterly was the presence of the other resented.

March came, and with it, to the intense amazement

of Anderson Crow, the ever-mysterious thousand dollars, a few weeks late. On a certain day the old marshal took Rosalie to Boggs City, and the guardianship proceedings were legally closed. Listlessly she accepted half of the money he had saved, having refused to take all of it. She was now her own mistress, much to her regret if not to his.

"I may go on living with you, Daddy Crow, may I not?" she asked wistfully as they drove home through the March blizzard. "This doesn't mean that I cannot be your own little girl after to-day, does it?"

"Don't talk like that, Rosalie Gray, er I'll put you to bed 'thout a speck o' supper," growled he in his most threatening tones, but the tears were rolling down his cheeks at the time.

"Do you know, daddy, I honestly hope that the big city detective won't find out who I am," she said after a long period of reflection.

"Cause why?"

"Because, if he doesn't, you won't have any excuse for turning me out."

"I'll not only send you to bed, but I'll give you a tarnation good lickin' besides if you talk like——"

"But I'm twenty-one. You have no right," said she so brightly that he cracked his whip over the horse's back and blew his nose twice for full measure of gratitude.

"Well, I ain't heerd anything from that fly detective lately, an' I'm beginnin' to think he ain't sech a long sight better'n I am," said he proudly.

"He isn't half as good!" she cried.

"I mean as a detective," he supplemented apologetically.

"So do I," she agreed earnestly; but it was lost on him.

There was a letter at home for her from Edith Bonner. It brought the news that Wicker was going South to recuperate. His system had "gone off" since the accident, and the March winds were driving him away temporarily. Rosalie's heart ached that night, and there was a still, cold dread in its depths that drove sleep away. He had not written to her, and she had begun to fear that their month had been a trifle to him, after all. Now she was troubled and grieved that she should have entertained the fear. Edith went on to say that her brother had seen the New York detective, who was still hopelessly in the dark, but struggling on in the belief that chance would open the way for him.

Rosalie, strive as she would to prevent it, grew pale and the roundness left her cheek as the weeks went by. Her every thought was with the man who had gone to the Southland. She loved him as she loved life, but she could not confess to him then or thereafter unless Providence made clear the purity of her birth to her and to all the world. When finally there came to her a long, friendly, even dignified letter from the far South, the roses began to struggle back to her cheeks and the warmth to her heart. Her response brought a prompt answer from him, and the roses grew faster than the spring itself. Friendship, sweet and loyal, marked every word that passed between them, but there was a dear world in each epistle—for her, at least, a world of comfort and hope. She was praying, hungering, longing for June to come —sweet June and its tender touch—June with its bitter-sweet and sun clouds. Now she was forgetting the wish which had been expressed to Anderson Crow on the drive home from Boggs City. In its place grew the fierce hope that the once despised detective might clear away the mystery and give her the right to stand among others without shame and despair.

"Hear from Wick purty reg'lar, don't you, Rosalie?" asked Anderson wickedly, one night while Blootch was there. The suitor moved uneasily, and Rosalie shot a reproachful glance at Anderson, a glance full of mischief as well.

"He writes occasionally, daddy."

"I didn't know you corresponded reg'larly," said Blootch.

"I did not say regularly, Blucher."

"He writes sweet things to beat the band, I bet," said Blootch with a disdain he did not feel.

"What a good guesser you are!" she cried tormentingly.

"Well, I guess I'll be goin'," exploded Blootch wrathfully; "it's gittin' late."

"He won't sleep much to-night," said Anderson, with a twinkle in his eye, as the gate slammed viciously behind the caller. "Say, Rosalie, there's somethin' been fidgetin' me fer quite a while. I'll blurt it right out an' have it over with. Air you in love with Wick Bonner?"

She started, and for an instant looked at him with wide open eyes; then they faltered and fell. Her breath came in a frightened, surprised gasp and her cheeks grew warm. When she looked up again, her eyes were soft and pleading, and her lips trembled ever so slightly.

"Yes, Daddy Crow, I love him," she almost whispered.

"An' him? How about him?"

"I can't answer that, daddy. He has not told me."

"Well, he ought to, doggone him!"

"I could not permit him to do so if he tried."

"What! You wouldn't permit? What in tarnation do you mean?"

"You forget, daddy, I have no right to his love. It would be wrong—all wrong. Good-night, daddy," she cried, impulsively kissing him and dashing away before he could check her, but not before he caught the sound of a half sob. For a long time he sat and stared at the fire in the grate. Then he slapped his knee vigorously, squared his shoulders and set his jaw like a vise. Arising, he stalked upstairs and tapped on her door. She opened it an inch or two and peered forth at him—a pathetic figure in white.

"Don't you worry, Rosalie," he gulped. "It will be all right and hunky dory. I've just took a solemn oath down stairs."

"An oath, daddy?"

"Yes, sir; I swore by all that's good and holy I'd find out who your parents are ef it took till doomsday. You shall be set right in the eyes of everybody. Now,

"'I BEG YOUR PARDON,' HE SAID HUMBLY"

if I was you, I'd go right to sleep. There ain't nothin'
to worry about. I've got another clew."

She smiled lovingly as he ambled away. Poor old
Anderson's confidence in himself was only exceeded by
his great love for her.

At last June smiled upon Rosalie and she was off
for Boston. Her gowns were from Albany and her
happiness from heaven—according to a reverential
Tinkletown impression. For two weeks after her departure, Anderson Crow talked himself hoarse into
willing ears, always extolling the beauty of his erstwhile ward as she appeared before the family circle in
each and every one of those wonderful gowns.

This humble narrative has not to do with the glories
and foibles of Boston social life. It has to deal with
the adventures of Anderson Crow and Rosalie Gray
in so far as they pertain to a place called Tinkletown.
The joys and pleasures that Rosalie experienced during that month of June were not unusual in character.
The loneliness of Anderson Crow was not a novelty,
if one stops to consider how the world revolves for
every one else. Suffice to say that the Bonners, *mère,
fils* and *fille,* exerted themselves to make the month an
unforgetable one to the girl—and they succeeded.
The usual gaiety, the same old whirl of experiences,
came to her that come to any other mortal who is
being entertained, fêted and admired. She was a success—a pleasure in every way—not only to her hosts
but to herself. If there was a cloud hanging over her
head through all these days and nights, the world was
none the wiser; the silver lining was always visible.

Once while she was driving with the Bonners she saw a man whom she knew, but did not expect to ever look upon again. She could not be mistaken in him. It was Sam Welch, chief of the kidnapers. He was gazing at her from a crowded street corner, but disappeared completely before Bonner could set the police on his trail.

Commencement Day at Cambridge brought back hundreds of the old men—the men famous in every branch of study and athletics. Among them was handsome Tom Reddon. He came to see her at the Bonner home. Elsie Banks was to return in September from Honolulu, and they were to be married in the fall. Wicker Bonner eagerly looked for the confusion of love in her eyes, but none appeared. That night she told him, in reply to an impulsive demand, that she did not care for Reddon, that she never had known the slightest feeling of tenderness for him.

"Have you ever been in love, Rosalie?" he asked ruthlessly.

"Yes," she said after a moment, looking him bravely in the eyes.

"And could you never learn to love any one else?"

"I think not, Wicker," she said ever so softly.

"I beg your pardon," he said humbly, his face white and his lips drawn. "I should not have asked."

And so he remained the blind man, with the light shining full into his eyes.

CHAPTER XXIX

The Mysterious Questioner

JULY brought Rosalie's visit to an end, and once more Tinkletown basked in her smiles and yet wondered why they were so sad and wistful. She and Bonner were much nearer, far dearer to one another than ever, and yet not one effort had been made to bridge the chasm of silence concerning the thing that lay uppermost in their minds. She only knew that Anderson Crow had not "run down" his clew, nor had the New York sleuth reported for weeks. Undoubtedly, the latter had given up the search, for the last heard of him was when he left for Europe with his wife for a pleasure trip of unknown duration. It looked so dark and hopeless to her, all of it. Had Bonner pressed his demands upon her at the end of the visit in Boston, it is possible—more than possible—that she would have faltered in her resolution. After all, why should she deprive herself of happiness if it was held out to her with the promise that it should never end?

The summer turned steaming hot in the lowlands about Tinkletown, but in the great hills across the river the air was cool, bright, and invigorating. People began to hurry to their country homes from the distant cities. Before the month was old, a score or more of beautiful places were opened and filled with the sons and daughters of the rich. Lazily they drifted and drove and walked through the wonderful hills, famed throughout the world, and lazily they wondered why the rest of the world lived. In the hills now were the Randalls, the Farnsworths, the Brackens, the Brewsters, the Van Wagenens, the Rolfes and a host of others. Tinkletown saw them occasionally as they came jaunting by in their traps and brakes and automobiles—but it is extremely doubtful if they saw Tinkletown in passing.

Anderson Crow swelled and blossomed in the radiance of his own importance. In his old age he was becoming fastidious. Only in the privacy of his own back yard did he go without the black alpaca coat; he was beginning to despise the other days, when he had gone coatless from dawn till dark, on the street or off. His badges were pinned neatly to his lapel and not to his suspenders, as in the days of yore. His dignity was the same, but the old sense of irritation was very much modified. In these new days he was considerate —and patronising. Was he not one of the wealthiest men in town—with his six thousand dollars laid by? Was he not its most honoured citizen, not excepting the mayor and selectmen? Was he not, above all, a close friend of the Bonners?

The Bonners were to spend August in the Congressman's home across the big river. This fact alone was enough to stir the Crow establishment to its most infinitesimal roots. Rosalie was to be one of the guests at the house party, but her foster-sisters were not the kind to be envious. They revelled with her in the preparations for that new season of delight.

With the coming of the Bonners, Anderson once more revived his resolution to unravel the mystery attending Rosalie's birth. For some months this ambition had lain dormant, but now, with the approach of the man she loved, the old marshal's devotion took fire and he swore daily that the mystery should be cleared "whether it wanted to be or not."

He put poor old Alf Reesling through the "sweat box" time and again, and worthless Tom Folly had many an unhappy night, wondering why the marshal was shadowing him so persistently.

"Alf," demanded Anderson during one of the sessions, "where were you on the night of February 18, 1883? Don't hesitate. Speak up. Where were you? Aha, you cain't answer. That looks suspicious."

"You bet I c'n answer," said Alf bravely, blinking his blear eyes. "I was in Tinkletown."

"What were you doin' that night?"

"I was sleepin'."

"At what time? Keerful now, don't lie."

"What time o' night did they leave her on your porch?" demanded Alf in turn.

"It was jest half past 'leven."

"You're right, Anderson. That's jest the time I was asleep."

"C'n you prove it? Got witnesses?"

"Yes, but they don't remember the night."

"Then it may go hard with you. Alf, I still believe you had somethin' to do with that case."

"I didn't, Anderson, so help me."

"Well, doggone it, somebody did," roared the marshal. "If it wasn't you, who was it? Answer that, sir."

"Why, consarn you, Anderson Crow, I didn't have any spare children to leave around on doorsteps. I've allus had trouble to keep from leavin' myself there. Besides, it was a woman that left her, wasn't it? Well, consarn it, I'm not a woman, am I? Look at my whiskers, gee whiz! I——"

"I didn't say you left the baskit, Alf; I only said you'd somethin' to do with it. I remember that there was a strong smell of liquor around the place that night." In an instant Anderson was sniffing the air. "Consarn ye, the same smell as now—yer drunk."

"Tom Folly drinks, too," protested Alf. "He drinks Martini cocktails."

"Don't you?"

"Not any more. The last time I ordered one was in a Dutch eatin' house up to Boggs City. The waiter couldn't speak a word of English, an' that's the reason I got so full. Every time I ordered 'dry Martini' he brought me three. He didn't know how to spell it. No, sir, Anderson; I'm not the woman you want. I was at home asleep that night. I remember jest as well as anything, that I said before goin' to bed that it was a good night to sleep. I remember lookin' at the kitchen clock an' seein' it was jest eighteen minutes after eleven. 'Nen I said——"

"That'll be all for to-day, Alf," interrupted the questioner, his gaze suddenly centering on something down the street. "You've told me that six hundred times in the last twenty years. Come on, I see the boys pitchin' horseshoes up by the blacksmith shop. I'll pitch you a game fer the seegars."

"I cain't pay if I lose," protested Alf.

"I know it," said Anderson; "I don't expect you to."

The first day that Bonner drove over in the automobile, to transplant Rosalie in the place across the river, found Anderson full of a new and startling sensation. He stealthily drew the big sunburnt young man into the stable, far from the house. Somehow, in spite of his smiles, Bonner was looking older and more serious. There was a set, determined expression about his mouth and eyes that struck Anderson as new.

"Say, Wick," began the marshal mysteriously, "I'm up a stump."

"What? Another?"

"No; jest the same one. I almost got track of somethin' to-day—not two hours ago. I met a man out yander near the cross-roads that I'm sure I seen aroun' here about the time Rosalie was left on the porch. An' the funny part of it was, he stopped me an' ast me about her. Doggone, I wish I'd ast him his name."

"You don't mean it!" cried Bonner, all interest. "Asked about her? Was he a stranger?"

"I think he was. Leastwise, he said he hadn't been aroun' here fer more'n twenty year. Y' see, it was this way. I was over to Lem Hudlow's to ask if he had any hogs stole last night—Lem lives nigh the poorhouse, you know. He said he hadn't missed any an' ast me if any hogs had been found. I tole him no, not that I knowed of, but I jest thought I'd ask; I thought mebby he'd had some stole. You never c'n tell, you know, an' it pays to be attendin' to business all the time. Well, I was drivin' back slow when up rode a feller on horseback. He was a fine-lookin' man 'bout fifty year old, I reckon, an' was dressed in all them new-fangled ridin' togs. 'Ain't this Mr. Crow, my old friend, the detective?' said he. 'Yes, sir,' said I. 'I guess you don't remember me,' says he. I told him I did, but I lied. It wouldn't do fer him to think I didn't know him an' me a detective, don't y' see?

"We chatted about the weather an' the crops, him ridin' longside the buckboard. Doggone, his face was familiar, but I couldn't place it. Finally, he leaned over an' said, solemn-like: 'Have you still got the little girl that was left on your porch?' You bet I jumped when he said that. 'Yes,' says I, 'but she ain't a little girl now. She's growed up.' 'Is she purty?' he ast. 'Yes,' says I, 'purty as a speckled pup!' 'I'd like to see her,' he said. 'I hear she was a beautiful baby. I hope she is very, very happy.' 'What's that to you?' says I, sharp-like. 'I am very much interested in her, Mr. Crow,' he answered. 'Poor child, I have had her in mind for a long time,' he went on very solemn. I begin to suspect right away that he had a lot to do with her affairs. Somehow, I couldn't help thinkin' I'd seen him in Tinkletown about the time she was dropped—left, I mean.

" 'You have given her a good eddication, I hope,' said he. 'Yes, she's got the best in town,' said I. 'The thousand dollars came all right every year?' 'Every February.' 'I should like to see her sometime, if I may, without her knowin' it, Mr. Crow.' 'An' why that way, sir?' demanded I. 'It would probably annoy her if she thought I was regardin' her as an object of curiosity,' said he. 'Tell her fer me,' he went on' gittin' ready to whip up, 'that she has an unknown friend who would give anything he has to help her.' Goshed, if he didn't put the gad to his horse an' gallop off 'fore I could say another word. I was goin' to ask him a lot of questions, too."

"Can't you remember where and under what circumstances you saw him before?" cried Bonner, very much excited.

"I'm goin' to try to think it up to-night. He was a rich-lookin' feller an' he had a heavy black band aroun' one of his coat sleeves. Wick, I bet he's the man we want. I've made up my mind 'at he's her father!"

Bonner impatiently wormed all the information possible out of the marshal, especially as to the stranger's looks, voice, the direction taken when they parted company and then dismally concluded that an excellent opportunity had been hopelessly lost. Anderson said, in cross-examination, that the stranger had told him he "was leavin' at once fer New York and then going to Europe." His mother had died recently.

"I'll try to head him off at Boggs City," said Bonner; and half an hour later he was off at full speed in the big machine for the county seat, a roundabout way to Bonner Place. The New York train had gone, but no one had seen a man answering the description of Anderson's interviewer.

"I'm sorry, Rosalie," said Bonner some time later. He was taking her for a spin in the automobile. "It was a forlorn hope, and it is also quite probable that Mr. Crow's impressions are wrong. The man may have absolutely no connection with the matter. I'll admit it looks interesting, his manner and his questions, and there is a chance that he knows the true story. In any event, he did not go to New York to-day and he can't get another train until to-morrow. I'll pick up Mr. Crow in the morning and we'll run up here to have a look at him if he appears."

"I think it is a wild goose chase, Wicker," Rosalie said despairingly. "Daddy Crow has done such things before."

"But this seems different. The man's actions were

"It was a wise, discreet old oak"

curious. He must have had some reason for being interested in you. I am absolutely wild with eagerness to solve this mystery, Rosalie. It means life to me."

"Oh, if you only could do it," she cried so fervently, that his heart leaped with pity for her.

"I love you, Rosalie. I would give my whole life to make you happy. Listen, dearest—don't turn away from me! Are you afraid of me?" He was almost wailing it into her ear.

"I—I was only thinking of the danger, Wicker. You are not watching the road," she said, flushing a deep red. He laughed gaily for the first time in months.

"It is a wide road and clear," he said jubilantly. "We are alone and we are merely drifting. The machine is alive with happiness. Rosalie—Rosalie, I could shout for joy! You *do* love me? You will be my wife?"

She was white and silent and faint with the joy of it all and the pain of it all. Joy in the full knowledge that he loved her and had spoken in spite of the cloud that enveloped her, pain in the certainty that she could not accept the sacrifice. For a long time she sat staring straight down the broad road over which they were rolling.

"Wicker, you must not ask me now," she said at last, bravely and earnestly. "It is sweet to know that you love me. It is life to me—yes, life, Wicker. But, don't you see? No, no! You must not expect it. You must not ask it. Don't, don't, dear!" she cried, drawing away as he leaned toward her, passion in his eyes, triumph in his face.

"But we love each other!" he cried. "What matters the rest? I want you—*you!*"

"Have you considered? Have you thought? I have, a thousand times, a thousand bitter thoughts. I cannot, I will not be your—your wife, Wicker, until——"

In vain he argued, pleaded, commanded. She was firm and she felt she was right if not just. Underneath it all lurked the fear, the dreadful fear that she may have been a child of love, the illegitimate offspring of passion. It was the weight that crushed her almost to lifelessness; it was the bar sinister.

"No, Wicker, I mean it," she said in the end resolutely. "Not until I can give you a name in exchange for your own."

"Your name shall one day be Bonner if I have to wreck the social system of the whole universe to uncover another one for you."

The automobile had been standing, by some extraordinary chance, in the cool shade of a great oak for ten minutes or more, but it was a wise, discreet old oak.

CHAPTER XXX

The Hemisphere Train Robbery

ANDERSON CROW lived at the extreme south end of Tinkletown's principal thoroughfare. The "cala-boose" was situated at the far end of Main Street, at least half a mile separating the home of the law and the home of the lawless. Marshal Crow's innate love for the spectacular alone explains the unneighbourli-ness of the two establishments. He felt an inward glory in riding or walking the full length of the street, and he certainly had no reason to suspect the populace of disregarding the outward glory he presented.

The original plan of the merchantry comprehended the erection of the jail in close proximity to the home of its chief official, but Mr. Crow put his foot flatly and ponderously upon the scheme. With the dignity which made him noticeable, he said he'd "be dog-goned ef he wanted to have people come to his own dooryard to be arrested." By which, it may be in-ferred, that he expected the evil-doer to choose his own arresting place.

Mr. and Mrs. Crow were becoming thrifty, in view of the prospect that confronted them, to wit: The pos-sible marriage of Rosalie and the cutting off of the yearly payments. As she was to be absent for a full month or more, Anderson conceived the idea of ad-vertising for a lodger and boarder. By turning Roscoe out of his bed, they obtained a spare room that looked down upon the peony beds beyond the side "portico."

Mr. Crow was lazily twisting his meagre chin whiskers one morning soon after Rosalie's departure. He was leaning against the town pump in front of the post-office, the sun glancing impotently off the bright badge on the lapel of his alpaca coat. A stranger

came forth from the post-office and approached the marshal.

"Is this Mr. Crow?" he asked, with considerable deference.

"It is, sir."

"They tell me you take lodgers."

"Depends."

"My name is Gregory, Andrew Gregory, and I am

here to canvass the neighbourhood in the interest of the Human Life Insurance Company of Penobscot. If you need references, I can procure them from New York or Boston."

The stranger was a tall, lean-faced man of forty or forty-five, well dressed, with a brusque yet pleasant manner of speech. His moustache and beard were black and quite heavy. Mr. Crow eyed him quietly for a moment.

"I don't reckon I'll ask fer references. Our rates are six dollars a week, board an' room. Childern bother you?"

"Not at all. Have you any?"

"Some, more or less. They're mostly grown."

"I will take board and room for two weeks, at least," said Mr. Gregory, who seemed to be a man of action.

For almost a week the insurance agent plied his vocation assiduously but fruitlessly. The farmers and the citizens of Tinkletown were slow to take up insurance. They would talk crops and politics with the obliging Mr. Gregory, but that was all. And yet, his suavity won for him many admirers. There were not a few who promised to give him their insurance if they concluded to "take any out." Only one man in town was willing to be insured, and he was too old to be comforting. Mr. Calligan was reputed to be one hundred and three years of age; and he wanted the twenty-year endowment plan. Gregory popularised himself at the Crow home by paying for his room in advance. Moreover, he was an affable chap with a fund of good stories straight from Broadway. At the post-office and in Lamson's store he was soon established as a mighty favourite. Even the women who came to make purchases in the evening,—a hitherto unknown custom,—lingered outside the circle on the porch, revelling in the second edition of the "Arabian Nights."

"Our friend, the detective here," he said, one night at the close of the first week, "tells me that we are to have a show in town next week. I haven't seen any posters."

"Mark Riley's been goin' to put up them bills sence day 'fore yesterday," said Anderson Crow, with exasperation in his voice, "an he ain't done it yet. The agent fer the troupe left 'em here an' hired Mark, but he's so thunderation slow that he won't paste 'em up 'til after the show's been an' gone. I'll give him a talkin' to to-morrer ."

"What-fer show is it?" asked Jim Borum.

"Somethin' like a circus on'y 'tain't one," said Anderson. "They don't pertend to have animals."

"Don't carry a menagerie, I see," remarked Gregory.

" 'Pears that way," said Anderson, slowly analysing the word.

"I understand it is a stage performance under a tent," volunteered the postmaster.

"That's what it is," said Harry Squires, the editor, with a superior air. "They play 'As You Like It,' by Shakespeare. It's a swell show. We got out the hand bills over at the office. They'll be distributed in town to-morrow, and a big batch of them will be sent over to the summer places across the river. The advance agent says it is a high-class performance and will appeal particularly to the rich city people up in the mountains. It's a sort of open-air affair, you know." And then Mr. Squires was obliged to explain to his fellow-townsmen all the known details in connection with the approaching performance of "As You Like It" by the Boothby Company, set for Tinkletown on the following Thursday night. Hapgood's Grove had been selected by the agent as the place in which the performance should be given.

"Don't they give an afternoon show?" asked Mrs. Williams.

"Sure not," said Harry curtly. "It isn't a museum."

"Of course not," added Anderson Crow reflectively. "It's a troupe."

The next morning, bright and early, Mark Riley fared forth with paste and brush. Before noon, the board fences, barns and blank walls of Tinkletown flamed with great red and blue letters, twining in and about the portraits of Shakespeare, Manager Boothby, Rosalind, Orlando, and an extra king or two in royal robes. A dozen small boys spread the hand bills from the *Banner* presses, and Tinkletown was stirred by the excitement of a sensation that had not been experienced since Forepaugh's circus visited the county seat three years before. It went without saying that Manager Boothby would present "As You Like It" with an "unrivalled cast." He had "an all-star production," direct from "the leading theatres of the universe."

When Mark Riley started out again in the afternoon

for a second excursion with paste and brush, "slapping up" small posters with a celerity that bespoke extreme interest on his part, the astonished populace feared

that he was announcing a postponement of the performance. Instead of that, however, he was heralding the fact that the Hemisphere Trunk Line and Express Company would gladly pay ten thousand dollars reward for the "apprehension and capture" of the men who robbed one of its richest trains a few nights before, seizing as booty over sixty thousand dollars in money, besides killing two messengers in cold blood. The great train robbery occurred in the western part of the State, hundreds of miles from Tinkletown, but nearly all of its citizens had read accounts of the deed in the weekly paper from Boggs City.

"I seen the item about it in Mr. Gregory's New York paper," said Anderson Crow to the crowd at Lamson's.

"Gee whiz, it must 'a' been a peach!" said Isaac Porter, open-mouthed and eager for details. Whereupon Marshal Crow related the story of the crime which stupefied the world on the morning of July 31st. The express had been held up in an isolated spot by a half-dozen masked men. A safe had been shattered and the contents confiscated, the perpetrators vanishing as completely as if aided by Satan himself. The authorities were baffled. A huge reward was offered in the hope that it might induce some discontented underling in the band to expose his comrades.

"Are you goin' after 'em, Anderson?" asked old Mr. Borton, with unfailing faith in the town's chief officer.

"Them fellers is in Asia by this time," vouchsafed Mr. Crow scornfully, forgetting that less than a week had elapsed since the robbery. He flecked a fly from his detective's badge and then struck viciously at the same insect when it straightway attacked his G. A. R. emblem.

"I doubt it," said Mr. Lamson. "Like as not they're right here in this State, mebby in this county. You can't tell about them slick desperadoes. Hello, Harry! Has anything more been heard from the train robbers?" Harry Squires approached the group with something like news in his face.

"I should say so," he said. "The darned cusses robbed the State Express last night at Vanderskoop and got away with thirteen hundred dollars. Say, they're wonders! The engineer says they're only five of them."

"Why, gosh dern it, Vanderskoop's only the fourth station west of Boggs City!" exclaimed Anderson Crow, pricking up his official ear. "How in thunder do you reckon they got up here in such a short time?"

"They probably stopped off on their way back from Asia," drily remarked Mr. Lamson; but it passed unnoticed.

"Have you heard anything more about the show, Harry?" asked Jim Borum. "Is she sure to be here?" What did Tinkletown care about the train robbers when a "show" was headed that way?

"Sure. The press comments are very favourable," said Harry. "They all say that Miss Marmaduke, who plays Rosalind, is great. We've got a cut of her and, say, she's a beauty. I can see myself sitting in the front row next Thursday night, good and proper."

"Say, Anderson, I think it's a dern shame fer Mark Riley to go 'round pastin' them reward bills over the show pictures," growled Isaac Porter. "He ain't got a bit o' sense."

With one accord the crowd turned to inspect two adjacent bill boards. Mark had either malignantly or insanely pasted the reward notices over the nether extremities of Rosalind as she was expected to appear in the Forest of Arden. There was a period of reflection on the part of an outraged constituency.

"I don't see how he's goin' to remove off them reward bills without scraping off her legs at the same time," mused Anderson Crow in perplexity. Two housewives of Tinkletown suddenly deserted the group and entered the store. And so it was that the train robbers were forgotten for the time being.

But Marshal Crow's reputation as a horse-thief taker and general suppressor of crime constantly upbraided him. It seemed to call upon him to take steps toward the capture of the train robbers. All that afternoon he reflected. Tinkletown, seeing his mood, refrained from breaking in upon it. He was allowed to stroke his whiskers in peace and to think to his heart's content. By nightfall his face had become an inscrutable mask, and then it was known that the President of Bramble County's Horse-Thief Detective Association was determined to fathom the great problem. Stealthily he went up to the great attic in his home and inspected his "disguises." In some far-off period of his official career he had purchased the most amazing collection of false beards, wigs and garments that any stranded comedian ever disposed of at a sacrifice. He tried each separate article, seeking for the best individual effect; then he tried them collectively. It would certainly have been impossible to recognise him as Anderson Crow. In truth, no one could safely have identified him as a human being.

"I'm goin' after them raskils," he announced to Andrew Gregory and the whole family, as he came down late to take his place at the head of the supper table.

"Ain't you goin' to let 'em show here, pop?" asked Roscoe in distress.

"Show here? What air you talkin' about?"

"He means the train robbers, Roscoe," explained the lad's mother. The boy breathed again.

"They are a dangerous lot," volunteered Gregory, who had been in Albany for two days. "The papers are full of their deeds. Cutthroats of the worst character."

"I'd let them alone, Anderson," pleaded his wife. "If you corner them, they'll shoot, and it would be jest like you to follow them right into their lair."

"Consarn it, Eva, don't you s'pose that I c'n shoot, too?" snorted Anderson. "What you reckon I've been keepin' them loaded revolvers out in the barn all these years fer? Jest fer ornaments? Not much! They're to shoot with, ef anybody asks you. Thunderation, Mr. Gregory, you ain't no idee how a feller can be handicapped by a timid wife an' a lot o' fool childern. I'm almost afeard to turn 'round fer fear they'll be skeered to death fer my safety."

"You cut yourself with a razor once when ma told you not to try to shave the back of your neck by yourself," said one of the girls. "She wanted you to let

Mr. Beck shave it for you, but you wouldn't have it that way."

"Do you suppose I want an undertaker shavin' my neck? I'm not that anxious to be shaved. Beck's the undertaker, Mr. Gregory."

"Well, he runs the barber shop, too," insisted the girl.

During the next three days Tinkletown saw but little of its marshal, fire chief and street commissioner. That triple personage was off on business of great import. Early, each morning, he mysteriously stole away to the woods, either up or down the river, carrying a queer bundle under the seat of his "buckboard." Two revolvers, neither of which had been discharged for ten years, reposed in a box fastened to the dashboard. Anderson solemnly but positively refused to allow any one to accompany him, nor would he permit any one to question him. Farmers coming to town spoke of seeing him in the lanes and in the woods, but he had winked genially when they had asked what he was trailing.

"He's after the train robbers," explained all Tinkletown soberly. Whereupon the farmers and their wives did not begrudge Anderson Crow the chicken dinners he had eaten with them, nor did they blame him for bothering the men in the fields. It was sufficient that he found excuse to sleep in the shade of their trees during his still hunt.

"Got any track of 'em?" asked George Ray one evening, stopping at Anderson's back gate to watch the marshal unhitch his thankful nag. Patience had ceased to be a virtue with George.

"Any track of who?" asked Mr. Crow with a fine show of innocence.

"The robbers."

"I ain't been trackin' robbers, George."

"What in thunder have you been trackin' all over the country every day, then?"

"I'm breakin' this colt," calmly replied the marshal, with a mighty wink at old Betty, whom he had driven to the same buckboard for twenty years. As George departed with an insulted snort, Andrew Gregory came from the barn, where he had been awaiting the return of Mr. Crow."

"I'm next to something big," he announced in a low tone, first looking in all directions to see that no one was listening.

"Gosh! Did you land Mr. Farnsworth?"

"It has nothing to do with insurance," hastily explained the agent. "I've heard something of vast importance to you."

"You don't mean to say the troupe has busted?"

"No—no; it is in connection with—with—" and here Mr. Gregory leaned forward and whispered something in Anderson's ear. Mr. Crow promptly stopped dead still in his tracks, his eyes bulging. Betty, who was being led to the water trough, being blind and having no command to halt, proceeded to bump forcibly against her master's frame.

CHAPTER XXXI

"As You Like It"

YOU—don't—say—so! Whoa! dang ye! Cain't you
see where you're goin', you old rip?" Betty was
jerked to a standstill. "What have you heerd?"
asked Anderson, his voice shaking with interest.

"I can't tell you out here," said the other cautiously.
"Put up the nag and then meet me in the pasture out
there. We can sit down and talk and not be over-
heard."

"I won't be a minute. Here, you Roscoe! Feed
Betty and water her first. Step lively, now. Tell
your ma we'll be in to supper when we git good an'
ready."

Anderson and Andrew Gregory strode through the
pasture gate and far out into the green meadow.
Once entirely out of hearing, Gregory stopped and
both sat down upon a little hillock. The agent was
evidently suppressing considerable excitement.

"Those train robbers are in this neighbourhood," he
said, breaking a long silence. Anderson looked behind involuntarily. "I don't mean that they are in
this pasture, Mr. Crow. You've been a good friend
to me, and I'm inclined to share the secret with you.
If we go together, we may divide the ten-thousand-
dollar reward, because I'm quite sure we can land
those chaps."

"What's your plan?" asked Anderson, turning a little pale at the thought. Before going any further into the matter, Gregory asked Anderson if he would sign a paper agreeing to divide the reward equally with him. This point was easily settled, and then the insurance man unfolded his secret.

"I have a straight tip from a friend in New York and he wouldn't steer me wrong. The truth about him is this: He used to work for our company, but took some money that didn't belong to him. It got him a sentence in the pen. He's just out, and he knows a whole lot about these robbers. Some of them were in Sing Sing with him. The leader wanted him to join the gang and he half-way consented. His duty is to keep the gang posted on what the officers in New York are doing. See?"

"Of course," breathed Anderson.

"Well, my friend wants to reform. All he asks is a slice of the reward. If we capture the gang, we can afford to give him a thousand or so, can't we?"

"Of course," was the dignified response.

"Here's his letter to me. I'll read it to you." In the gathering dusk Gregory read the letter to the marshal of Tinkletown. "Now, you see," he said, at the close of the astounding epistle, "this means that if we observe strict secrecy, we may have the game in our hands. No one must hear a word of this. They may have spies right here in Tinkletown. We can succeed only by keeping our mouths sealed."

"Tighter'n beeswax," promised Anderson Crow.

Briefly, the letter to Andrew Gregory was an exposure of the plans of the great train-robber gang, together with their whereabouts on a certain day to come. They were to swoop down on Tinkletown on the night of the open-air performance of "As You Like It," and their most desperate coup was to be the result. The scheme was to hold up and rob the entire audience while the performance was going on. Anderson Crow was in a cold perspiration. The performance was but three days off, and he felt that he required three months for preparation.

"How in thunder are we goin' to capture that awful gang, jest you an' me?" he asked, voicing his doubts and fears.

"We'll have to engage help, that's all."

"We'll need a regiment."

"Don't you think it. Buck up, old fellow, don't be afraid."

"Afeerd? Me? I don't know what it is to be skeered. Didn't you ever hear about how I landed them fellers that kidnaped my daughter Rosalie? Well, you jest ast some one 'at knows about it. Umph! I guess that was a recommend fer bravery. But these fellers will be ready fer us, won't they?"

"We can trick them easily. I've been thinking of a plan all afternoon. We don't know just where they are now, so we can't rake them in to-night. We'll have to wait until they come to us. My plan is to have a half-dozen competent private detectives up from New York. We can scatter them through the audience next Thursday night, and when the right time comes we can land on every one of those fellows like hawks on spring chickens. I know the chief of a big private agency in New York, and I think the best plan is to have him send up some good men. It won't cost much, and I'd rather have those fearless practical men here than all the rubes you could deputise. One of 'em is worth ten of your fellow-citizens, Mr. Crow, begging your pardon for the remark. You and I can keep the secret and we can do the right thing, but we would be asses to take more Tinkletown asses into our confidence. If you'll agree, I'll write to Mr. Pinkerton this evening. He can have his men here, disguised and ready for work, by Thursday afternoon. If you don't mind, I'd like to have you take charge of the affair, because you know just how to handle thieves, and I don't. What say you?"

Anderson was ready and eager to agree to anything, but he hesitated a long time before concluding to take supreme charge of the undertaking. Mr. Gregory at once implored him to take command. It meant the success of the venture; anything else meant failure.

"But how'n thunder am I to know the robbers when I see 'em?" demanded the marshal, nervously pulling bluegrass up by the roots.

"You'll know 'em all right," said Andrew Gregory.

Thursday came and with it the "troupe." Anderson Crow had not slept for three nights, he was so full of thrills and responsibility. Bright and early that morning he was on the lookout for suspicious characters. Gregory was to meet the detectives from New York at half-past seven in the evening. By previous arrangement, these strangers were to congregate casually at Tinkletown Inn, perfectly disguised as gentlemen, ready for instructions. The two arch-plotters had carefully devised a plan of action. Gregory chuckled secretly when he thought of the sensation Tinkletown was to experience—and he thought of it often, too.

The leading members of Boothby's All Star Company "put up" at the Inn, which was so humble that it staggered beneath this unaccustomed weight of dignity. The beautiful Miss Marmaduke (in reality, Miss Cora Miller) was there, and so were Miss Trevanian, Miss Gladys Fitzmaurice, Richmond Barrett (privately Jackie Blake), Thomas J. Booth, Francisco Irving, Ben Jefferson and others. The Inn was glorified. All Tinkletown looked upon the despised old "eating house" with a reverence that was not reluctant.

The manager, a busy and preoccupied person, who looked to be the lowliest hireling in the party, came to the Inn at noon and spread the news that the reserved seats were sold out and there was promise of a fine crowd. Whereupon there was rejoicing among the All Star Cast, for the last legs of the enterprise were to be materially strengthened.

"We won't have to walk back home," announced Mr. Jackie Blake, that good-looking young chap who played Orlando.

"Glorious Shakespeare, thou art come to life again," said Ben Jefferson, a barn-stormer for fifty years. "I was beginning to think you were a dead one."

"And no one will seize our trunks for board," added Miss Marmaduke cheerfully. She was a very pretty young woman and desperately in love with Mr. Orlando.

"If any one seized Orlando's trunks, I couldn't appear in public to-night," said Mr. Blake. "Orlando possesses but one pair of trunks."

"You might wear a mackintosh," suggested Mr. Booth.

"Or borrow trunks of the trees," added Mr. Irving.

"They're off," growled Mr. Jefferson, who hated the puns he did not make.

"Let's dazzle the town, Cora," said Jackie Blake; and before Tinkletown could take its second gasp for breath, the leading man and woman were slowly promenading the chief and only thoroughfare.

"By ginger! she's a purty one, ain't she?" murmured Ed Higgins, sole clerk at Lamson's. He stood in the doorway until she was out of sight and remained there for nearly an hour awaiting her return. The men of Tinkletown took but one look at the pretty young woman, but that one look was continuous and unbroken.

"If this jay town can turn up enough money to-night to keep us from stranding, I'll take off my hat to it for ever more," said Jackie Blake.

"Boothby says the house is sold out," said Miss Marmaduke, a shade of anxiety in her dark eyes. "Oh, how I wish we were at home again."

"I'd rather starve in New York than feast in the high hills," said he wistfully. The idols to whom

Tinkletown was paying homage were but human, after all. For two months the Boothby Company had been buffeted from pillar to post, struggling hard to keep its head above water, always expecting the crash. The "all-stars" were no more than striving young Thespians, who were kept playing throughout the heated term with this uncertain enterprise, solely because necessity was in command of their destinies. It was not for them to enjoy a summer in ease and indolence.

"Never mind, dear," said she, turning her green parasol so that it obstructed the intense but complimentary gaze of no less than a dozen men; "our luck will change. We won't be barn-storming for ever."

"We've one thing to be thankful for, little woman," said Jackie, his face brightening. "We go out again this fall in the same company. That's luck, isn't it? We'll be married as soon as we get back to New York and we won't have to be separated for a whole season, at least."

"Isn't it dear to think of, Jackie sweetheart? A whole season and then another, and then all of them after that? Oh, dear, won't it be sweet?" It was love's young dream for both of them.

"Hello, what's this?" exclaimed Orlando the Thousandth, pausing before a placard which covered the lower limbs of his pictorial partner. "Ten Thousand Dollars reward! Great Scott, Cora, wouldn't I like to catch those fellows? Great, eh? But it's a desperate gang! The worst ever!"

Just then both became conscious of the fact that

some one was scrutinising them intently from behind. They turned and beheld Anderson Crow, his badges glistening.

"How are you, officer?" said Jackie cheerily. Miss Marmaduke, in her happiness, beamed a smile upon the austere man with the chin whiskers. Anderson was past seventy, but that smile caused the intake of his breath to almost lift him from the ground.

"First rate, thanks; how's yourself? Readin' the reward notice? Lemme tell you something. There's goin' to be somethin' happen tarnation soon that will astonish them fellers ef—" but here Anderson pulled up with a jerk, realising that he was on the point of betraying a great secret. Afraid to trust himself in continued conversation, he abruptly said: "Good afternoon," and started off down the street, his ears tingling.

"Queer old chap, isn't he?" observed Jackie, and immediately forgot him as they strolled onward.

That evening Tinkletown swarmed with strangers. The weather was fine, and scores of the summer dwellers in the hills across the river came over to see the performance, as the advance agent had predicted. Bluff Top Hotel sent a large delegation of people seeking the variety of life. There were automobiles, traps, victorias, hay-racks, and "sundowns" standing all along the street in the vicinity of Hapgood's Grove. It was to be, in the expansive language of the press agent, "a cultured audience made up of the élite of the community."

Late in the afternoon, a paralysing thought struck in upon the marshal's brain. It occurred to him that this band of robbers might also be engaged to carry off Rosalie Gray. After all, it might be the great dominant reason for their descent upon the community. Covered with a perspiration that was not caused by heat, he accosted Wicker Bonner, the minute that gentleman arrived in town. Rosalie went, of course, to the Crow home for a short visit with the family.

"Say, Wick, I want you to do me a favour," said Anderson eagerly, taking the young man aside. "I cain't tell you all about it, 'cause I'm bound by a deathless oath. But, listen, I'm afraid somethin's goin' to happen to-night. There's a lot o' strangers here, an' I'm nervous about Rosalie. Somebody might try to steal her in the excitement. Now I want you to take good keer of her. Don't let 'er out o' your sight, an' don't let anybody git 'er away from you. I'll keep my eye on her, too. Promise me."

"Certainly, Mr. Crow. I'll look out for her. That's what I hope to do all the rest of——"

"Somethin' 's liable to happen," Mr. Crow broke in, and then quietly slipped away.

Bonner laughed easily at the old man's fears and set them down as a part of his whimsical nature. Later, he saw the old man near the entrance as the party passed inside the inclosure. The Bonner party occupied prominent seats in front, reserved by the marshal. There were ten in the group, a half-dozen young Boston people completing the house party.

The side walls of a pavilion inclosed the most beautiful section of the grove. In one end were the seats, rapidly filling with people. At the opposite end, upon Mother Earth's green carpet, was the stage, lighted dimly by means of subdued spot lights and a few auxiliary stars on high. There was no scenery save that provided by Nature herself. An orchestra of violins broke through the constant hum of eager voices.

Anderson Crow's heart was inside the charmed inclosure, but his person was elsewhere. Simultaneously, with the beginning of the performance of "As

You like It," he was in his own barn-loft confronting Andrew Gregory and the five bewhiskered assistants from New York City. Gregory had met the detectives at the Inn and had guided them to the marshal's barn, where final instructions were to be given. For half an hour the party discussed plans with Anderson Crow, speaking in low, mysterious tones that rang in the marshal's ears to his dying day.

"We've located those fellows," asserted Mr. Gregory firmly. "There can be no mistake. They are already in the audience over there, and at a signal

will set to work to
hold up the whole
crowd. We must
get the drop on
them, Mr. Crow.
Don't do that!
You don't need a
disguise. Keep
those yellow whis-
kers in your
pocket. The rest
of us will wear
disguises. These
men came here dis-
guised because the
robbers would be
onto them in a minute if they didn't. They know
every detective's face in the land. If it were not for
these beards and wigs they'd have spotted Pinkerton's
men long ago. Now, you know your part in the
affair, don't you?"

"Yes, sir," respectfully responded Anderson, his
chin whisker wobbling pathetically.

"Then we're ready to proceed. It takes a little
nerve, that's all, but we'll soon have those robbers
just where we want them," said Andrew Gregory.

The second act of the play was fairly well under way
when Orlando, in the "green room," remarked to the
stage director:

"What's that old rube doing back here, Ramsay?
Why, hang it, man, he's carrying a couple of guns.

Is this a hold-up?" At the same instant Rosalind and two of the women came rushing from their dressing tent, alarmed and indignant. Miss Marmaduke, her eyes blazing, confronted the stage director.

"What does this mean, Mr. Ramsay?" she cried. "That old man ordered us out of our dressing-room at the point of a revolver, and—see! There he is now doing the same to the men."

It was true. Anderson Crow, with a brace of horse pistols, was driving the players toward the centre of the stage. In a tremulous voice he commanded them to remain there and take the consequences. A moment later the marshal of Tinkletown strode into the limelight with his arsenal, facing an astonished and temporarily amused audience. His voice, pitched high with excitement, reached to the remotest corners of the inclosure. Behind him the players were looking on, open-mouthed and bewildered. To them he loomed up as the long-dreaded constable detailed to attach their personal effects. The audience, if at first it laughed at him as a joke, soon changed its view. Commotion followed his opening speech.

CHAPTER XXXII

The Luck of Anderson Crow

"Don't anybody attempt to leave this tent!" commanded Mr. Crow, standing bravely forth with his levelled revolvers. The orchestra made itself as small as possible, for one of the guns wavered dangerously. "Don't be alarmed, ladies and gentlemen. The train robbers are among you."

There were a few feminine shrieks, a volume of masculine "Whats!" a half-hearted and uncertain snigger, and a general turning of heads.

"Keep your seats!" commanded Anderson. "They can't escape. I have them surrounded. I now call upon all robbers present to surrender in the name of the law. Surrender peaceful and you will not be damaged; resist and we'll blow you to hell an' gone, even at the risk of injurin' the women and childern. The law is no respecter of persons. Throw up your hands!"

He waited impressively, but either through stupefaction or obstinacy the robbers failed to lift their hands.

"You're cornered, you golderned scamps!" shouted Anderson Crow, "an' you might jest as well give up! Twenty Pinkerton men are here from New York City, an' you can't escape! Throw up your hands!"

"The damned old fool is in earnest," gasped Judge Brewster, from across the river.

"He's crazy!" cried Congressman Bonner.

"Let everybody in this crowd throw up their hands!" called a firm, clear voice from the entrance. At the same instant five bewhiskered individuals appeared as if by magic with drawn revolvers, dominating the situation completely. The speaker was Andrew Gregory, the insurance agent.

"Now, what have you got to say?" cried Anderson gaily. "I guess me an' the detectives have you cornered all right, ain't we?"

The audience sat stupefied, paralysed. While all this was going on upon the inside, a single detective on the outside was stealthily puncturing the tires of every automobile in the collection, Mr. Bracken's huge touring car being excepted for reasons to be seen later on.

"Good heavens!" groaned old Judge Brewster. A half dozen women fainted and a hundred men broke into a cold perspiration.

"Hands up, everybody!" commanded Andrew Gregory. "We can take no chances. The train robbers are in this audience. They came to hold up the entire crowd, but we are too quick for you, my fine birds. The place is surrounded!"

"Mr. Gregory, the insurance——" began Anderson Crow, but he was cut short.

"Mr. Crow deserves great credit for this piece of detective work. His mere presence is a guaranty of safety to those of you who are not thieves. You all have your hands up? Thanks. Mr. Crow, please keep those actors quiet. Now, ladies and gentlemen, it is not always an easy matter to distinguish thieves from honest men. I will first give the desperadoes a chance to surrender peaceably. No one steps forward? Very well. Keep your hands up, all of you. The man who lowers his hands will be instantly regarded as a desperado and may get a bullet in his body for his folly. The innocent must suffer with the guilty. Mr. Crow, shall we proceed with the search?"

"Yes, sir; go right ahead, and be quick," replied Anderson Crow.

"Very well, then, in the name of the law, my men will begin the search. They will pass among you, ladies and gentlemen, and any effort to retard their progress will be met with instant—well, you know."

Before the petrified audience could fully realise what was taking place, three of the detectives were swiftly passing from person to person, stripping the women of their jewels, the men of their money and their watches. A half-hearted protest went up to Anderson Crow, but it was checked summarily by the "searching party." It was well for the poor marshal that he never knew what the audience thought of him at that ghastly moment.

It was all over in five minutes. The detectives had searched every prosperous-looking person in the audience, under the very nose and guns of Marshal Crow, and they were sardonically bidding the assemblage a fond good-bye from the flapping doorway in the side wall. Andrew Gregory addressed the crowd, smiling broadly.

"We found a good many more robbers in the crowd than we could conveniently handle, ladies and gentlemen. In fact, I never came across such a rare collection of hold-up men outside of Wall Street. The only perfectly honest man in Tinkletown to-night is Anderson Crow, your esteemed marshal. Believe me, he is ridiculously honest. He may be a damn fool, but he is honest. Don't blame him. Thanking you, one and all, for your generous help in our search for the train robbers, we bid you an affectionate farewell. We may meet again if you travel extensively on express trains. Good-night!"

With a taunting laugh, Andrew Gregory dropped the flap and leaped after his companions. Bracken's chauffeur lay senseless by the roadside, and one of the "detectives" sat in his seat. Even as the audience opened its collective mouth to shout its wrath and surprise, the big touring car, with six armed men aboard, leaped away with a rush. Down the dark road it flew like an express train, its own noise drowning the shouts of the multitude, far behind.

Bonner, recovering from his stupefaction and rage, led the pursuit, first commanding Rosalie to hurry home with the women and lock herself safely indoors.

Anderson Crow, realising what a dupe he had been in the hands of the clever scoundrels, was covered with fear and shame. The outraged crowd might have killed him had not his escape been made under cover of darkness. Shivering and moaning in abject misery, the pride of Tinkletown fled unseeing, unthinking into the forest along the river. He was not to know until afterward that his "detectives" had stripped the rich sojourners of at least ten thousand dollars in money and jewels. It is not necessary to say that the performance of "As You Like It" came to an abrupt end, because it was not as they liked it. Everybody knew by this time that they had seen the celebrated "train robbers."

Jackie Blake was half dressed when he leaped to his feet with an exclamation so loud that those preceding it were whispers.

"Holy smoke!" fell from his lips; and then he dashed across the green to the women's dressing tent. "Cora! Cora! Come out!"

"I can't," came back in muffled tones.

"Then good-bye; I'm off!" he shouted. That brought her, partially dressed, from the tent. "Say, do you remember the river road we walked over to-day? Well, those fellows went in that direction, didn't they? Don't you see? Aren't you on? The washout! If they don't know about it the whole bunch is at the bottom of the ravine or in the river by this time! Mum's the word! There's a chance, darling; the reward said 'dead or alive!' I'm off!"

She tried to call him back, but it was too late. With his own revolver in his hand, the half Orlando, half Blake, tore down the rarely travelled river road south. Behind him Tinkletown raved and wailed over the great calamity, but generally stood impotent in the face of it all. But few felt inclined to pursue the robbers. Blake soon had the race to himself. It was a mile or more to the washout in the road, but the excitement made him keen for the test. The road ran through the woods and along the high bluff that overlooked the river. He did not know it, but this same road was a "short cut" to the macadam pike farther south. By taking this route the robbers gave Boggs City a wide berth.

Blake's mind was full of the possibilities of disaster to the over-confident fugitives. The washout was fresh, and he was counting on the chance that they were not aware of its existence. If they struck it even at half speed the whole party would be hurled a hundred feet down to the edge of the river or into the current itself. In that event, some, if not all, would be seriously injured.

As he neared the turn in the road, his course pointed out to him by the stars above, he was startled half out of his boots by the sudden appearance of a man, who staggered from the roadside and wobbled painfully away, pleading for mercy.

"Halt, or I'll shoot!" called Jackie Blake, and the pathetic figure not only halted, but sat down in the middle of the road.

"For the Lord's sake, don't shoot!" groaned a hoarse voice. "I wasn't in cahoots with them. They fooled me—they fooled me." It was Anderson Crow, and he would have gone on interminably had not Jackie Blake stopped him short.

"You're the marshal, eh? The darned rube——"

"Yes, I'm him. Call me anything, only don't shoot. Who are you?" groaned Anderson, rising to his knees. He was holding his revolvers by the muzzles.

"Never mind who I am. I haven't time. Say, you'd better come with me. Maybe we can head off those villains. They came this way and——"

"Show 'em to me," roared Anderson, recognising a friend. Rage surged up and drove out the shame in his soul. "I'll tackle the hull caboodle, dang 'em!" And he meant it, too.

Blake did not stop to explain, but started on, commanding Mr. Crow to follow. With rare forethought the marshal donned his yellow beard as he panted in the trail of the lithe young actor. The latter remembered that the odds were heavily against him. The marshal might prove a valuable aid in case of resistance, provided, of course, that they came upon the robbers in the plight he was hoping for.

"Where the dickens are you a-goin'?" wheezed the marshal, kicking up a great dust in the rear. The other did not answer. His whole soul was enveloped in the hope that the washout had trapped the robbers. He was almost praying that it might be so. The reward could be divided with the poor old marshal if——

He gave a yell of delight, an instant later, and then began jumping straight up and down like one demented. Anderson Crow stopped so abruptly that his knees were stiff for weeks. Jackie Blake's wild dream had come true. The huge automobile had struck the washout, and it was now lying at the base of the bluff, smashed to pieces on the rocks! By the

dim light from the heavens, Blake could see the black hulk down there, but it was too dark to distinguish other objects. He was about to descend to the river bank when Anderson Crow came up.

"What's the matter, man?" panted he.

"THE HUGE AUTOMOBILE HAD STRUCK THE WASHOUT"

"They're down there, don't you see it? They went over the bluff right here—come on. We've got 'em!"

"Hold on!" exclaimed Anderson, grasping his arm. "Don't rush down there like a danged fool. If they're alive they can plug you full of bullets in no time. Let's be careful."

"By thunder, you're right. You're a wise old owl, after all. I never thought of that. Let's reconnoitre."

Tingling with excitement, the two oddly mated pursuers descended stealthily by a roundabout way. They climbed over rocks and crept through underbrush until finally they came to a clear spot not twenty feet from where the great ma-chine was lying, at the very edge of the swift, deep current. They heard groans and faint cries, with now and then a pite-ous oath. From their hiding place they counted the forms of four men lying upon the rocks, as if dead. The two held a whis-pered consultation of war, a plan of action resulting.

"S u r r e n d e r !" s h o u t e d Jackie

Blake, standing forth. He and Anderson had their pistols levelled upon the prostrate robbers. For answer there were louder groans, a fiercer oath or two and then a weak, pain-struck voice came out to them:

"For God's sake, get this machine off my legs. I'm dying. Help! Help! We surrender!"

Ten minutes later, the jubilant captors had released the miserable Andrew Gregory from his position beneath the machine, and had successfully bound the hands and feet of five half-unconscious men. Gregory's legs were crushed and one other's skull was cracked. The sixth man was nowhere to be found. The disaster had been complete, the downfall of the great train robbers inglorious. Looking up into the face of Anderson Crow, Gregory smiled through his pain and said hoarsely:

"Damned rotten luck; but if we had to be taken, I'm glad you did it, Crow. You're a good fool, anyway. But for God's sake, get me to a doctor."

"Dang it! I'm sorry fer you, Mr. Gregory——" began Anderson, ready to cry.

"Don't waste your time, old man. I need the doctor. Are the others dead?" he groaned.

"I don't know," replied Jackie Blake. "Some of them look like it. We can't carry you up that hill, but we'll do the next best thing. Marshal, I'll stay here and guard the prisoners while you run to the village for help—and doctors."

"And run fast, Anderson," added Gregory. "You always were so devilish slow. Don't walk—trot."

Soon afterward, when Anderson, fagged but overjoyed, hobbled into the village, the excited crowd was ready to lynch him, but with his first words the atmosphere changed.

"Where is Jackie Blake?" sobbed a pretty young woman, grasping the proud marshal's arm and shaking him violently.

"Derned if I know, ma'am. Was he stole?"

She made him understand, and together, followed by the actors, the audience and the whole town, they led the way to the washout, the fair Rosalind dragging the overworked hero of the hour along at a gait which threatened to be his undoing.

Later on, after the five bandits had been carried to the village, Jackie Blake gladly informed his sweetheart that they could have easy sailing with the seven thousand dollars he expected. Anderson Crow had agreed to take but three thousand dollars for his share in the capture. One of the robbers was dead. The body of the sixth was found in the river weeks afterward.

"I'm glad I was the first on the ground," said Blake, in anticipation of the reward which was eventually to be handed over to him. "But Anderson Crow turned out to be a regular trump, after all. He's a corker!" He was speaking to Wicker Bonner and a crowd of New Yorkers.

Tinkletown began to talk of a monument to Anderson Crow, even while he lived. The general opinion was that it should be erected while he was still able to enjoy it and not after his death, when he would not know anything about its size and cost.

"By gosh! 'Twas a great capture!" swelling perceptibly. "I knowed they couldn't escape me. Dang 'em! they didn't figger on me, did they? Pshaw! it was reediculus of 'em to think they c'd fool me entirely, although I'll have to confess they did fool me at first. It was a desprit gang an' mighty slick."

"You worked it great, Anderson," said George Ray. "Did you know about the washout?"

"Did I know about it?" snorted Anderson witheringly. "Why, good Gosh a'mighty, didn't I purty near run my legs off to git there in time to throw down the barricade before they could get there with Mr. Bracken's automobile? Thunderation! What a fool question!"

CHAPTER XXXIII

Bill Briggs Tells a Tale

TINKLETOWN fairly bubbled with excitement. At last the eyes of the world were upon it. News of the great sensation was flashed to the end of the earth; every detail was gone into with harrowing minuteness. The Hemisphere Company announced by telegraph that it stood ready to hand over the ten thousand dollars; and the sheriff of Bramble County with all the United States deputy marshals within reach raced at once to Tinkletown to stick a finger in the pie.

The morning after the "great pavilion robbery," as it was called in the *Banner,* Anderson Crow and Bonner fared forth early to have a look at the injured desperadoes, all of whom were safely under guard at the reincarnated calaboose. Fifty armed men had stood guard all night long, notwithstanding the fact that one robber was dead and the others so badly injured that they were not expected to survive the day.

A horseman passed the marshal and his friend near the post-office, riding rapidly to the north. He waved his crop pleasantly to them and Bonner responded. Anderson stopped stock still and tried to speak, but did not succeed for a full minute; he was dumb with excitement.

"That's him!" he managed to gasp. "The feller I saw the other day—the man on horseback!"

"That?" cried Bonner, laughing heartily. "Why, that is John E. Barnes, the lawyer and probably a United States Senator some day. Good heavens, Mr. Crow, you've made a bad guess of it this time! He is staying with Judge Brewster, his father-in-law."

"What! Well, by Geminy! I thought I knowed him," cried Anderson. "They cain't fool me long, Wick—none of 'em. He's the same feller 'at run away with Judge Brewster's daughter more'n twenty year ago. 'y Gosh, I was standin' right on this very spot the first time I ever see him. He sold me a hoss and buggy—but I got the money back. I arrested him the same day."

"Arrested John Barnes?" in amazement.

"Yep—fer murder—only he wasn't the murderer. We follered him down the river—him an' the girl— to Bracken's place, but they were married afore we got there. Doggone, that was a busy day! Some blamed good detective work was did, too. I——"

"And Mr. Barnes was interested in Rosalie?" asked Bonner suddenly. "How could he have known anything about her?"

"That's what puzzles me. She came here about two years after the elopement more er less, but I don't remember ever seein' him after that time."

"It's very strange, Mr. Crow," reflected Bonner soberly. "He has a son, I know. His wife died a year or so after the boy's birth. Young Barnes is about twenty-one, I think at this time. By George! I've heard it said that Barnes and his wife were not hitting it off very well. They say she died of a broken heart. I've heard mother speak of it often. I wonder—great heavens, it isn't possible that Rosalie can be connected in any way with John Barnes? Anderson Crow, I—I wonder if there is a possibility?" Bonner was quivering with excitement, wonder—and—unbelief.

"I'm workin' on that clew," said Anderson as calmly as his tremors would permit. He was thrilled by the mere suggestion, but it was second nature for him to act as if every discovery were his own. "Ever sence I saw him on the road up there, I've been trackin' him. I tell you, Wick, he's my man. I've got it almost worked out. Just as soon as these blamed robbers are moved to Boggs City, er buried, I'm goin' over an' git the truth out of Mr. Barnes. I've been huntin' him fer twenty-one years." Anderson, of course, was forgetting that Barnes had slipped from his mind completely until Bonner nudged his memory into life.

"It's a delicate matter, Mr. Crow. We must go about it carefully," said Bonner severely. "If Mr. Barnes is really interested in her, we can't find it out by blundering; if he is not interested, we can't afford to drag him into it. It will require tact——"

"Thunderation, don't you suppose I know that?" exploded Anderson. "Detectives are allers tackin'. They got to, y' see, ef they're goin' to foller half a dozen clews at oncet. Gee whiz, Wick, leave this thing to me! I'll git at the bottom of it inside o' no time."

"Wait a few days, Mr. Crow," argued Bonner, playing for time. "Don't hurry. We've got all we can do now to take care of the fellows you and that young actor captured last night." The young man's plan was to keep Anderson off the trail entirely and give the seemingly impossible clew into the possession of the New York bureau.

"I don't know what I'd 'a' done ef it hadn't been fer that young feller," said the marshal. "He was right smart help to me last night." Bonner, who knew the true story, suppressed a smile and loved the old man none the less for his mild deception.

They entered the "calaboose," which now had all the looks and odours of a hospital. A half-dozen doctors had made the four injured men as comfortable as possible. They were stretched on mattresses in the jail dining-room, guarded by a curious horde of citizens.

"That's Gregory!" whispered Anderson, as they neared the suffering group. He pointed to the most distant cot. "That's jest the way he swore last night. He must 'a' shaved in the automobile last night," though Gregory had merely discarded the false whiskers he had worn for days.

"Wait!" exclaimed Bonner, stopping short beside the first cot. He stooped and peered intently into the face of the wounded bandit. "By George!"

"What's up?"

"As I live, Mr. Crow, this fellow was one of the gang that abducted Rosalie Gray last winter. I can swear to it. Don't you remember the one she tried to intercede for? Briggs! That's it! Briggs!"

The injured man slowly opened his eyes as the name

was half shouted. A sickly grin spread slowly over his pain-racked face.

"She tried to intercede fer me, did she?" he murmured weakly. "She said she would. She was square."

"You were half decent to her," said Bonner. "How do you happen to be with this gang? Another kidnaping scheme afloat?"

"No—not that I know of. Ain't you the guy that fixed us? Say, on the dead, I was goin' to do the right thing by her that night. I was duckin' the gang when you slugged me. Honest, mister, I was goin' to put her friends next. Say, I don't know how bad I'm hurt, but if I ever git to trial, do what you can fer me, boss. On the dead, I was her friend."

Bonner saw pity in Anderson's face and rudely dragged him away, although Bill's plea was not addressed to the old marshal.

"Wait for me out here, Mr. Crow," said he when they reached the office. "You are overcome. I'll talk to him." He returned at once to the injured man's cot.

"Look here, Briggs, I'll do what I can for you, but I'm afraid it won't help much. What do the doctors say?"

"If they ain't lyin', I'll be up an' about in a few weeks. Shoulder and some ribs cracked and my legs stove up. I can't move. God, that was an awful tumble!" He shuddered in memory of the auto's leap.

"Is Sam or Davy in this gang?"

"No; Davy's at Blackwell's Island, an' Sam told me he was goin' to Canada fer his health. Jim Courtney is the leader of this gang. He sailed under the name of Gregory. That's him swearin' at the rubes."

"The thing for you to do is to make a clean breast of it, Briggs. It will go easier with you."

"Turn State's evidence? What good will that do when we was all caught with the goods?"

"If you will tell us all of the inside facts concerning the abduction I'll guarantee that something can be done to lighten your sentence. I am Congressman Bonner's nephew."

"So? I thought you was the swellest hold-up man I ever met, that night out in the woods. You'd do credit to Sam Welch himself. I'll tell you all I know, pardner, but it ain't a great deal. It won't do me any good to keep my mouth shut now, an', if you say so, it may help me to squeal. But, fer the Lord's sake, have one of these rotten doctors give me something to make me sleep. Don't they know what morphine is for?"

Growling and cursing at the doctors, Bill was moved into the office. Anderson came in from the dining-room at that juncture, visibly excited.

"I've got a confession from Gregory," he said. "He confesses that he oughter be hung."

"What!"

"That's what he said—'y ginger. Here's his very words, plain as day: 'I oughter be hung half a dozen times.' 'What fer?' says I. 'Fer bein' sech a damned ass,' said he. 'But that ain't a hangable offence,' said

I. You know, I kinder like Gregory, spite of all. 'It's the worst crime in the world,' said he. 'Then you confess you've committed it?' said I, anxious to pin him right down to it, y' see.' 'You bet I do. Ef they hang me it'll be because I'm a drivelling idiot, an' not because I've shot one er two in my time. Nobody but an ass could be caught at it, an' that's why I feel so infernal guilty. Look here, Mr. Crow, ever' time you see a feller that's proved himself a downright ass, jest take him out an' lynch him. He deserves it, that's all I've got to say. The greatest crime in the world is criminal neglect.' Don't bother me now, Wick; I'm going to write that down an' have him sign it."

"Look here, pard," said Bill Briggs, laboriously breaking in upon their conversation; "I want to do the right thing by you an' her as fer as I can. You've been good to me, an' I won't fergit it. Besides, you said you'd make things easy fer me if I told you what I knowed about that job last winter. Well, I'd better tell it now, 'cause I'm liable to pass in my checks before these doctors git through with me. An' besides, they'll be haulin' me off to the county seat in a day or two. Now, this is dead straight, I'm goin' to give you. Maybe it won't help you none, but 'll give you a lead."

"Go on," cried Bonner breathlessly.

"Well, Sam Welch come to me in Branigan's place one night—that's in Fourt' Avenue—an' says he's got a big job on. We went over to Davy Wolfe's house an' found him an' his mother—the old fairy, you remember. Well, to make it short, Sam said it was a kidnaping job an' the Wolfes was to be in on it because they used to live in this neighbourhood an' done a lot of work here way back in the seventies. There was to be five thousand dollars in the job if we got that girl safe on board a ship bound fer Europe. Sam told us that the guy what engineered the game was a swell party an' a big boy in politics, finance, society an' ever'thin' else. He could afford to pay, but he didn't want to be seen in the job. Nobody but Sam ever seen his face. Sam used to be in politics some. Jest before we left New York to come up here, the swell guy comes around to Davy's with another guy fer final orders. See? It was as cold as h—— as the dickens—an' the two of 'em was all muffled up so's we couldn't get a pipe at their mugs. One of 'em was old—over fifty, I guess—an' the other was a young chap. I'm sure of that.

"They said that one or the other of 'em would be in this neighbourhood when the job was pulled off; that one thousand dollars would be paid down when we started; another thousand when we got 'er into the cave; and the rest when we had 'er at the dock in New York—alive an' unhurt. See? We was given to understand that she was to travel all the rest of 'er life fer 'er health. I remember one thing plain: The old man said to the young 'un: 'She must not know a thing of this, or it will ruin everything.' He wasn't referrin' to the girl either. There was another woman in the case. They seemed mighty anxious to pull the job off without this woman gettin' next.

"Well, we got ready to start, and the two parties coughed up the thousand plunks—that is, the young 'un handed it over to Sam when the old 'un told him to. Sam took three hundred and the rest of us two hundred a piece. When they were lookin' from the winder to see that nobody on the streets was watchin' the house, I asked Sam if he knowed either of them by name. He swore he didn't, but I think he lied. But jest before they left the house, I happened to look inside of the old boy's hat—he had a stiff dicer. There was a big gilt letter in the top of it."

"What was that letter?" demanded Bonner eagerly.

"It was a B."

Bonner looked at Anderson as if the floor were being drawn from under his feet.

"The young chap said somethin' low to the old 'un about takin' the night train back to the University an' comin' down again Saturday."

"To the University? Which one? Did he mention the name?" cried Bonner.

"No. That's all he said."

"Good heavens, if it should be!" said Bonner as if to himself.

"Well, we come up here an' done the job. You know about that, I guess. Sam saw the young feller one night up at Boggs City, an' got instructions from him. He was to help us git 'er away from here in an automobile, an' the old man was to go across the ocean with 'er. That's all I know. It didn't turn out their way that time, but Sam says it's bound to happen."

Bonner, all eagerness and excitement, quickly looked around for Anderson, but the marshal had surreptitiously left the room.   Then, going over to the door, he called for Anderson Crow.   Bud Long was there.

"Anderson left five minutes ago, Mr. Bonner, hurryin' like the dickens, too," he said.   "He's gone to hunt up a feller named Barnes.   He told me to tell you when you came out."

CHAPTER XXXIV

Elsie Banks Returns

BONNER, considerably annoyed and alarmed by the marshal's actions, made every effort to turn him back before he could ruin everything by an encounter with Mr. Barnes. He sent men on bicycles and horseback to overtake him; but the effort was unsuccessful. Mr. Crow had secured a "ride" in an automobile which had brought two newspaper correspondents over from Boggs City. They speeded furiously in order to catch a train for New York, but agreed to drop the marshal at the big bridge, not more than a mile from Judge Brewster's place.

Chagrined beyond expression, he made ready to follow Anderson with all haste in his own machine. Rosalie hurriedly perfected preparations to accompany him. She was rejoining the house party that day, was consumed by excitement over the situation, and just as eager as Bonner to checkmate the untimely operations of poor old Anderson Crow.

The marshal had more than half an hour's start of them. Bonner was his own chauffeur and he was a reckless one to-day. Luck was against him at the outset. The vigorous old detective inspired to real speed, for the first time in his lackadaisacal life, left the newspaper men at the bridge nearly three-quarters of an hour before Bonner passed the same spot, driving furiously up the hill toward Judge Brewster's.

"If your bothersome old daddy gets his eyes on Barnes before I can head him off, dearest, the jig will be up," groaned Bonner, the first words he had spoken in miles. "Barnes will be on his guard and ready for anything. The old—pardon me, for saying it—the old jay ought to know the value of discretion in a case like this."

"Poor old daddy," she sighed, compassion in her heart. "He thinks he is doing it for the best. Wicker, I hope it is—it is not Mr. Barnes," she added, voicing a thought which had been struggling in her mind for a long time.

"Why not, dearest?"

"It would mean one of two things. Either he does not want to recognise me as his child—or cannot, which is even worse. Wicker, I don't want to know the truth. I am afraid—I am afraid."

She was trembling like a leaf and there was positive distress in her eyes, eyes half covered by lids tense with alarm.

"Don't feel that way about it, dear," cried he, recovering from his astonishment and instantly grasping the situation as it must have appeared to her. "To tell you the truth, I do not believe that Mr. Barnes is related to you in any way. If he is connected with the case at all, it is in the capacity of attorney."

"But he is supposed to be an honourable man."

"True, and I still believe him to be. It does not

seem possible that he can be engaged in such work as this. We are going altogether on supposition—putting two and two together, don't you know, and hoping they will stick. But, in any event, we must not let any chance slip by. If he is interested, we must bring him to time. It may mean the unravelling of the whole skein, dear. Don't look so distressed. Be brave. It doesn't matter what we learn in the end, I love you just the same. You shall be my wife."

"I *do* love you, Wicker. I will always love you."

"Dear little sweetheart!"

They whirled up to the lodge gate at Judge Brewster's place at last, the throbbing machine coming to a quick stop. Before he called out to the lodge keeper, Bonner impulsively drew her gloveless hand to his lips.

"Nothing can make any difference now," he said.

The lodge keeper, in reply to Bonner's eager query, informed them that Mr. Barnes had gone away ten or fifteen minutes before with an old man who claimed to be a detective, and who had placed the great lawyer under arrest.

"Good Lord!" gasped Bonner with a sinking heart.

"It's an outrage, sir! Mr. Barnes is the best man in the world. He never wronged no one, sir. There's an 'orrible mistake, sir," groaned the lodge keeper. "Judge Brewster is in Boggs City, and the man wouldn't wait for his return. He didn't even want to tell Mr. Barnes what 'e was charged with."

"Did you ever hear of anything so idiotic?" roared Bonner. Rosalie was white and red by turn. "What direction did they take?"

"The constable told Mr. Barnes he'd 'ave to go to Tinkletown with 'im at once, sir, even if he 'ad to walk all the way. The old chap said something, sir, about a man being there who could identify him on sight. Mr. Barnes 'ad to laugh, sir, and appeared to take it all in good humour. He said he'd go along of 'im, but he wouldn't walk. So he got his own auto out, sir, and they went off together. They took the short cut, sir, by the ferry road, 'eaded for Tinkletown. Mr. Barnes said he'd be back before noon, sir—if he wasn't lynched."

"It's all over," groaned Bonner dejectedly. Something had slipped from under his feet and he was dangling in space, figuratively speaking. "There's nothing to do, Rosalie, except to chase them down. Mr. Crow has ruined everything. I'll leave you at Bonner Place with mother and Edith, and I'll hurry back to Tinkletown."

The excitement was too much for Rosalie's nerves. She was in a state of physical collapse when he set her down at his uncle's summer home half an hour later. Leaving her to explain the situation to the curious friends, he set speed again for Tinkletown, inwardly cursing Anderson Crow for a meddling old fool.

In the meantime Tinkletown was staring openmouthed upon a new sensation. The race between Anderson and Bonner was hardly under way when down the main street of the town came a jaded team and surrey. Behind the driver sat a pretty young woman with an eager expression on her pale face, her gaze bent intently on the turn in the street which hid

Anderson Crow's home from view. Beside the young woman lounged another of her sex, much older, and to all appearances, in a precarious state of health. The young men along the street gasped in amazement and then ventured to doff their timid hats to the young woman, very much as if they were saluting a ghost. Few of them received a nod of recognition from Elsie Banks, one-time queen of all their hearts.

Roscoe Crow bounded out to the gate when he saw who was in the carriage, first shouting to his mother and sisters, who were indoors receiving congratulations and condolences from their neighbours.

Miss Banks immediately inquired if she could see Rosalie.

"She ain't here," said Roscoe. "She's away fer a month—over at the Bonners'. He's her feller, you know. Ma! Here's Miss Banks! Edner! Sue!" Mrs. Crow and the girls flew out to the gate, babbling their surprise and greetings.

"This is my mother," introduced the young lady. "We have just come from New York, Mrs. Crow. We sail for England this week, and I must see Rosalie before we go. How can we get to Mr. Bonner's place?"

"It's across the river, about twelve miles from here," said Mrs. Crow. "Come in and rest yourselves. You don't have to go back to-day, do you? Ain't you married yet?"

"No, Mrs. Crow," responded Elsie, with a stiff, perfunctory smile. "Thank you, we cannot stop. It is necessary that we return to New York to-night, but

I must see Rosalie before going. You see, Mrs. Crow, I do not expect to return to America. We are to live in London forever, I fear. It may be the last chance I'll have to see Rosalie. I must go on to Bonner Place to-day. But, dear me, I am so tired and hot, and it is so far to drive," she cried ruefully. "Do you know the way, driver?" The driver gruffly admitted that he did not. Roscoe eagerly bridged the difficulty by offering to act as pathfinder.

At first Mrs. Banks tried to dissuade her daughter from undertaking the long trip, but the girl was obstinate. Her mother then flatly refused to accompany her, complaining of her head and heart. In the end the elder lady decided to accept Mrs. Crow's invitation to remain at the house until Elsie's return.

"I shall bring Rosalie back with me, mother," said Elsie as she prepared to drive away. Mrs. Banks, frail and wan, bowed her head listlessly and turned to follow her hostess indoors. With Roscoe in the seat with the driver, the carriage started briskly off down the shady street, headed for the ferry road and Bonner Place.

To return to Anderson Crow and his precipitancy. Just as the lodge keeper had said, the marshal, afoot and dusty, descended upon Mr. Barnes without ceremony. The great lawyer was strolling about the grounds when his old enemy arrived. He recognised the odd figure as it approached among the trees.

"Hello, Mr. Crow!" he called cheerily. "Are you going to arrest me again?" He advanced to shake hands.

"Yes, sir; you are my prisoner," said Anderson, panting, but stern. "I know you, Mr. Barnes. It won't do you any good to deny it."

"Come in and sit down. You look tired," said Barnes genially, regarding his words as a jest; but Anderson proudly stood his ground.

"You can't come any game with me. It won't do you no good to be perlite, my man. This time you don't git away."

"You don't mean to say you are in earnest?" cried Barnes.

"I never joke when on duty. Come along with me. You c'n talk afterward. Your hirelin' is in jail an' he c'n identify you; so don't resist."

"Wait a moment, sir. What is the charge?"

"I don't know yet. You know better'n I do what it is."

"Look here, Mr. Crow. You arrested me the first time I ever saw you, and now you yank me up again, after all these years. Haven't you anything else to do but arrest me by mistake? Is that your only occupation?"

Anderson sputtered indignantly. Driven to it, he informed John Barnes that he was charged with kidnaping, attempted murder, polygamy, child desertion, and nearly everything else under the sun. Barnes, at first indignant, finally broke into a hearty laugh. He magnanimously agreed to accompany his captor to Tinkletown. Not only that, but he provided the means of transportation. To the intense dismay of the servants, he merrily departed with Mr. Crow, a prisoner operating his own patrol wagon. The two were smoking the captive's best cigars.

"It's mighty nice of you, Mr. Barnes, to let us use your autermobile," said Anderson, benignly puffing away as they bowled off through the dust. "It would 'a' been a long walk. I'll speak a good word fer you fer this."

"Don't mention it, old chap. I rather enjoy it. It's been uncommonly dull up here. I did not get away as soon as I expected, you see. So I am charged with being Rosalie's father, eh? And deserting her? And kidnaping her? By jove, I ought to be hung for all this!"

" 'Tain't nothin' to laugh at, my friend. You ought to be ashamed of yourself. I was onto you the day you stopped me in the road an' ast about her. What a fool you was. Reg'lar dead give-away."

"See here, Mr. Crow, I don't like to upset your hopes and calculations," said Barnes soberly. "I did that once before, you remember. That was years ago. You were wrong then, and you are wrong now. Shall I tell you why I am interested in this pretty waif of yours?"

"It ain't necessary," protested the marshal.

"I'll tell you just the same. My son met her in New York while he was at school. He heard her story from mutual friends and repeated it to me. I was naturally interested, and questioned you. He said she was very pretty. That is the whole story, my dear sir."

"That's all very purty, but how about the B in your hat?"

"I don't understand. Oh, you mean the political bee?"

"Politics, your granny! I mean the 'nitial that Briggs saw. No; hold on! Don't answer. Don't say anything that'll incriminate yourself."

"I never had an initial in my hat, and I don't know Briggs. Mr. Crow, you are as crazy as a loon." He prepared to bring the machine to a standstill. "I'm going home. You can ride back with me or get out and walk on, just as you please."

"Hold on! Don't do that! I'll see that you're paid fer the use of the machine. Besides, consarn ye, you're my prisoner." This was too much for Barnes. He laughed long and loud, and he did not turn back.

Just beyond the ferry they turned aside to permit a carriage to pass. A boy on the box with the driver shouted frantically after them, and Anderson tried to stop the machine himself.

"Stop her!" he cried; "that's Roscoe, my boy. Hold on! Who's that with him? Why, by cracky, it's Miss Banks! Gee whiz, has she come back here to teach again? Whoa! Turn her around, Mr. Barnes. They are motionin' fer us to come back. 'Pears to be important, too."

Barnes obligingly turned around and ran back to where the carriage was standing. An hour later the automobile rolled into the driveway at Bonner Place, and Anderson Crow, a glorious triumph in his face, handed Miss Banks from the tonneau and into the arms of Rosalie Gray, who at first had mistaken the automobile for another. Pompous to the point of explosion, Anderson waved his hand to the party assembled on the veranda, strolled around to Mr. Barnes's seat and acquired a light for his cigar with a nonchalance that almost overcame his one-time prisoner, and then said, apparently to the whole world, for he addressed no one in particular:

"I knowed I could solve the blamed thing if they'd jest give me time."

CHAPTER XXXV

The Story is Told

ELSIE BANKS had a small and select audience in Mrs. Bonner's room upstairs. She had come from New York—or from California, strictly speaking—to furnish the narrative which was to set Rosalie Gray's mind at rest forever-more. It was not a pleasant task; it was not an easy sacrifice for this spirited girl who had known luxury all her life. Her spellbound hearers were Mrs. Bonner and Edith, Wicker Bonner, Anderson Crow, Rosalie, and John E. Barnes, who, far from being a captive of the law, was now Miss Gray's attorney, retained some hours before by his former captor.

"I discharge you, sir," Anderson had said, after hearing Miss Bank's statement in the roadway. "You are no longer a prisoner. Have you anything to say, sir?"

"Nothing, Mr. Crow, except to offer my legal services to you and your ward in this extraordinary matter. Put the matter in my hands, sir, and she shall soon come into her own, thanks to this young lady. I may add that, as I am not in the habit of soliciting clients, it is not my intention in this instance to exact a fee from your ward. My services are quite free, given in return, Mr. Crow, for the magnanimous way in which you have taken me into your confidence ever since I have known you. It is an honour to have been arrested by you; truthfully it is no disgrace."

In the privacy of Mrs. Bonner's sitting-room, Elsie Banks, dry-eyed and bitter, told the story of her life. I cannot tell it as she did, for she was able to bring tears to the eyes of her listeners. It is only for me to relate the bare facts, putting them into her words as closely as possible. Rosalie Gray, faint with astonishment and incredulity, a lump in her throat that would not go down, and tears in her eyes, leaned back in an easy-chair and watched her unhappy friend.

"I shall provide Mr. Barnes with proof of everything I say," said Miss Banks. "There can be no difficulty, Rosalie dear, in confirming all that I have to tell. If you will permit me to relate the story without interruption and afterward let me go my way without either pity or contempt, I shall be, oh, so grateful to you all—especially to you, dear Rosalie. Believe me I love you with my whole soul.

"I have come to you voluntarily, and my mother, who is in Tinkletown, in resigning herself to the calls of conscience, is now happier than she has ever been before. A more powerful influence than her own will or her own honour, an influence that was evil to the core, inspired her to countenance this awful wrong. It also checkmated every good impulse she may have had to undo it in after years. That influence came from Oswald Banks, a base monster to whom my mother was married when I was a year old. My mother was the daughter of Lord Abbott Brace, but married my own father, George Stuart, who was a brilliant but radical newspaper writer in London, against her father's wish. For this he cast her off and disinherited her. Grandfather hated him and his views, and he could not forgive my mother even after my father died, which was two years after their marriage.

"Lord Richard Brace, my mother's only brother, married the daughter of the Duchess of B——. You, Rosalie, are Lady Rosalie Brace of Brace Hall, W——shire, England, the true granddaughter of General Lord Abbott Brace, one of the noblest and richest men of his day. Please let me go on; I cannot endure the interruptions. The absolute, unalterable proof of what I say shall be established through the confession of my own mother, in whose possession lies every document necessary to give back to you that which she would have given to me.

"Your mother died a few weeks after you were born, and Sir Richard, who loved my mother in the face of his father's displeasure, placed you in her care, while he rushed off, heart-broken, to find solace in Egypt. It is said that he hated you because you were the cause of her death. On the day after your birth, old Lord Brace changed his will and bequeathed a vast amount of unentailed property to you, to be held in trust by your father until you were twenty-one years of age. I was almost two years old at the time, and the old man, unexpectedly compassionate, inserted a provision which, in the event that you were to die before that time, gave all this money to me on my twenty-first birthday. The interest on this money, amounting to five thousand pounds annually, was to go to you regularly, in one case, or to me, in the other. Oswald Banks was an American, whom my mother had met in London several years prior to her first marriage. He was the London representative of a big Pennsylvania manufacturing concern. He was ambitious, unscrupulous and clever beyond conception. He still is all of these and more, for he is now a coward.

"Well, it was he who concocted the diabolical scheme to one day get possession of your inheritance. He coerced my poor mother into acquiescense, and she became his wretched tool instead of an honoured wife and helpmate. One night, when you were three weeks old, the house in which we lived was burned to the ground, the inmates narrowly escaping. So narrow was the escape, in fact, that you were said to have been left behind in the confusion, and the world was told, the next day, that the granddaughter of Lord Brace had been destroyed by the flames.

"The truth, however, was not told. My stepfather did not dare to go so far as to kill you. It was he who caused the fire, but he had you removed to a small hotel in another part of the city some hours earlier, secretly, of course, but in charge of a trusted maid. My mother was responsible for this. She would not listen to his awful plan to leave you in the house. But you might just as well have died. No one was the wiser and you were given up as lost. A week later, my mother and Mr. Banks started for America. You and I were with them, but you went as the daughter of a maid-servant—Ellen Hayes.

"This is the story as my mother has told it to me after all these years. My stepfather's plan, of course, was to place you where you could never be found, and then to see to it that our grandfather did not succeed in changing his will. Moreover, he was bound and determined that he himself should be named as trustee—when the fortune came over at Lord Brace's death. That part of it turned out precisely as he had calculated. Let me go on a few months in advance of my story. Lord Brace died, and the will was properly probated and the provisions carried out. Brace Hall and the estates went to your father and the bequest came to me, for you were considered dead. My stepfather was made trustee. He gave bond in England and America, I believe. In any event, the fortune was to be mine when I reached the age of twenty-one, but each year the income, nearly twenty-five thousand dollars, was to be paid to my stepfather as trustee, to be safely invested by him. My mother's name was not mentioned in the document, except once, to identify me as the beneficiary. I can only add to this phase of the hateful conspiracy, that for nineteen years my stepfather received this income, and that he used it to establish his own fortune. By investing what was supposed to be my money, he has won his own way to wealth.

"Mr. Banks decided that the operations were safest from this side of the Atlantic. He and my mother took up their residence in New York, and it has been their home ever since. He spent the first half year after your suspected death in London, solely for the pur-

pose of establishing himself in Lord Brace's favour.
Within a year after the death of Lord Brace your
father was killed by a poacher on the estate. He had
but lately returned from Egypt, and was in full control of the lands and property attached to Brace Hall.
If my stepfather had designs upon Brace Hall, they
failed, for the lands and the title went at once to your
father's cousin, Sir Harry Brace, the present lord.

"So much for the conditions in England then and
now. I now return to that part of the story which
most interests and concerns you. My poor mother
was compelled, within a fortnight after we landed in
New York, to give up the dangerous infant who was
always to hang like a cloud between fortune and
honour. The maid-servant was paid well for her
silence. By the way, she died mysteriously soon after
coming to America, but not before giving to my
mother a signed paper setting forth clearly every detail in so far as it bore upon her connection with the
hateful transaction. Conscience was forever at work
in my mother's heart; honour was constantly struggling to the surface, only to be held back by fear of
and loyalty to the man she loved.

"It was decided that the most humane way to put
you out of existence was to leave you on the doorstep
of some kindly disposed person, far from New York.
My stepfather and my mother deliberately set forth
on this so-called mission of mercy. They came north,
and by chance, fell in with a resident of Boggs City
while in the station at Albany. They were debating
which way to turn for the next step. My mother was

firm in the resolve that you should be left in the care of honest, reliable, tender-hearted people, who would not abuse the trust she was to impose. The Boggs City man said he had been in Albany to see about a bill in the legislature, which was to provide for the erection of a monument in Tinkletown—where a Revolutionary battle had been fought. It was he who spoke of Anderson Crow, and it was his stories of your goodness and generosity, Mr. Crow, that caused them to select you as the man who was to have Rosalie, and, with her, the sum of one thousand dollars a year for your trouble and her needs.

"My mother's description of that stormy night in February, more than twenty-one years ago, is the most pitiful thing I have ever listened to. Together they made their way to Tinkletown, hiring a vehicle in Boggs City for the purpose. Mr. Banks left the basket on your porch while mother stood far down the street and waited for him, half frozen and heartsick. Then they hurried out of town and were soon safely on their way to New York. It was while my stepfather was in London, later on, that mother came up to see Rosalie and make that memorable first payment to Mr. Crow. How it went on for years, you all know. It was my stepfather's cleverness that made it so impossible to learn the source from which the mysterious money came.

"We travelled constantly, always finding new places of interest in which my mother's conscience could be eased by contact with beauty and excitement. Gradually she became hardened to the conditions, for, after all, was it not her own child who was to be enriched by the theft and the deception? Mr. Banks constantly forced that fact in upon her mother-love and her vanity. Through it all, however, you were never neglected nor forgotten. My mother had your welfare always in mind. It was she who saw that you and I were placed at the same school in New York, and it was she who saw that your training in a way was as good as it could possibly be without exciting risk.

"Of course, I knew nothing of all this. I was rolling in wealth and luxury, but not in happiness. Instinctively I loathed my stepfather. He was hard, cruel, unreasonable. It was because of him that I left school and afterward sought to earn my own living. You know, Rosalie, how Tom Reddon came into my life. He was the son of William Reddon, my stepfather's business partner, who had charge of the Western branch of the concern in Chicago. We lived in Chicago for several years, establishing the business. Mr. Banks was until recently president of the Banks & Reddon Iron Works. Last year, you doubtless know, the plant was sold to the great combine and the old company passed out of existence. This act was the result of a demand from England that the trust under which he served be closed and struck from the records. It was his plan to settle the matter, turn the inheritance over to me according to law, and then impose upon my inexperience for all time to come. The money, while mine literally, was to be his in point of possession.

"But he had reckoned without the son of his partner.

Tom Reddon in some way learned the secret, and he was compelled to admit the young man into all of his plans. This came about some three years ago, while I was in school. I had known Tom Reddon in Chicago. He won my love. I cannot deny it, although I despise him to-day more deeply than I ever expect to hate again. He was even more despicable than my stepfather. Without the faintest touch of pity, he set about to obliterate every chance Rosalie could have had for restitution. Time began to prove to me that he was not the man I thought him to be. His nature revealed itself; and I found I could not marry him. Besides, my mother was beginning to repent. She awoke from her stupor of indifference and strove in every way to circumvent the plot of the two conspirators, so far as I was concerned. The strain told on her at last, and we went to California soon after my ridiculous flight from Tinkletown last winter. It was not until after that adventure that I began to see deep into the wretched soul of Tom Reddon.

"Then came the most villainous part of the whole conspiracy. Reddon, knowing full well that exposure was possible at any time, urged my stepfather to have you kidnaped and hurried off to some part of the world where you could never be found. Even Reddon did not have the courage to kill you. Neither had the heart to commit actual murder. It was while we were at Colonel Randall's place that the abduction took place, you remember. Mr. Banks and Tom Reddon had engaged their men in New York. These desperadoes came to Boggs City while Tom was here to watch their operations. All the time Mr. Crow was chasing us down Reddon was laughing in his sleeve, for he knew what was to happen during the marshal's absence. You know how successfully he managed the job. It was my stepfather's fault that it did not succeed.

"My mother, down in New York, driven to the last extreme, had finally turned on him and demanded that he make restitution to Rosalie Gray, as we had come to know her. Of course, there was a scene and almost a catastrophe. He was so worried over the position she was taking, that he failed to carry out his part of the plans, which were to banish Rosalie forever from this country. You were to have been taken to Paris, dear, and kept forever in one of those awful sanitoriums. They are worse than the grave. In the meantime, the delay gave Mr. Bonner a chance to rescue you from the kidnapers.

"Shortly after reaching New York I quarrelled with Thomas Reddon, and my mother and I fled to California. He followed us and sought a reconciliation. I loathed him so much by this time, that I appealed to my mother. It was then that she told me this miserable story, and that is why we are in Tinkletown today. We learned in some way of the plot to kidnap you and to place you where you could not be found. The inhuman scheme of my stepfather and his adviser was to have my mother declared insane and confined in an asylum, where her truthful utterances could never be heard by the world, or if they were, as the ravings of a mad woman.

"The day that we reached New York my mother *placed* the documents and every particle of proof in her possession in the hands of the British Consul. The story was told to him and also to certain attorneys. A member of his firm visited my stepfather and confronted him with the charges. That very night Mr. Banks disappeared, leaving behind him a note, in which he said we should never see his face again. Tom Reddon has gone to Europe. My mother and I expect to sail this week for England, and I have come to ask Rosalie to accompany us. I want her to stand at last on the soil which knows her to be Rosalie Brace. The fortune which was mine last week is hers to-day. We are not poor, Rosalie dear, but we are not as rich as we were when we had all that belonged to you."

CHAPTER XXXVI

Anderson Crow's Resignation

SOME days later Anderson Crow returned to Tinkletown from New York, where he had seen Rosalie Bonner and her husband off for England, accompanied by Mrs. Banks and Elsie, who had taken passage on the same steamer. He was attired in a brand-new suit of blue serge, a panama hat, and patent-leather shoes which hurt his feet. Moreover, he carried a new walking stick with a great gold head and there was a huge pearl scarf-pin in his necktie Besides all this, his hair and beard had been trimmed to perfection by a Holland House barber. Every morning his wife was obliged to run a flatiron over his trousers to perpetuate the crease. Altogether Anderson was a revelation not only to his family and to the town at large, but to himself as well. He fairly staggered every time he got a glimpse of himself in the shop windows.

All day long he strolled about the street, from store to store, or leaned imposingly against every post that presented itself conveniently. Naturally he was the talk of the town.

"Gee-mi-nently!" ejaculated Alf Reesling, catching sight of him late in the day. "Is that the president?"

"It's Anderson Crow," explained Blootch Peabody.

"Who's dead?" demanded Alf.

"What's that got to do with it?"

"Why, whose clothes is he wearin'?" pursued Alf, utterly overcome by the picture.

"You'd better not let him hear you say that," cautioned Isaac Porter. "He got 'em in New York. He says young Mr. Bonner give 'em to him fer a weddin' present. Rosalie give him a pearl dingus to wear in his cravat, an' derned ef he don't have to wear a collar all the time now. That lawyer Barnes give him the cane. Gee whiz! he looks like a king! don't he?"

At that moment Anderson approached the group in front of Lamson's store. He walked with a stateliness that seemed to signify pain in his lower extremities more than it did dignity higher up.

"How fer out do you reckon they are by this time, Blootch?" he asked earnestly.

"'Bout ten miles further than when you asked while ago," responded Blootch, consulting his watch.

"Well, that ought to get 'em to Liverpool sometime soon then. They took a powerful fast ship. Makes it in less 'n six days, they say. Let's see. They sailed day before yesterday. They must be out sight o' land by this time."

"Yes, unless they're passin' some islands," agreed Blootch.

"Thunderation! What air you talkin' about?" said Anderson scornfully. "Cuby an' Porty Rico's been passed long ago. Them islands ain't far from Boston. Don't you remember how skeered the Boston people were durin' the war with Spain? Feared the Spanish shells might go a little high an' smash up the town? Islands nothin'! They've got away out into deep water by this time, boys. 'y Gosh, I'm anxious about Rosalie. S'posin' that derned boat struck a rock er upset er somethin'! They never could swim ashore."

"Oh, there's no danger, Anderson," said Mr. Lamson. "Those boats are perfectly safe. I suppose they're going to telegraph you when they land."

"No, they're goin' to cable, Wick says. Doggone, I'm glad it's all settled. You don't know how hard I've worked all these years to find out who her parents was. Course I knowed they were foreigners all the time, but Rosalie never had no brogue, so you c'n see how I was threw off the track. She talked jest as good American as we do. I was mighty glad when I finally run Miss Banks to earth." The crowd was in no position to argue the point with him. "That Miss Banks is a fine girl, boys. She done the right thing. An' so did my Rosalie—I mean Lady Rosalie. She made Elsie keep some of the money. Mr. Barnes is goin' to England next week to help settle the matter for Lady Rosalie. He says she's got nearly a million dollars tied up some'eres. It's easy sailin', though, 'cause Mrs. Banks says so. Did you hear what Rosalie said when she got convinced about bein' an English lady?"

"No; what did she say?"

"She jest stuck up that derned little nose o' hern an' said: 'I am an American as long as I live.' "

"Hooray!" shouted Alf Reesling, throwing Isaac Porter's new hat into the air. The crowd joined in the cheering.

"Did I ever tell you how I knowed all along that it was a man who left Rosalie on the porch?" asked Anderson.

"Why, you allus told me it was a woman," said Alf. "You accused me of bein' her."

"Shucks! Woman nothin'! I knowed it was a man, Here's somethin' you don't know, Alf. I sized up the foot-prints on my front steps jest after she—I mean he—dropped the basket. The toes turned outward, plain as day, right there in the snow." He paused to let the statement settle in their puzzled brains. "Don't you know that one hunderd percent of the women turn their toes in when they go upstairs? To keep from hookin' into their skirts? Thunder, you oughter of thought of that, too!"

Some one had posted Anderson on this peculiarly feminine trait, and he was making the best of it. Incidentally, it may be said that every man in Tinkletown took personal observations in order to satisfy himself.

"Any one seen Pastor MacFarlane?" went on Anderson. "Wick Bonner give me a hunderd dollar bill to give him fer performin' the ceremony up to our house that night. G'way, Ed Higgins! I'm not goin' 'round showin' that bill to people. If robbers got onto the fact I have it, they'd probably try to steal it. I don't keer if you ain't seen that much money in one piece. That's none of my lookout. Say, are you comin' to the town meetin' to-night?"

They were all at the meeting of the town board that night. It was held, as usual, in Odd Fellows' Hall, above Peterson's dry-goods store, and there was not so much as standing room in the place when the clerk read the minutes of the last meeting. Word had gone forth that something unusual was to happen. It was not idle rumour, for soon after the session began, Anderson Crow arose to address the board.

"Gentlemen," he said, his voice trembling with emotion, "I have come before you as I notified you I would. I hereby tender my resignation as marshal of Tinkletown, street commissioner and chief of the fire department—an' any other job I may have that has slipped my mind. I now suggest that you app'int Mr. Ed Higgins in my place. He has wanted the job fer some time, an' says it won't interfere with his business any more than it did with mine. I have worked hard all these years an' I feel that I ought to have a rest. Besides, it has got to be so that thieves an' other criminals won't visit Tinkletown on account o' me, an' I think the town is bein' held back considerable in that way. What's the use havin' a marshal an' a jail ef nobody comes here to commit crimes? They have to commit 'em in New York City er Chicago nowadays, jest because it's safer there than it is here. Look at this last case I had. Wasn't that arranged in New York? Well, it shouldn't be that way. Even the train robbers put up their job in New York. I feel that the best interests of the town would be served ef I resign an' give the criminals a chance. You all know Ed Higgins. He will ketch 'em if anybody kin. I move that he be app'inted."

The motion prevailed, as did the vote of thanks,

which was vociferously called for in behalf of Anderson Crow.

"You honour me," said the ex-marshal, when the "ayes" died away. "I promise to help Marshal Higgins in ever' way possible. I'll tell him jest what to do in everything. I wish to say that I am not goin' out of the detective business, however. I'm goin' to open an agency of my own here. All sorts of detective business will be done at reasonable prices. I had these cards printed at the *Banner* office to-day, an' Mr. Squires is goin' to run an ad. fer me fer a year in the paper."

He proudly handed a card to the president of the board and then told the crowd that each person present could have one by applying to his son Roscoe, who would be waiting in the hallway after the meeting. The card read:

"Anderson Crow, Detective.
All kinds of cases Taken and Satisfaction
Guaranteed.
Berth mysteries a Specialty."

Mrs. Bonner, upon hearing of his resignation the next day, just as she was leaving for Boston, drily remarked to the Congressman:

"I still maintain that Anderson Crow is utterly impossible."

No doubt the entire world, aside from the village of Tinkletown, agrees with her in that opinion.

The End